ALABAMA NOIR

ALABAMA NOIR

ALABAMA NOIR

EDITED BY DON NOBLE

BROOKLYN, NEW YORK, USA
BALLYDEHOB, CO. CORK, IRELAND

This collection consists of works of fiction. All names, characters, places, and incidents are the product of the authors' imaginations. Any resemblance to real events or persons, living or dead, is entirely coincidental.

Published by Akashic Books
©2020 Akashic Books

Series concept by Tim McLoughlin and Johnny Temple
Alabama map by Sohrab Habibion

ISBN: 978-1-61775-808-9
Library of Congress Control Number: 2019943616

First printing

Akashic Books
Brooklyn, New York, USA
Ballydehob, Co. Cork, Ireland
Twitter: @AkashicBooks
Facebook: AkashicBooks
E-mail: info@akashicbooks.com
Website: www.akashicbooks.com

To my friend Dr. David K. Jeffrey, lover of noir

ALSO IN THE AKASHIC NOIR SERIES

FORTHCOMING

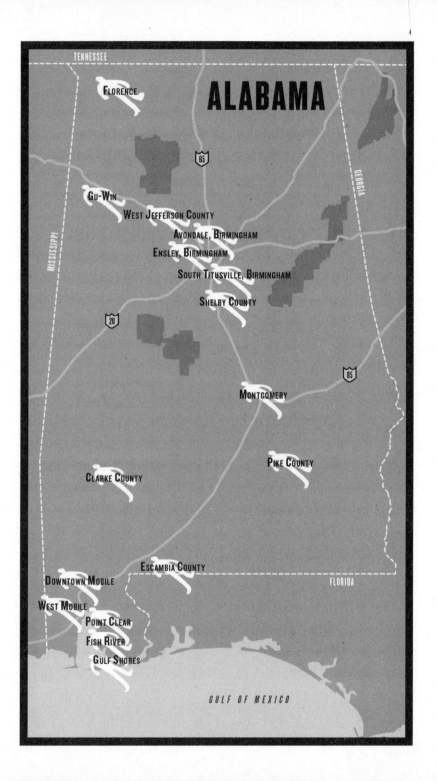

TABLE OF CONTENTS

INTRODUCTION
TROUBLES AND FOIBLES

There must be places like Hawaii where the idea of noir would be difficult to accommodate. Sunshine, drinks in a coconut, warm beaches, and leis do not generate the fear, darkness, and despair on which noir thrives.

Alabama also has plenty of sunshine, some lovely beaches, and only a few foggy waterfronts where miscreants lurk, but it has been a famously dark place. Americans of a certain age read in their daily papers about the burning of the Freedom Riders' bus in Anniston and about the KKK beating those riders at the Birmingham and Montgomery bus stations in May 1961, with the silent cooperation of law enforcement. Americans actually watched, on the evening news, the German shepherds and fire hoses used on demonstrators in Birmingham and the violence at the Edmund Pettus Bridge in Selma.

These days, Alabama has truly turned a corner on race, but the past will not, should not, and in fact *cannot* be forgotten. We are aware of the past here on a daily basis.

In Montgomery, the public interest lawyer Bryan Stevenson has overseen the creation of the National Memorial for Peace and Justice, which features more than eight hundred hanging steel slabs, each representing an American county, with the names of lynching victims inscribed. It also features hundreds of jars of earth, taken from the sites of murders, from underneath tree limbs, and from places where shootings occurred. A walk through the memorial is sobering, chilling.

One might expect that many of the stories in this collection would focus on racial injustice, and indeed some do. Anthony Grooms sets his story in a period of violence from an unusual African American point of view—that of a professor at the historically black school Miles College.

The news these days is full of stories concerning the inadequacies and dangers of the Alabama prison system, where homicides and suicides abound. Ravi Howard sets his story in Holman Prison, where executions are carried out, and tells of one person's maneuver to mitigate that cruelty. Both Thom Gossom Jr. and D. Winston Brown place their stories inside black communities; racial prejudice is always present but not exactly the catalyst for action.

It is perfectly appropriate that racial injustice permeates *Alabama Noir*. But of course, so do many other themes and obsessions of traditional noir, those based on the violent and dark side of human nature. Noir has been enjoying a strong resurgence in the past few years, nationwide, even worldwide, in fiction and in film, and aficionados understand that its roots are to be found in many places: *Black Mask* magazine stories, for example, or the novels of James M. Cain and others. But perhaps the best-known noir novel of all time is Dashiell Hammett's *The Maltese Falcon,* and it serves amazingly well as a model or template for the form.

In *The Maltese Falcon*, Sam Spade, private detective, exasperated, declares, "When a man's partner is killed, he's supposed to do something about it." Revenge in myriad forms has always been a staple of noir fiction and this volume is no exception. In Michelle Richmond's story, a dead husband is avenged; in Carolyn Haines's, it is a father. In the story by Anthony Grooms, an assault on an innocent black man will bring retribution; in D. Winston Brown's story, it is the death of an unborn child. And less somber, perhaps, but no less fatal, Winston Groom's story tells of a man furious over unfair treatment by the state tax commissioner.

Violence not sparked by revenge is often sparked by love and/or lust in noir, often generated by the "femme fatale." In *The Maltese Falcon,* that femme was Brigid O'Shaughnessy. In *Alabama Noir,* there are several strong and deadly females, each seeking and achieving retribution, but there is only one ferociously sexy female consciously using her wiles like the *Falcon*'s immortal Brigid.

When Brigid enters Spade's office she is described as "tall and pliantly slender, without angularity anywhere. Her body was erect and high-breasted, her legs long . . ." The heroine of Wendy Reed's "Custom Meats," Cassie DeBardelaiwin, drives simple Jimbo Sutt crazy from the second she enters his deer-processing room. Her eyes are the same color as her denim skirt; she smells like green apples and she "strutted right up to him until she stopped with her crotch at his face." Suzanne Hudson's Misty Smith, "with long hair streaked blond, animated green eyes, and [a] distinctive laugh," ensorcells poor Gary Wright and wrecks the fragile life he and Yoder Everett live on Fish River.

The men in both these stories don't stand a chance. Gullible, susceptible, they utterly lack Sam Spade's sophistication and his cynicism. Neither could ever manage "We didn't exactly believe your story . . . We believed your two hundred dollars."

Violence not generated by revenge or lust is likely to be the child of greed. Several of these stories are, like Hammett's, tales of criminal schemes gone bad. To say there is no honor among these thieves is a hopeless understatement.

In *Falcon,* Spade realizes the power of this greed in a character like Kasper Gutman, and uses it against him. Of course, obsessed lowlifes will double-cross one another, feed one another to the wolves or the police. In negotiations over the missing statuette, the fat man Gutman reveals the lengths he will go to in order to obtain the bird he has been pursuing for seventeen years. He explains to his young gunman Wilmer, "I want you to know that I couldn't be any fonder of you if you were my own son; but—well by Gad!—if you lose a son, it's possible to get another—but there's only one Maltese falcon."

In Kirk Curnutt's story, a collection of lowlifes seek their fortune in drugs and, God help us, Confederate coins. Anita Miller Garner has based her story on Chaucer's "The Pardoner's Tale," in which a simple double cross would not be enough. Trust in noir stories is in short supply.

In both these stories and others, the action is fueled by serious drinking and drug abuse. Alabama, despite or perhaps because of dry counties and cities, has historically been a place of alcoholism and, in keeping with the times, drug addiction—meth, OxyContin, heroin, all of it. There were and still are moonshiners and bootleggers.

Sometimes these noir stories are not explicitly violent. They explore powerful emotions rather than actions—the emotions of extreme stress, fear, terror, and despair. Tom Franklin shows a mother, heartbroken, still cleaning up her son's mess. The heroine in Thom Gossom Jr.'s tale has her life ruined by a very modern kind of stalker.

Sometimes the violence is offstage, or is to come immediately after the curtain falls. We don't get to watch it, but we know no power on earth can stop it. The different men in Daniel Wallace's three short-shorts are on the edge, or perhaps have gone over it. One is obsessed with coffin building—before there is a corpse. Life is fragile, as are relationships, especially marriage. The men in the woods are wifeless, be-coming like feral cats, but their lifestyle is oddly compelling.

Any discussion of the dark side of human nature will eventually deal with the debate between nature and nurture, whether a character is innately evil or has been twisted by cruel experiences. Brad Watson's little creature Betty, mal-formed and bitter, is capable of premeditated, cold-blooded violence, but a reader might feel justified in cheering her on in her flight to freedom. In Ace Atkins's story, which will remind readers of one of America's most famous child murder cases, one bent soul meets another; it might be difficult to figure out which of the two characters is more damaged.

Some locales seem to come with their own soundtrack. Don Ho and his tiny bubbles provide the background music for Hawaii, Edith Piaf for Paris. The reggae of Bob Marley evokes Jamaica. The soundtrack for Alabama is without ques-tion provided by our troubled troubadour Hank Williams. The 2016 biography *Hank* by Mark Ribowsky paints a dark picture of the musician's short, alcoholic, drug-filled life: a life of loneliness and pain. He goes so far as to call Hank's life story "noir-ish."

Alabamians' love for and identification with Hank was expressed in the 2012 memoir of columnist Rheta Grimsley Johnson, *Hank Hung the Moon . . . and Warmed Our Cold, Cold Hearts*. She writes that Williams was "an Alabamian . . . whose music had a beat like that of our own hearts." He was "in our minds as a distant cousin or close friend who had died far too soon. He spoke our language and knew our secrets and made us feel better about our troubles and foibles."

Marlin Barton's tale takes place at the Hank Williams grave in Oakwood Cemetery in Montgomery, a spot that has become "sacred" and where ceremonies and rituals of different sorts are performed by visitors, often late at night, similar to those performed at Jim Morrison's grave in Père Lachaise Cemetery in Paris. Barton's twisted lovers are caught in a perfectly deadly folie à deux, and with them we end the collection.

In *Alabama Noir* we encounter "troubles and foibles" galore, darkness in many forms. The stories range from the deadly grim to some that are actually mildly humorous. We see desperate behavior on the banks of the Tennessee River, in the neighborhoods of Birmingham, in the affluent suburbs of Mobile, in a cemetery in Montgomery, and even on the deceptively pleasant beaches of the Gulf of Mexico.

Fans of noir should all find something to enjoy.

Don Noble
Cottondale, Alabama
January 2020

PART I

Cold, Cold Heart

PART I

EXHAUSTION

BY Anita Miller Garner

Florence

I t's late, even for young guys like me and Ray and DC. So late, it's early. The rest of the bars done closed down and we the only ones left just outside the city limits at the Hollywood where life don't start till after midnight. People been stopped playing pool and gone. Ol' Skunk—tired ol' black man, walks slow, got a big white streak in the hair on top of his head—Skunk's getting tired, shuffling back to where we're shooting nine-ball and cut-throat. White folks other than me call him Edsel. They slap him on the back, shake his hand, talk like they're black for about thirty seconds. *Hey, Edsel. Man. What up?* they say, think they cool. I call him Skunk just like Ray and DC do. We all call him Skunk. I can tell he's tired of asking us if we need more beers. He's too busy slow-mopping behind the bar, stacking chairs one by one on the table, making a little bit of noise so we get the message, but not so much noise that Ray gets mad. Skunk wants us to leave, but he's too scared to say nothing.

We done hustled three drunk dudes for most they paychecks. Don't nobody look us in the eye or give us lip when we take the money. The men leave us alone and the few chicks all sit on the far side of the bar, far away from us as they can get. But they're looking, the chicks are. I catch the chicks looking at me sideways-like, acting like they're not looking. Me and Ray and DC, we're just what they want. We just what they need, baby. Hard ride. Hard six-pack ride with our big shoulders. Some nights I walk over and pick one out. Like that last white girl I had with the sweet face like she loves me. She wants me bad like I'm G-Eazy/Yelawolf. Tonight ain't that kinda night, though. Tonight's a business night. A player's gonna play when he wants to play.

Ol' Skunk finally rattles over our way, dragging a nasty sour mop and bucket on wheels. *Sun comin' up*, he says. *Watch out for the sheriff deputy down by the bridge*, he says, like talkin' is gonna get us to leave. *They catch you they put you under the jail till you cough up the big bucks.* Which is bullshit. We walked here. Didn't nobody drive. Walked to the Hollywood through the woods from where Ray's girlfriend Yolanda stays. Cold weather like this, you see them green and orange outside lights of the Hollywood from Yolanda's front porch. Just walk down a steep hill and don't get caught up in no raggedy saw brier vines in the dark, cross over a footbridge, then walk back up a hill and you'll be right at the Hollywood's back door. Nobody see you coming. Nobody see you going. We way too smart for that fat cracker sheriff deputy.

Ol' Skunk's still talking. *Y'all go on over to Poochie's. He open all the time for whoever show up whenever. Poochie a good man.*

Poochie serves whoever shows up all right, but Poochie's just a bootleg man. Last time we were sitting in Poochie's front room, some man nobody ever seen before come up to DC and knocked DC out cold with a chair. Man never seen DC before.

Ol' Skunk's getting braver now, looking us in the eye, smiling. *I seen you boys back here scammin'*, he says, like he's up on us. Then he stands there like he's 'bout to stick his hand out like maybe he wants a piece of the action just because he thinks he knows something. *That Raeburn boy you took for a hunderd, his cousin work down at the jail,* Skunk says.

I don't know where this motha thinks he's going with this line, but before he can put together his own low deal, Ray's up off his stool and got this motha choked up against the wall, Ray holding his chalky pool stick with both hands across Ol' Skunk's throat so Skunk can't breathe/talk/nothing. Ol' Skunk's right eye pretty much popping out of his head.

Most of the time Ray's easygoing, but when the money-man comes after Ray, Ray gets nervous. I need to say something to soothe Ray down. "Hey." I start talking and think fast since I need a plan to get us out of this fast. "Hey man," I say, "we're a team. Me and you and DC makes three. Ain't that right?"

But what I'm thinking is this: money from Skunk's cash box ain't enough to help. Ray baby needs more than the skanky jingle in Ol' Skunk's cash box. Ray's in deep to the money-man this time. Way deep. Not even Ray's fault, but that don't matter.

Skunk is light-skinned enough that his face turns red. Other eye looks like it's about to pop too. I can tell Skunk wants to ask something, but that's hard to do with your throat mashed against a wall so hard your jaw's hanging loose.

Ray speaks up, talking low and regular, like he's at the Dairy Queen down on Court Street, trying to decide what flavor Blizzard he wants. "I'm gonna let you down nice and easy like, and you gonna tell me what I want to know."

And I'm thinking: *What the shit?* Ray's not even asked Skunk nothing I can hear, so how is Skunk gonna tell Ray what Ray wants to know? What's that shit mean? Ray keeps Skunk held up pretty much slammed against the wall, letting him down slow, letting that chalky stick fall, bouncing off the floor. Skunk's not fighting back, either. He's just held up by

Ray's big arms, blue skull and flower on top of muscle, the name of Ray's dead Texas friend in black on the other arm on Ray's light skin. Almost as light as my skin. Ink looking good on Ray.

Ol' Skunk tries to talk. Just air comes out. Then he says, like a whisper, *I got no part in that deal.*

Skunk's right hand moving and Ray is holding Skunk's collar with his right and reaching for what Skunk's reaching for with his left. Metal flashes back up on Skunk's throat.

Ray talks easy: "You gonna tell me what I wanna know?"

Skunk's talk is still full of air: *I got no part of that deal, man.*

Ray takes the knife edge and nicks Skunk's throat like shaving. "You gonna tell me what I wanna know." But Ray is telling this time, not asking.

DC looks at me like he's thinking: *What the shit? Ol' Skunk give us Orange Crush when we kids. Skunk opened up the Hollywood during Handy Fest Week and paid that famous Muscle Shoals trumpet man to teach kids like us how to blow without spitting.* DC says out loud, "Hey man, Skunk got no money. Just chump change over in the cash box."

But Ray pays DC no mind and cuts Skunk's cheek—not deep, just enough to make it bleed.

Skunk never pisses his pants or nothing. Looking sad, he says, *Boy, what you lookin' at is being dead, ain't it?*

Ray takes the point of Skunk's own knife and makes like to stick Skunk's ribs. "You see this on my arm?" he says right in Skunk's face, breathing the man's nasty breath. "I'm already dead, man."

The way Ray says it, Skunk's gotta know Ray means it. Ray lets him go, and me and Ray and DC leaving slow. Because we want to leave. Not because we struck out. Ray and me and DC make three, picking up our shit real slow while Skunk doubles over and rubs his face.

We're almost out the door when Skunk gets his voice back enough to yell out at us: *You wanna die, just go past that sheriff deputy and take the trail that starts at the willow!*

Ray doesn't even act like he hears. We out the door, and me and DC go back down the hill. We're headed back to Ray's girl's place, back to chill and catch a buzz, hanging, maybe Ray and Yo knock it in the next room and me and DC turn up the tunes loud 'fore my own stick gets hard just listening. Whatever it takes to chill Ray down.

"Hold up," Ray says.

"What?" DC says. "What you wanna go hustle Ol' Skunk for?"

"I'm goin' back to Yolanda's house," I say, heading to that big bottle of cognac mostly full we left sitting on YoGirl's table.

But Ray don't move. "You wi' me or not?" He's serious. Not the same Ray played tight end last year Friday nights hoping somebody see his excellent shit and give him a ticket out.

DC done had enough. "Look, man, whatever shit you in, count me out." He starts on up the hill toward the cognac.

"Don't work that way," Ray call to him. "If I go down, *all* go down."

DC starts back down the hill. Me and DC are all ears.

"Won't waste me first," Ray says.

And then we see the scam. Ray don't pay up, his friends and fam be the first to get whacked. And he ain't got no family 'cept his mama that nobody know of. That's the money-man's way to let folks know the money-man means business. Dead dude can't pay like a scared dude can. A scared dude is what you call *motivated.*

So me and DC follow Ray through the edge the woods by the road, Ray walking like a ghost he's so quiet, me and DC stepping on sticks and dry-ass leaves and all kinda shit making racket. When we see the sheriff deputy car hid behind brush down low on the side road, Ray motions us to get down and we squat there till the gray daylight is enough for the sheriff deputy to think night is over and he takes his dumb-ass self back to his office. Sheriff deputy thinks he knows what's going on. Sheriff deputy don't know squat.

Ray starts up the willow path just like Skunk says not to do unless we wanna die, and we're right behind. Light's coming fast now. Before we know it, we're standing on the edge of this big-ass rock, looking way down on Buzzard Creek below. Real name is Cypress Creek, runs right into the Tennessee River, but we all call it Buzzard Creek since the old garbage dump and the new garbage dump both right on the creek so that on and off you can see fifty or more buzzards in the trees here, right here at this rock where the trail ends. Me and DC looking at each other, studying what's next. Ray sits down in the beat-down dead yellow grass under a big pine. I sit down myself and lean up 'gainst the pine. When my eyes shut, my head spins, so I open them quick-like again.

"What we looking for?" I ask. I'm thinking: kilos, cash money. Maybe ice, Oxy.

Ray's not saying nothing for a minute. Then: "Maybe we lookin' for the shit got ripped off me. Or maybe we lookin' for cash-money."

DC's making water off the rock edge, seeing how far he can shoot his stream in the creek way down below. He's looking around, looking across the creek, looking up in the air, as he makes water. "What's that?" he asks.

"What's *what*?" I ask.

"That," he says, and points up in the pine tree.

So that's how me and Ray and DC come to be hunkered down behind some needle-ass-stabbing green bush on the coldest day of the year, feet numb, snot running out my nose, hungover, waiting to kill somebody I ain't never seen before when they come back to get their black L.L.Bean backpack stacked full of hundred-dollar bills. Ray had taken it down, looked at it, then grabbed the black plastic rope and pulled it back up there, back up in that tall ol' pine tree.

First off, Ray says it could be a trap by the police trying to sucker some poor unsuspectings like us to take the money so's they would have somebody to put in jail and make the police look good, pretend like they're making the world safe. Nothing in the world makes rich folk feel better than to read in the paper that people like me/Ray/DC been caught doing some something and headed for jail. Even if it's something made up, like DC's uncle that paid his child support but they claim it ain't been paid and he's got no paper says he did pay it so he's back in jail. Always some piece of paper, somewhere, with words saying you messed up. Ray says it's all fixed, it's all a trap.

Then, after 'bout an hour of talking that shit, Ray up and changes his mind and says, "Maybe this is the money due to me, the money made off what got stole from me. Maybe *I'm* the rightful owner of this money."

"One thing for sure," says DC, "you not the one throwed that prep-ass backpack up in that pine tree with that rope tied to it. Whoever did that, they comin' back for it."

Even Ray can't deny that. "This is life or death. *Our* life or death. We have to watch who comes back for this." He starts coughing like he's about to cough out a lung.

I let him catch his breath. "And when we see 'em?" I ask.

"Then we find out if they on the up-and-up. See if it's one dude or a crew. My guess is one dude. Alone. Us three find out easy from one dude what we need to know. That cash money gonna be ours. Pay off the money-man and let the rest sit around just waitin' till the time is right. Then we invest. In product."

DC speaks up: "Somebody talks. Somebody gonna know it's us. Then payback come knockin'.'"

Ray laughs. Then he's quiet, talking low: "Nobody will be in no shape to talk."

"But Ol' Skunk's the one told us to come here. Ol' Skunk knows," DC says.

Ray looks at me and DC and raises up his left eyebrow and I know he means Skunk, too, will be in no shape to talk when Ray finishes with him.

I feel sick enough to puke, and DC don't look no better. Ray's eyes are leaking water. And when Ray's feeling sick, he only gets meaner.

Then Ray starts in on the money: "How much you think is in that pack?"

We take turns guessing just before we take turns telling what all we gonna do and buy with all that money. I think: *Ray's gonna tell how he will be the man for Yo, provide for her and all.* But all he says is: Yo's just a trick and he's gonna leave her ass, maybe go to LA where he's got cousins. Take me and DC with him. "We gonna make so much money scammin'," he says, "that this money in this pack will look like chump change."

The sun is full up now, not that we can see it. The gray just got lighter is all. "Lord," DC says, "I'm tired. I'm past tired. Exhausted."

I, too, feel like sleeping. Just too cold and hungry and in pain.

Ray is coughing more, seems to be comin' down with a bad cough.

The air feels warmer now, but the wind when it kicks up cuts like a knife. My belly growls loud as a man talking, and I could use something to drink. DC looks sleepy. A squirrel rustles the dry grass and leaves, and Ray jerks, like he's scared by the racket. He smiles a mean rusty saw-blade smile.

"I'm hungry," DC whines too loud.

Ray's face is dark.

"How you sure somebody gonna come?" DC asks.

Ray looks like he wants to waste DC now.

Finally DC says he's cold and hungry and can't sit out under no bush with stickers on it no more.

"What we need," Ray whispers, "is somethin' to eat and drink, somethin' to warm us up." Only his mouth is smiling. Eyes not smiling. Then he says to me, "Get down to the creek and follow it back to Yolanda. Can't use no path. And don't let nobody see you. Bring back some good stuff."

"What if somebody comes while I'm gone?"

"Me and DC handle it." Still, just his mouth smiling.

So I pick my way down the hill, almost falling it's so steep, and walk alongside the creek, under the bridge, back up to where I know good the way up the hill to find Yo's place. I knock and knock before she comes to the door. She's sleepy-eyed in a big soft pink thing wrapped around her, nothing under that, far as I can tell. Just the pink thing wrapped around Yo's smooth skin. She's sweet like a sleeping baby, her voice tiny.

"Where's Ray?" she asks.

I come in and tell her no more than she makes me tell. She's been with Ray long enough to know better than to ask too much. I go in Yo's kitchen and start looking in the fridge and in the cabinets. "Ray needs this," I say, grabbing a plastic bag and throwing shit in it like crackers, cheese, meat.

She sits down in a raggedy-ass chair and puts her head in her hands. When she looks up at me, one big tear rolls down her cheek.

"He's in trouble?" she asks in that tiny voice.

"Naw," I say, "we just hungry."

"So why did he not come himself?"

"He's busy. Comin' by later. Just to see you." And no sooner I say it I know it's a lie. Soon as that money is Ray's and he thinks nobody can trace him, he leaves town and never sees Yo again. Truth is, Ray's not taking me or DC to LA either. Then who is left around for the money-man to whack? Everbody—Yo, police, everbody—will think me and DC are responsible for whatever's stole, whoever's dead. And we'll be too dead to stand up for ourself.

I grab the cognac off the table, pull out the cork, and take a big two-gulp swallow that burns like fire. Yo is still sitting at the table when I go into the bathroom and sit the cognac on the sink and close the door and put up the seat to be nice-like. I'm feeling gray and dirty, and I smell my own self. I'm not looking in the mirror because there's nothing there I want to see. That ol' cognac bottle sits on the sink, right below the medicine shelf, so when I zip up, I open up that mirror door and look inside. Cough stuff, rubbing alcohol, cotton balls, a bottle of stuff YoGirl takes off her fake nails with, deodorant. Usual stuff. I'm just standing there with both hands on the sink, leaning and thinking, when it comes to me. I take the cork out the cognac, drink down a whole bunch more, and then I take the top off the rubbing alcohol and pour some in that cognac bottle. Then I take the cough stuff bottle, open it up, pour some of it down the sink to make room, and then pour some of that nasty-smelling nail-remover shit in there with the cough stuff.

I shake it all up real good.

When I come back out, I can see more of Yo's tears streaking down her face. I hold up the bottle of cough stuff. "I'm takin' this to Ray," I say.

"He sick?" she asks in that sweet little voice.

"Naw. Just coughing a little," I say. Then I find in the fridge a blue Pepsi can for DC. Me and DC go way back to when we played Little League down at McFarland Bottoms, then middle school, then high school. Him pitcher, me catcher, but we could only do that when the rich coach's own son got too tired to pitch. When I get back to that pine tree and hand DC that blue Pepsi can and look him in the eye a certain way, I tell you this much: he'll know just what I mean. If DC don't see me drink no cognac, he won't be drinking no cognac neither. We read each other minds, me and DC. That's my plan. First get Ray to drink a bunch of that cough stuff that probably tastes like poison anyway. When he says it tastes bad, I'll tell him he must be coming down with a cold, and that's when I hand him the bottle and tell him the best thing to do for a cold is to drink a big swig of cognac. Soon after that, he'll be so sick we'll have to take him to the hospital. He'll be safe there. And me and DC can figure out what to do.

I didn't even know I'd warmed up at YoGirl's till I hit the outside again and the cold air slaps my face still too numb from cognac to hurt too bad. Air racing around with what my grandma call hominy snow in it, like little-bitty sleet but not enough to stick or pile up white on the ground. Bits of hominy snow caught in the dead leaves my boots push around trying not to fall down in the creek on the way back. Dead leaves covering the rocks make me stumble once and make a big racket, but I slow down and wait and listen. Sky still gray and the wind slows down. Creek runs slow, just a tinkle. Everything nice and quiet. I pick my way soft-like back to DC and Ray. Maybe the man has done come back for his prep-ass pack and is lying there dead, Ray and DC gone already. God knows what I'll be walking up on, so I think I'd best be easing up that hill, one step, another step. I take so long and am so careful the wind starts back up, rattling all the dead leaves again, so I get off the trail and walk below the big rock DC pissed off of before. Then I start crawling up the side the hill, hanging that plastic bag on one wrist. When I get near the top, I look up and it is still there, that black backpack up in the tree, so I ease on up, thinking Ray and DC are still squatted back behind that prickly bush.

But what I see: DC lying there in a lump behind the prickly bush, not looking like he's asleep but something worse, one leg twisted up under him. A cold clear feeling runs through me like I'm in a bad dream and I'm just now waking up to something worse. The backpack man has done sneaked up, I'm thinking. The backpack man might be *two* men. Somebody sure laid DC out like this.

I throw down the plastic bag and head to DC as quick as I can. I need to straighten him out, see if he's still breathing, thinking I myself might be jumped any second, when Ray scares the shit out me, runs up from where the trail starts.

"What happened?" I ask.

"DC fell. Hit his head. I went lookin' for you."

About this time I see a big rock in Ray's hand. I look down and feel the lump on the side of DC's head and too much blood. When I start to move DC, blood is all under him. Then Ray comes at me. My head goes *boom* and my neck cracks, and I fall down hard over DC.

I try to get up and my head gets whacked again. I try to get up but my arms and legs are not doing what I say. My head hurts hot like part of it's gone. I'm trying to tell my hand to feel my head but mostly my arm goes limp. I pass out and then a loud noise wakes me up and I know again that I'm lying on DC, which don't seem right. Something tells me DC is dead and then me too if I can't drag my ass up from here. But I can't even pick my head up. My one eye is open, though. My one eye is seeing it all.

Ol' Skunk standing by Ray, and Ray down on the ground. Half of Ray's head gone. Skunk holding a pistol like it's a snake. Skunk looking over to me.

Then another voice. Right behind me. "Come on over here, Edsel, and put that pistol in this white boy's hand here. This boy ought to knowed not to hang out with these others."

My one eye sees a shiny deputy boot toe-tap my hand, showing Skunk where to put it.

"Use this," the voice behind me says. Voice throws a white rag over to Skunk. "Wipe it clean."

The white rag and pistol now in Skunk's hand. White top of Skunk's head in my face when he bends down.

And then I'm light and free. Rising in the air, slow. Like I'm caught in some cold rising breeze. First I'm circling low just looking around, looking down at myself on the ground on top of DC, watching the sheriff deputy reach a hand down to his pocket, take out his radio, hear him say, "Derrick, you my backup, ain't you?" before he says, "Well, get your ass on up here then."

And Ol' Skunk edging down the creek bank, whispering to himself, whispering low but I hear him. I hear it all now, from the loud right on down to the tiny sound every ripple in the creek makes. I hear Skunk whispering stuff makes no sense, like another language, and then: *Don't mess wi' me. Don't mess wi' me. Don't mess wi' me. I'm OG. OG. I seen they kind. I seen they kind.*

And then I'm higher and higher, higher and higher, watching Ol' Skunk's white head-top moving down the creek, crossing the footbridge, heading back to the Hollywood, hominy snow falling harder and hitting all the dry leaves, sounding loud now, flakes getting bigger and fluffy, and then me higher still, like a balloon somebody let go of, rising in the open sky where the flakes are falling thick now, sky soft and full of it. I look down and there the creek flows into the Tennessee River, and there are the miles and miles of cotton fields out Gunwaleford Road all frozen but with raggedy cotton lint like more snow. Higher still now, soft snow, flakes like cotton. Till the whole world's looking exactly like nothing at all but white.

DEEPWATER, DARK HORIZONS

BY SUZANNE HUDSON

Fish River

Gary Wright, in his expert, know-it-all way, insisted that what was happening on Turkey Branch was a crime. "A goddamned crime, you stubborn old coot. You can get fined for it. I've done googled it. The county site says five hundred dollars a day for every day you let them turds roll down in the branch yonder." The man jabbed his pointer finger with every few syllables.

Yoder Everett ran his fingers through thinning hair, hair that had once upon a time been a thick home to the ladies' painted fingernails that combed through it, now gone limp and thin as he traversed his sixties, alone but for this one pathetic friend. "You're always so goddamned sure of yourself, Gary."

It had finally come to a head, after months of back and forth, after Gary first noticed the oozing fissures in the grass, soil becoming a sloosh of fetid, foul stink. Yoder, tight with a dollar and loath to spend from the thousands he had hoarded over the years, managed to deny, pretend, and scoff his way out of taking any action, until Gary drilled down into something like research. Any fool could find out what was what, it seemed, on the Internet.

Now the two men stood beneath one of the massive live oaks that thrust their mossy arms to the summer sky across Yoder's six acres of waterfront on a branch of the Fish River, studying the patch of yard gone to shit swamp. When breezes lifted, along with the undeniable stench, a chorus of clatters and clacks and tinklings and knockings rose and fell from the scores of wind chimes hanging from branches, from hooks on porches, from posts on the wharf and the pier, from the trash-can corral Gary had built to keep away the raccoons, armadillos, and possums. Gary was handy that way.

The noisy mobiles, though, were all fashioned by Yoder's own hands, inspired by a fragmenting mind, that willy-nilly mishmash of chimes, along with paintings on plywood, palettes of muddy browns, reds, oranges; even murals painted onto the asbestos-shingled sides of his river house. His gnarled but nimble fingers strung together the cacophonous orchestra of objects tied onto lengths of fishing lines, knotted through the boards of driftwood or stripped sapling limbs or guitar necks or whatever, from which the lines dangled. He used all sorts of materials too, for the chimes themselves: old costume jewelry, a deconstructed clarinet, wooden kitchenware, beer cans, women's stilettos, anything at all. "I make art out of junk," he liked to boast. "I'm environmentally friendly that way."

But here was Gary Wright's dumb ass claiming Yoder was a major polluter, right up there with the goddam BP criminals who had ruined the gulf this past spring. Now into full-bore summer, the beaches from NOLA to Apalachicola were so gummed up with the crude that business owners along the coast were yelling bloody murder.

"It's right there in black and white, son," Gary went on. "It's right there on the damn website. You know, that branch runs out to the river and the river runs to the bay and the bay—"

"Hell, Gary, don't you think I know about geography and watersheds and currents and all? And don't call me *son*."

"And the bay goes to the Gulf of Mexico and then out to the whole goddamned world. You're polluting the world with that rusted-out old septic system."

"I told you I've fixed it. I worked on it all day yesterday, down in the bowels of it. Ha!"

"Naw, crawling down in the empty old thing and squirting a hosepipe through it ain't fixed a damn thing about it. You've done broke so many laws I can't count 'em."

"Why don't you google them up, then, the laws?" Yoder shot back. "Google is God now, I guess. Google is the eyes of Dr. T.J. Eckleburg looking down on the Valley of Ashes."

"What the hell?"

"Forget it. Why read a book when you have the Google machine to impart life's truths to your stupid ass."

"It's the law, that's all I'm talking about. You can't let a steady stream of turds and piss-water keep rolling down that hill and into that branch. You've got to call a septic service or I'm gonna have to turn you in to the county. You're the property owner. It's *your* responsibility."

Yoder, clench-fisted, tight-toothed, gritted out, "Get off my property, then. I've a good mind to evict you."

But they both knew it was an empty threat. They had a long history of disputes, even fistfights, going back to when they were young, potent warriors of the gridiron, back when women liked their looks and a loop around the town of Foley, Alabama, from drive-in diners to picture shows in a Ford Mustang, when a make-out chick in the front seat was the pinnacle of a life promising to be all downhill from there.

They were an odd couple, all right: Yoder, well-educated, creative, once-charming-now-cautious, carrying several DSM-referenced labels; and Gary, low of IQ, naive, spur-of-the-moment. Yoder taught art education in a community college before the mental meltdown that had him on disability by the time he was forty. Gary, no hope of a deferment, found himself, straight out of high school, chasing Charlie in the jungles of Vietnam. He spoke of it from time to time, though not with enough depth or detail to satisfy the curiosity Yoder kept in check.

"I seen some shit there, over yonder, in itty-bitty-titty land. Nobody ought to see them things." He would fall silent for several beats, then, "I seen nothing BUT shit all my life," he would repeat, to the air, to the nights, to anybody or nobody, "and shit don't cool for folks like me."

"You think you're the only one that had it so damn bad?" Yoder would toss out, as a challenge, their routine one-upmanship of misery, on twilit evenings when they sat on the dock, working their way through a case of Budweiser. "Hell, my stepmother was cold and wicked and hated my guts," and he would recount tales about how his real mama took the cancer when he was only six, went downhill fast, and how it was clear to everyone that his daddy had "Miss Dinah" waiting in the wings long before the cancer ever even hit.

His memories of his real mama, Janine, were warm and conjured something like reassurance, despite the odd quirks she had, the rituals, a prominent one being the taking of the castor oil, every single Friday evening of every single week. "Folks just believed in it back then, believed it kept you regular, like it was good for you. Mama was the queen of poop."

Yoder couldn't remember a time in his life, post–potty training, when his mother did not insist on inspecting his bowel movements, to see if his excrement was healthy or if it demanded more attention. He and Gary sometimes had a good laugh about Yoder's fecal foundation. "No sir, I wasn't allowed to flush, not until Mama checked—and she'd say things like, *Oh, that one looks real good, Yodie,* or, *No wiggle worms to be found,* or, *That one's a pretty picture of health.* I didn't think anything about it—that was just how our routines went along, until she got the cancer."

When Miss Dinah took over, her two brats in tow, she showed no inclination to study Yoder's bowel movements. In fact, when, all of seven years old and eager to please his new parent, he finally offered to show her what he had landed in the toilet bowl, she scrunched up her face, shuddered, and said, "Why on God's green earth would I want to look at anybody's BM? Let alone *yours.*" And it was the way she said it, *yours,* that planted her hatred of him in his mind, hardening him to her, young though he was, and by adolescence the reciprocal disdain was set in his soul.

"She was my ruination," he would lament, blaming her for his bad luck with women. "And yeah, I had to call the bitch *Miss Dinah,* just like my daddy did. He was one goddamned pussy-whipped somebitch. But she sure did pretend-dote on him, waiting on him, baking seven-layer cakes and all," and Yoder would recount how the chocolate confections were locked in the china cabinet, locked away from him in particular, locked away in such a way as he would have to see the sheen of the chocolate each time he passed by, lust after it, wish for it, but he never, ever gave her the satisfaction of doing something as brazen or pathetic as, say, asking for a piece of it. Even when she brought it out as an after-school treat for her own two children, his "steps," Yoder refused to ever ask to be included.

"Don't you want a little bit, baby?" she would singsong, if his daddy was there, and sometimes Yoder would accept a piece, sometimes not.

The two men shared a bottle of Jim Beam down at the

dock that evening, to chase behind the beer, as they typically did of a dusky sunset, having sprayed down with deet, thrown their feet up on footstools, spending hours swapping memories and disagreements, flicking cigarettes hissing into the low tide, the high tide, the ebb and the flow.

"I'll get some prices, then," Yoder said, finally, his way of acquiescing to his foe in the great septic dispute of 2010. "But you have to kick in something. You gonna take that panhandle gig? The one that gal Sissy or Missy or somebody told you about? Because I'll be wanting you to throw in on the new septic tank. It handles *your* shit just as much as it handles mine."

"It's *Misty*," Gary said. "Like the song. Like that Clint Eastwood movie, *Play Misty for Me*. And she says disaster money is almost like free money, depending."

Depending on what? Yoder wondered, thinking Gary might need a good lookout on this Misty person.

Gary and Misty had reconnected via the Internet, a landscape he had only begun exploring around 2007, when Yoder was threatening to put his desktop out with the trash. Yoder had bought the thing as he entered the twenty-first century in a feeble attempt at technology—an attempt that turned into his certainty and fear that the government was spying on him.

"There's a camera on the things, you know," he said, disengaging all manner of cables. "Ever since 9/11 they've been watching us all."

"Why don't they just watch them Islams?" Gary pushed back. "It's them Islams that's bombing themselves and all."

"Muslims," Yoder sighed. "Islam is the religion. Muslims are the practitioners of Islam."

"I don't understand. Baptist is Baptist, Cath'lic is Cath'lic, what the fuck?"

"Never mind."

"Okay. Never-minding."

But Gary took on the surfing of the Net with uncharac-teristic vigor, networking his way through Classmates.com, navigating over to the high schools of some of his old army buddies, reconnecting, flirting his way past a few former girl-friends, before finding Misty again, just after the explosion in the gulf. She talked him through the skyping process and schooled him on the larger landscape of the Internet. He boasted to her about his artist friend Yoder Everett, embel-lishing, "Yeah, he's a big deal around here. He gets big money for his wind chimes—well, he ought to be getting more."

"Is there a website where I can look at them?" Misty asked.

"Hell no—Yoder hardly never touches no computer. He thinks they're taking over the world."

"Ridiculous," Misty said. "You *have* to have a website these days, to advertise, to promote, to sell—you two boys need me. I can do all of that."

And that was the springboard for their planned reunion. After they rendezvoused in Florida, after the work for BP played out, they would haul her trailer back to Turkey Branch, and she would barter her promotional work on Yoder's art for something like rent.

Yoder, however, was skeptical. "Normal people don't do that, just pull up stakes, drive off to meet a stranger and start up a new life."

"Aw, she's a good ol' gal," Gary countered, filling Yoder in on how he had dated her briefly when he returned from 'Nam, during a short, drug-fueled stay on the West Coast. "She was one of them hippie chicks—you know, titties flap-ping and bouncing, hairy pits, the whole deal. Which I ain't minded no hairy pits at all—all I needed was that one little particular patch of hairs, you know? I was fresh out of the army, son. Horny as hell. And she was a wild thing, always into something. Hell, man, she wants to help you sell your wind chimes."

"What the hell? And don't call me *son*."

"Yeah, she's gonna make you a website. Says nobody can't do no kind of business without no website. Says she has real experience in all kinds of business doings, advertising and whatnot."

"Then what's she doing in a double-wide in Arkansas?"

"She's been hiding out from an ex-boyfriend, a mean one, a stalker type. She ran off from him in Portland, changed her looks and all—you know, like that movie, like Julia Roberts in *Sleeping with the Enemy*."

"That's even worse," Yoder said. "All we need is some stalker nutcase to come around here. Hell, somebody's likely to get killed."

"Naw, man, you got it all wrong. Her guy can't leave Portland, his job—and last Misty heard, he's done took up with a whole 'nother woman. It's cool."

"I don't know."

"Shit, man, think of her like the business manager you never had. Remember you always said the business side of art makes you want to puke? Well, Misty's a pro, knows computers, says she's a real, for sure, *people person*. Which you ain't, right?"

"Right."

"So let her manage the crap you hate—the crap you suck at—and see if your income gets better. Come on, man."

"Can't argue with that," Yoder mumbled, seeing a few dollar signs gathering in his future. He did, indeed, hate hauling the chimes around to all the fru-fru and chi-chi and cutesy-cute little galleries and shops in the Foley–Gulf Shores–Orange Beach area, making fake-nice with all the managers and artsy-arts folks. Even though his pieces were popular, unique, and sold quite well, he thought some of those "fancy ladies and gay boys," as he called them, the ones running the shops, might be overpricing and skimming their own special kind of slick off the top of his profits.

It was his mind-set, to be wary. The older he got, the less he trusted folks, even old friends. He had just about stripped away anyone who ever mattered to him, stripped away with suspicion, always, of ulterior motives. His two children were long estranged, radio silent for over a decade, and the ex-wives did not even bother to try anymore. Gary was all he had. And Gary, like him, had alienated his own set of friends and family, not with paranoia but with his scattershot approach to living, his sheer and utter unreliability.

Gary and Misty had skyped throughout May, June, and into July's haze, becoming more and more familiar, gestating the plans that would culminate in their reunion, in mere weeks, the revival of a long-ago hot second of a romance—all while the Deepwater Horizon vomited its ominous cloud of crude into the cesspit of the Gulf of Mexico, in ever-mounting numbers of gallons per day. It seemed like CNN had a picture of it on TV 24-7, the live, real-time movie of the slow murder of the gulf. And the numbers, the volume of the disaster, forever ticked upward.

"It's an awful thing," Gary told Misty's image on the computer screen, "a terrible thing—not just the folks killed but no telling what all else is gonna die. They say it'll kill the coral, even. Hell, I didn't know coral was alive to begin with."

"Well, that's what a lot of the free money is for, to help with that, so I'm going to get there as quick as I can—no later than July's end. Can't wait to see you in the real flesh, sweetie," she cooed.

Gary allowed that she had held up pretty well. She laid claim to the age of fifty-four but looked light of it, with long hair streaked blond, animated green eyes, and the distinctive laugh he remembered from all those years ago, "kind of a hoarse, horsey laugh," he always called it. And the once–braless teenybopper showed him her relatively new fake boobs. "I was dating a plastic surgeon in San Francisco for a while," she said, spreading her top open, unhooking her bra from the front, spilling them on out, right in his face, giving him the kinds of sexual itches he had not scratched in years. "The doc gave me these, plus an eye job, and a slight nose job—just got rid of that little bump. You remember that little bump on my nose?"

He did not. He was preoccupied with the not-little boobs.

"What do you think, daddy? Nice, huh? It's a D-cup size."

Gary was done for.

They spent more and more hours skyping, which soon became elaborate cyber-sexcapades full of dirty talk and all manner of autoeroticism the likes of which Gary had never imagined himself doing. "She sure does know about some variety," he confided to Yoder one humid evening. "But hell," and he took a long pull from the bottle, "why jerk off to a nudie mag when you can see everything right there, just a-writhin' along with you?"

"Can't argue with that," Yoder exhaled his cheap cigarette. "Just seems kind of weird to me, having romantic doings like that."

"You're being old-fashioned, man. This is how it's done these days—everything's on the Internet line."

"Can't argue," Yoder said again.

* * *

Elite Septic Systems sent a "technician" to Turkey Branch the day after Gary headed out for Blountstown, to his new, big-boobed love, and the cleanup job, armed with booze and Viagra.

"This one's a doozey, one of the worst I ever seen. Gonna need new field lines too," Ronny, the self-proclaimed *turd wrestler*, insisted. "This thing is a dinosaur, that's all there is to it. We got to put in all new. Run you a few thousand dollars."

"Nothing here to work with at all?" Yoder responded.

"Zero. Zip. You're lucky you ain't had the EPA and the Corps of Engineers and any government regulator you can think of out here. The money you'll save in fines could install a boatload of septic systems."

Yoder seethed and silently vowed to garnish Gary's British Petroleum wages or government money or whatever. And he didn't have to wait long. After only three weeks on the job, sans Turkey Branch commute, not a trailer but a pop-up camper on the back of a Toyota pickup following Gary's own truck came rolling up to his property, which one Misty Smith hit with the force of Hurricane Katrina.

"I'm moving in with Gary," she squealed. "My man. My destiny."

Gary blushed. "If it's no never mind to you, that is," nodding at Yoder.

"Of course he doesn't mind!" Misty was possessed of grand movements, physically—large swoops of arms, long strides of legs, and she had a booming voice to match, a voice she exercised with the looseness of one who was possessed of few boundaries. "The only way I can get the work done is to set up office space. Not going to happen in a camper, that's for sure. And Yoder, I promise, I *guarantee* you, that I'll get you noticed, get the bucks rolling in. As your agent, I'll negotiate for higher prices, and as your advertiser and website administrator I'll handle it *all*. My sweetie here explained your dilemma in detail. And it's so typical of artist types. You just need to be left alone to do the art. You deserve to be known, and I'm making your fame my mission in life, along with loving up this guy," nudging Gary, who blushed again, with her elbow. "Oh! Where's my camera? Look on the front passenger seat, honey, and grab it for me." But she strode her long legs past Gary, arms flailing a pricey digital camera out of her vehicle and commenced striding, bounding all over the property snapping pictures of individual wind chimes, studying them, making a show of her professional eye. It wore Yoder out already, her energy, but, he told himself, she obviously was a worker bee, and it was, after all, for him.

"What happened to the cleanup job?"

"Aw, man, it was bullshit—walking up and down the beach scooping up tar balls, wearing these dinky, cheap-ass rubber gloves and neon vests. All Misty had to do was hand out water all the livelong day; said she was definitely overqualified for that."

"Can't disagree."

"But after I got hit with that fog a few times, I was thinking I had enough."

"Fog?"

"Yeah, man, that shit they been spraying all out over the water from planes. To bust up the oil."

"Dispersant? I saw something about that on the news, I think. Breaks up the oil and sinks it to the bottom of the gulf." Yoder tapped out a cigarette and lit it. "You say you got hit with it?"

"Lots of folks got hit with it—anybody on the beach—

'cause the damn planes would be maybe a hundred, two hundred yards out, and that gulf wind blowed it all up on the beach, in the air, smelling like a bitch, burning our eyes and all. Nasty stuff. It ate clean through them cheap-ass gloves they gave us. And them stupid lawn-mowin' masks ain't no kinda protection."

"Damn, Gary, that can't be good. It's bound to have had some kinds of physical effects on you. Did you get nauseous or light-headed?"

"Not really. It was just a nasty stink, mostly—my eyes got okay. It's just those damn ate-up gloves, man. That's some toxic shit. Poison."

Gary's utter lack of concern beyond the stupid gloves frustrated Yoder to no end. Gary had taken the same blasé attitude when Yoder had questioned him about Agent Orange, years earlier. *It wasn't no big deal*, Gary had said, *they used it all the time.*

"It *was* a big deal," Yoder said now, under his breath.

That afternoon, while Misty flitted about the place clicking chime images and Gary lazed on the hanging bed in one of the screened-in porches on the outbuilding, Yoder drove into Foley, to the public library, and began sifting through the reference section.

The septic system was to be installed on October 1, but the existing tank and lines had to be yanked before that. Due to scheduling there would be lag time, so they would have to make do with a porta-potty in between. Ironically, the Elite Septic System folks scheduled the euthanasia of the tank for September 19, the very same date that the Deepwater Horizon well was declared "effectively dead" by the national incident commander, some admiral or other. And it was on that exact date that Yoder began to move from suspicion to decision about one Misty Smith.

She had, indeed, created a website, an attractive one, featuring pictures of the wind chimes and some of the paintings on plywood, inflating prices, "just to see if they'll bite," she said. And even though Yoder couldn't argue with that, he was incrementally taking more and more offense to her intrusive, bossy ways. "You need to at least post something personal on your page," was one of the many *you-need-to* remarks he got from her.

"That's *your* job, isn't it? You're the administrator."

"Yes, but if you personalize it more, cultivate some fans, we'll add a Facebook page. The Facebook page is really where you'll find your numbers."

"Fans? Facebook? What the hell? Sounds like you want me to be somebody that doesn't even resemble me. Back off."

"Sure, I'm a pit bull," she allowed, "but you need a pit bull, somebody who will lock their jaws down hard for you—it's for *you*, after all!"

And Yoder would let it be. Gary seemed happy enough, though over the weeks his demeanor gradually became tinged with apathy. "She ain't so easy to live with," he conceded. "Kinda high strung, you know. But she's driven. *Them* kinds of folks—folks that's driven—tend to be high strung is what I think."

"So is it worth it, the sex?"

Gary smirked. "Always, man."

In the meantime, Yoder's library research into the benzene component of oil, and into the Corexit 9500 and Corexit 9527 used in the cleanup, was causing him to filter government conspiracies through his brain. The toxic brew of Corexit was banned in the United Kingdom, he discovered, and health professionals in general were definitely not fans. Why would the US be willing to put such a chemical into the already-poisonous soup that was the Gulf of Mexico? Did President Obama give the okay? If not, then who? Was it not enough to sacrifice the marine flora and fauna on the altar of tourism? Shouldn't someone calculate how many human lives were worth the salvaging of the sugar-white sands? It gave him a headache, the mulling of it.

Then, on the day of the septic tank killing, Misty rolled out some cockamamie idea about making Turkey Branch an incorporated entity, a move that would require a shared bank account, for business purposes, of course. "I can make this work," she insisted. "I've done it time after time!"

"Like when? Like where?" Yoder pressed.

"What the hell?" she shrieked. "Are you questioning my legitimacy? Do you hear him, Gary? Nobody appreciates a goddamn thing I'm doing around here! You two are a couple of witless idiots—you wouldn't even have a website if it wasn't for me!" And she strode off into the afternoon. By now both men knew that the snit would last for a few hours, possibly a day, with plenty of passive-aggressive behavior to dish out until said snit subsided.

But this day, Yoder pushed back: "Exactly what do you actually *know* about this chick?"

"Man, I know she's a great piece of ass. Which, I gotta tell you, I'm not looking to miss out on no nookie. What's *with* you?"

"I'm not looking to have her putting her paws all over my money, that's what."

"She ain't no thief. Come on, this is the first pussy I've had in years."

"Jesus."

"We'll work it out, man," Gary said. "I'll talk to her."

But for someone who was living it up with a great piece of tail, Yoder thought his friend didn't have much fight in him. No, not much fight at all.

It made him wonder: Why had Misty insisted on meeting up with Gary over in Blountstown? Why had she pushed so hard for him to sign on for cleanup? What the hell was her angle?

October blew in and so did a flatbed truck carrying the brand-new, sure enough state-of-the-art septic system that turd wrestler Ronny was so excited to sell him. Forget a rusting metal tank; this concrete one would last at least forty years, probably much longer, long past Yoder's life span.

Yoder set a folding lawn chair out near the work site, brought along a cooler of beer, plenty of smokes, and settled in. He was loath to allow any repairman of any stripe—electrical, carpentry, refrigerator, whatever—to work without being under his supervisory gaze; he trusted no one to do the job "right."

He hollered at Gary, laid out on the hanging bed, to come out and join him.

"Naw, man," came a faint response.

"Why the hell not? Nookie time?" he joked, expecting a laugh he didn't get.

"No, Yodie—I'm lying down."

"What's the matter?"

"Nothing, man. Just feeling a little tired, like I'm running out of gas, that's all."

Misty joined him, though. She dragged an outdoor lounge chair up to his, and he offered her a beer. She declined, as she usually did. She rarely drank and never smoked and seemed to like the high moral ground it gave her, though she was never overt or verbal in her self-righteousness. *Hell,* Yoder thought, *she was a goddamn braless, LSD-taking, marijuana-smoking hippie back in the seventies, when she first fucked Gary.*

She didn't waste a second. "I wish you wouldn't be so stubborn about forming a real business. You need to look into it. Do some," she enunciated, "*research.*"

"Not real thrilled with anybody who uses the words *you need* with me. *You* need to cut that shit out."

"Well, I know what I know. And I know you *love* some *research.*"

"Just like Gary," he said automatically, "a goddamn know-it-all," certain she had just smugly tossed him some bait. He was baffled, but knew enough that he refused to take the minnow.

She pounced. "I have a limit, you know. I'll only go so far for people who have no appreciation for me."

"Does it count that you're living at my place?"

"Fuck you!" she cried out, catching the attention of the septic crew. "Tell you what. You like to do stupid fucking research. The old-school kind of research. So why don't you research *this,* for your friend, who's not doing so great. Yeah, research this: *black, tarry stool.* Goddamn research *that!*" She executed her dramatic stride to her camper truck and gravel-slung her way down the driveway.

Yoder took a sip of beer, narrowed his eyes, wondering how she knew so much about his doings, making leapfrogging connections in his head, noting *dark* and *tarry.* "Hey, Ronny! You say that concrete tank's going to outlast *me?*"

"Damn right."

"It'll handle the waste?"

"Sure thing. 'Course, you got to treat it right. But you'd be surprised what folks put in these things that they ain't supposed to. Hell, tampons, paper towels, dead goldfish, even rodents."

"But it eventually breaks down, huh?"

"Long as it don't get too cluttered. I mean, the solids is gonna go to the bottom, the scum to the top, the liquid to the field lines. It all breaks down if it don't get backed up."

"You're a damn septic savant, Ronny. Not going to argue with that."

Yoder watched in fascination over Gary's shoulder as his computer-savvy buddy mouse-clicked through a series of websites, a virtual wizard at private investigation. Talk about a savant. He was a little surprised that Gary put up no resistance when Yoder, having abandoned his monitoring of the septic installation, shook him out of the hanging bed, demanding, "Get on that damn computer right now, asshole, and show me how to find out about this bitch you've hauled into our lives."

What they found, pretty quickly, was that there was no residence in Portland, ever, as far as they could tell. There *was* a series of marriages, even one to a plastic surgeon, but in Boulder, Colorado, not California. There were hefty divorce settlements, some unimaginative aliases, a few restraining orders against her, a couple of arrests, one for theft of property and another for harassment described as *hacking into a cell phone*. She moved often, every year or two at least. Employment records were nonexistent.

"Phone hacking, huh?"

"Yeah, you can track a person's whole life, where they are, what they're saying even, just by hacking in their phone. Misty told me she does it all the time."

"Well, that explains *that*."

"What?"

"Never mind, Gary."

"Okay," he sighed. "Never-minding."

The reality of the whole sorry business settled in on Yoder. "Holy crap, she's a bullshit artist," he said, "only without much artfulness to speak of. She played you, big-time. Sorry, Gary."

"Hell, I figured it was too good to last." Gary was pale, haggard, and Yoder only now realized just how hollowed-out he was, how that succubus of a criminal bitch had sucked the endangered life right out of him.

"What I don't understand is why you didn't check her out, research her, before you let her come here. I mean, you obviously know how."

Gary sighed, picked up a glass of whiskey. "Age-old story, ain't it?"

"I guess so."

"Well, I had me some pussy for a little while."

"Yes, you did."

"I reckon we're gonna have a knock-down drag-out when she gets back." Gary looked down at his hands. "I ain't got much use for that. Outta gas. Damnedest thing."

Yoder studied his friend's profile, the slump of his shoulders, the drop of his chin, his obvious fragility. "Don't worry, buddy. Don't you worry. You go lie down. I'll take care of it."

"I know. Thanks."

Gary slept fitfully that night, images of billowing clouds of smoke in thick jungles, huts ablaze, the screams of women as the planes came in low, misting the vegetation, aiming to strip away Charlie's cover. He half woke a few times, and reached to see if she was there, but he was alone with these fever dreams racing, like the spirits of dolphins chasing across the waves.

He caught a sleep-soaked glimpse of the moon, hanging

like the blade of a scythe in the clouds. It reminded him of the Vincent Price movie *The Pit and the Pendulum*, of the last, chilling scene, the torture dungeon being locked, the door shut forever on the evil Elizabeth, trapped, all alone yet still alive, in an "iron maiden." Then the dark closed over him, pushing through his consciousness, force-flashing images of dead baby dolphins washing up on the black-blotted sands of the gulf, seagulls stained slick with poison, and watercolors of pastel children picking at the tar balls between their toes. And he wondered, in his stormy dreams, if the coral really could die.

BUBBA AND ROMY'S PLATONIC BENDER

BY KIRK CURNUTT

Pike County

Romy's elbow was in Bubba's rhomboid when she said the name: Otis Owen. *Dr.* Otis Owen, she actually said, no *s* on the end. She started to add that even though she'd banged Dr. O when he taught her basic micro-computing her one semester of college, they were only friends now—no sex, no kissing, all touches strictly business. Before Romy could say that, though, Bubba, bare-bellied on her massage table, looked up with a hurt face.

"Otis Owen? You hang with that creep?"

"Dr. O comes here to work out the same kinks you do." She pushed Bubba's head into the table's fleece-lined face cradle. "I feel sorry for him. I'm the age he was when he'd fuck me in his office ten minutes before class. He was a god to me then, but not anymore—he's putty. I've never known a guy to go so squishy."

"What you do for him out of pity you won't do for me out of friendship?"

"I give you both what you want. Rejuvenation through humiliation."

Her elbow descended into Bubba's latissimus dorsi, grinding until his pancreas threatened to burst. He tried to ignore the discomfort, but her turquoise-painted toes entered his peripheral vision, along with the familiar smell of verbena and lavender, Romy's favorite lotion, and Bubba knew his aches and pangs were inescapable.

"Listen, I know things about Otis Owen. It's intel you should have, but intel's not free. Humor me, and afterward I'll not only pay your rip-off $85-per-hour rate, but I'll take you out for drinks. What you should know about Otis goes down better with tequila."

"No more humoring, Bubs. You're just hurting yourself, and I've got a license to lose if anybody ever peeked in my window."

She started to step back, but the only reliable man she'd ever known clutched her wrist. Lifting his torso, Bubba stared into her eyes, firm in need but weak with want.

"I had a manicure today," she pleaded. "You'll ruin it."

"We've been friends twenty-five years, Romy. You've always needed me as a big brother, maybe a dad. I care for you enough that unlike Dr. O I've never taken advantage of that. Never even tried. That's how much I respect our friendship. Otis Owen's pulled some snaky shit; I'm not protecting you if I don't tell you. But I need you first." Bubba released her arm. "I'll rest better too," he added, "if you lose those cutoffs."

Romy grunted at the obligation as Bubba recradled his face. He didn't want to watch her wriggle down her shorts, didn't want to know what she wore under them, two more tokens of respect for their friendship. He just liked the warmth of her—that part of Romy Bubba knew he was too good of a friend to ever get to experience—as she straddled his tailbone, her butt atop his. As her weight settled on his glutes she sank her nails into his skin, and he tensed in expectation. Then Romy raked her fingers along his spine in a long, euphoric scratch.

"Deeper," Bubba told her.

"The oil's getting scooped under my nails. Like ice cream. The skin's too slick to break."

"You've managed every time."

The second scrape was shorter but more intense. Bubba whinnied softly. Romy reached back and swatted a flank.

"Don't buck me, Seabiscuit. You do and no oats for you in the stable."

On the fourth try she drew blood. On the fifth Bubba gripped the table legs and chewed his lips. Romy clawed until her friend lost count of how many times she stopped to crack her knuckles and stretch her fingers. Perspiring, Bubba felt furrowed, carved, whittled.

"I'm all nubs." Romy lasted as long as she usually did, twenty minutes. "You're done too. Any more and you'll scar."

"How's it look?"

"Like you've been crosshatched."

"Then you're right. I'm done."

He jounced hard enough to pop Romy off his sacrum. She landed on one foot and had to slide the other across Bubba's greased thighs, holding his towel in place, he knew, so she didn't have to see his hairy rump. She told him to get dressed while she washed him out from under her manicure, then left. Bubba rolled off the table, dropping the towel, half hoping she'd walk in on him, fully knowing she wouldn't. He looked around the studio, spotting what he was after on the sideboard, tucked among flickering candles: a little Ganesha statue, new to the room since his last visit. Sure enough, when Bubba shook the porcelain figure, something inside rattled. He pried out the statue's rubber stopper and tipped its contents into his palm. "Got it," he said aloud, sliding an object into a front pocket of the jeans he pulled from the floor. He was adjusting the pen clipped to his shirt placket when Romy reappeared. Her blond shag was fashionably mussed and she wore a red shift with suede boots. She looked funky, like when she'd been jailbait.

"Sure," Bubba chuckled, "let's play dress-up, like tonight's a night at the opera." Blood driblets skied down his lumbar region. One rode over his coccyx and cascaded into his ass crack. "Because this fuckery Otis's pulled is straight-up operatic . . ."

They drove from the bohemian district where Bubba had bartended for thirty-three years to a lounge in Montgomery's black half. Exactly where black Montgomery began nobody could really say; it tended to start wherever white people started feeling uncomfortable. But Bubba liked black joints. He could name all the legendary ones from Montgomery's past: Club 400, the Ty-Juanna on Highland Avenue, Laicos. In a booth at G's he ordered four Agave Locos and shot two before an unamused Romy reminded him he still had to drive.

"And still a story to tell," Bubba noted. "Two things about Otis Owen: he's a bad drunk and a worse gambler. In two years he's lost $80,000 to Biloxi casinos, every cent he ever saved."

"He still has my $85-an-hour," shrugged Romy.

"I didn't say he's broke. I said he's blown his savings. To feed his beast he's had to cook up a profitable scam . . ."

Romy hiked her brows. "I gotta beg for deets?"

"I'll detail it—*after* you shoot that Loco. That's how this story unfolds. We come to a plot twist, you gotta drink to learn the next chapter."

Romy reluctantly drained a tequila and chewed the lime. Before she stopped puckering, Bubba flagged down a hostess and ordered another round—though not straight Agave Loco this time. This time the hostess brought three firecrackers: tequila with Goldschläger and Rumple Minze.

"Why you trying to get me drunk, Bubs?"

"Because it's the only way you'll believe this story."

He set his third empty down. The shot glasses on the tablecloth began resembling chess pieces.

"Bitcoins," he said.

"What's that?"

"Cryptocurrency, the fool's gold of the Internet. Other types exist—Monero, Ether, Ripple. Computer dorks pay real dollars in online exchanges for this 'money.' It's legal tender on the Darknet because transactions are untraceable. The problem is cryptocurrencies are easy to steal. Cryptopickpocketing's a billion-dollar industry."

"You're telling me Dr. O's an Internet safecracker?"

"Even Luddites like us can learn to five-finger Bitcoins. Websites galore teach how to hack into the virtual wallets where investors store this funny money, how to phish for logins to trading accounts."

"I've heard of phishing," Romy admitted. "But I thought only developed nations like Nigeria did it, not third world countries like Alabama."

Bubba grinned before pointing at her remaining shots. "You're behind three to one."

Romy knocked back her second Agave. "You drink too much, Bubs."

He ignored her. "Dr. O didn't plan on hacking on his lonesome. He aimed to start a big-time operation, maybe forty hackers mining cryptocurrency side by side. He couldn't post a *Help Wanted* ad for entry-level cryptocrooks, though. He needed a Fagin with a labor pool of Artful Dodgers—and that, my friend, is how Dr. Otis Owen ended up in business with Iv'ry Cole."

Romy flinched.

"So Otis's mentioned Iv'ry Cole to you," Bubba realized. "I wish he hadn't."

"His last appointment, he got a call. Clients usually ignore their phones, but Dr. O said he had to take it. He downplayed the call, claiming he was helping a former student—Iv'ry was all he said, no Cole—set up a computer network. But the conversation upset him. The rest of his hour he was twitchy."

"Former student? Maybe Dr. O taught Iv'ry Cole basic microcomputing like he taught you. Probably didn't fuck Iv'ry like he fucked you, however."

"Jealousy doesn't suit you, Bubs."

"Nothing does anymore, honestly. But about Iv'ry: he runs black Montgomery. Loansharking, coke, punani. All are big moneymakers, but nothing close to Darknet profits. Iv'ry's wanted into cyber-scamming for a while, but he lacked technical know-how until Otis the computer wiz came calling . . . You buy this story so far, Romy?"

She shrugged. "I buy that Iv'ry Cole's real, but only because I heard the name from Dr. O, not from you. Your motives remain suspect. Part of me thinks you're slandering Otis to make yourself look good."

Bubba raised his final firecracker in a mock toast. "I'm just the storyteller," he assured her, downing the shot. "Now finish yours so we can roll."

"Why? I like it here."

"Because Club G's is Iv'ry Cole's front. He owns this place like he owns Dr. O's ass. The first time Iv'ry heard of Bitcoins was in this room. Dr. O pitched his scheme two tables from where we sit. For all we know, Iv'ry and Otis are here now, watching our every move."

They drove to Highway 231, where Bubba hit a RaceWay for

vodka and OJ. He mixed screwdrivers in a jug and traded sips with Romy while an Emmylou Harris CD played. Three songs in Bubba realized he was lit. Five songs in Romy fell asleep, temple to the window. The farther south they drove and the drunker Bubba grew, the less he watched his rearview for headlights. Occasionally he plucked the pen off his shirt and pressed it against the dashboard speaker. Mostly his attention lingered over the landmarks along the two-lane blacktop. Highway 231 was littered with detritus from every Southern motel chain, service station, and diner to ever go bust. Bubba passed a collapsed Ponderosa, a demolished Gibson's Gas, skeletal remains of fruit and firecracker stands whose weather-warped planks looked like rib cages from rotted carcasses.

"Where are we?" Romy asked when he woke her. Bubba's truck idled in a cul-de-sac of sparkling new McMansions.

"In Troy."

"What the fuck for? I'm an hour from home now!"

Bubba circled the cul-de-sac, popping his high beams to spotlight each yard's freshly laid sod. In every verdant ocean bobbed the same customized landscaper flag. *Meisel's Lawn Care*, the flags read. *Tim "Tiny" Meisel, Proprietor. Let Us Do Your Dirty Work*.

"You gotta be blotto." Romy held the jug to the moonlight. According to the translucence, the vodka was three-quarters gone. "We get pulled over, you'll blow a 0.15. That's mandatory jail."

"I'm already doing hard time."

He took them to a bar called the Double Branch Lounge. Its wood exterior and checkered awning made it look more country-western than it was. Once upon a time Hank Williams commanded its stage, but nowadays the DB was a Top 40 dive for students at a nearby university. In the lot the wobbly bartender searched for his sea legs before retrieving a throw pillow and belt from his truck bed.

"Thirty-three years hoisting kegs . . ." Bubba stuffed the cushion into his back waistband. "Insurance covers steroid injections in my sacroiliac joints, only I don't have insurance. I treat sciatica with a goddamn pillow."

He made Romy embrace him from behind and guided her hands tightening the belt under his shirt around the cushion. Then, as onlookers gawked, he wrapped her arms across his chest, hoarding the rub of her body.

"That part about never taking advantage," Romy whispered. "You won't forget it, however shitfaced you get? I'm an hour from home without my own ride."

"Naw. This bender's entirely platonic."

Inside the Double Branch, Bubba ordered tomahawks—amaretto with cinnamon schnapps.

"Where were we? Oh yeah . . . so Iv'ry installed Otis in a warehouse to train two dozen budding hackers, mostly high school dropouts. In time the operation loots maybe $30,000, but that's nothing compared to the millions newspapers tell Iv'ry cryptokleptos are heisting. Meanwhile, Otis's reading about Bitcoin thieves pulling ten-year sentences. Otis starts stressing. Ulcers, insomnia. For all I know his sacroiliac joints lock up. Eventually he begs Iv'ry to pull the plug, but Iv'ry's got an investment to recoup. *You want out,* Iv'ry tells Otis, *pay me $100,000.* Dr. O's already blown $80k gambling. No way he—what's wrong?"

Romy was slumped in her chair, sullenly watching a band soundcheck. "If you don't get to the point, when the music starts I'll be dancing, not listening."

"This part's the best. The love story starts now . . . Has Otis talked lately about a woman?"

"He's mentioned in passing he's seeing someone. Her name's weird: Marcella."

"That's her—Marcella Meisel."

Romy turned toward Bubba. "Meisel? That's the name on those landscaper flags . . ."

"So you *are* paying attention!" He scooted a tomahawk at her. They had to sip these shots because their stomachs felt oily. The vague nausea didn't keep Bubba from ordering kamikazes—vodka with triple sec and lime juice.

"The Double Branch is Otis and Marcella's personal love shack. She first landed on him like a heat-seeking missile up in Montgomery, but she's from Troy, so once Otis's smitten he's burning rubber to Pike County every night. They party hard—Marcella's got a nose for coke. They fuck hard too. Otis hasn't made love in a long time. He's forgotten how wonderful women's bodies are, forgotten the pleasures of hands and holes, napes and crannies . . ."

"You're scaring the sorority girls."

"Dr. O's in love, but he's still Iv'ry Cole's bitch. Marcella can tell he's plagued. Takes her some time to coax the sad shebang from him. Then, in bed, right after a hot rut, she proposes a solution. Her ex-husband, this landscaper Tiny Meisel, inherited a coin collection worth $200k. Marcella won half in their divorce, but Tiny staged a bogus theft to avoid paying. He's buried the coins somewhere on his family's two-hundred-acre cotton farm. Marcella's bought a souped-up metal detector to find them. The thing's built like a rocket launcher, too heavy for her to lug. But if Otis can locate the coins, Marcella's willing to split the sale and buy his freedom from Iv'ry."

"So now we've gone from Bitcoins to *real* coins?"

"Not just any coins. We're talking *Confederate* half-dollars and nickels."

"I feel like I read this in a book once."

"For ten straight nights Otis humps this contraption over two hundred cotton acres. Guess what happens next."

"Dr. O is abducted by aliens."

Bubba laughed and celebrated by making Romy join him in shooting a kamikaze.

"What happens is the gizmo pings. Otis uncovers genuine Johnny Reb silver and copper. He can taste his freedom. He rushes to tell Marcella, only something awful's happened to her—"

"*She's* been abducted by aliens," suggested Romy.

"This gets serious now. Otis finds Marcella beaten raw. Tiny Meisel's been trailing his ex-wife, peeping through her blinds when she and Otis knock boots. He knows they're stealing his coins, so he fractures Marcella's jaw and blacks both eyes. Otis wants to go to the police, but Marcella refuses. Now that Otis found the coins, she's got a better idea."

"Take the money and run. Start a new life under a new name."

"Nope . . . Marcella wants Otis *to kill* her ex."

Romy pressed at her stomach. "I don't feel good. I need to eat."

Bubba agreed. It was time to move on anyway. He ordered his tab, but when the barkeep broke his hundred-dollar bill she had to make change with four rolls of quarters. The Double Branch was fresh out of dead presidents. *There are no accidents,* Bubba decided. *Only opportunities.* He squeezed a roll in each fist; the quarters felt like brass knuckles.

In the truck Romy asked if Bubba seriously expected her to believe that a prof she once banged would agree to kill somebody. "I have standards," she insisted.

"And I don't meet them," Bubba replied. "But Otis *did*

agree to shoot Tiny dead in his sleep. Marcella gave him a gun and a key to Tiny's house."

It'd happened less than twenty-four hours earlier, Bubba insisted. Otis emptied seventeen rounds from a 9mm Smith & Wesson M&P into Tiny's bedroom until something thumped to the floor.

"Guess what Otis discovered when he flipped on the light?"

Romy played along, indifferently. "Tiny Meisel's body."

"Nope . . . He discovered Iv'ry Cole's body."

From the DB they retraced seventeen miles on 231 to a greasy spoon called the BBQ House. Bubba's vision was fuzzy, but the shack couldn't be missed. Its driveway was marked with a pink neon pig in sunglasses kicking out a can-can leg over two flaming slices of Texas toast. "Nice tits," Romy said, observing the blinking ∞ on the sow's chest. Beside the pig sat a portable billboard with plastic letters: *In All Things Give God Your Gratitude*.

"When Southerners finally admit the contradictions splitting us down the middle," slurred Bubba, parking, "we won't call our impulses hell and heaven, or the agony and the ecstasy even. We'll call them *pork and pray*."

"You're gonna tell me Tiny Meisel loves this place," Romy predicted.

"Indeed. Tiny can eat the motherfucking love out of some pork."

Bubba ambled to the highway's edge. There was no oncoming traffic, but the rolls of quarters in his pocket weighed him down anyway. "Bitcoin, Confederate coin," he mumbled. "Always the coin of somebody's realm. I want free of money and pain." He hurled the quarters into the woods across the blacktop.

Inside he bought Romy a pulled pork platter and motioned her to a door that looked like a fire exit. "Not another one," she groaned as she crossed the threshold into a secluded bar. Bubba bought two final shots, straight Jack Daniel's.

"One drawback to this place," he said when they found a table, "the can's out back. Just in case you get sick."

"Can I get a side order of silence, please? I'm starving, but I'm fed up with your tall tale."

"It's almost done . . . Here's the deal: Otis didn't kill Iv'ry. Grazed his temple, that's all. The affair with Marcella was a setup to rob Iv'ry. Landscaping is Tiny Meisel's front. He really deals coke for the Sinaloa cartel. The Sinaloa boys want Iv'ry out of business so they can take over the Montgomery trade. Tiny offs Iv'ry, he gets promoted out of Troy to run it. So Marcella seduced out of Otis the info Tiny needed about Iv'ry's operation, and while Dr. O hunted buried Confederate treasure the Meisels were in Montgomery casing it. They stole Iv'ry's blow and kidnapped him to that house, duping Otis into taking him out. The coin collection never existed, of course. During the Civil War the Confederacy minted exactly four silver half-dollars and twelve copper nickels total. Dr. O should've known that . . ."

"I'm not listening," Romy said, tearing into her pulled pork.

"Iv'ry's alive, but he's out $250k in product. All he knows is his coke's buried somewhere outside Troy until the Meisels can transport it out of Alabama. Iv'ry overheard Tiny and Marcella talking when they shanghaied him. The location of the coke's marked with a GPS tracker. Won't be easy for Iv'ry to get to that tracker. Tiny hides it in the knee socket of the prosthetic leg he's worn since an IED blasted his off during the Iraq War."

Romy looked up from her plate of food. "A fake leg? That's it. Take me home. I can't take another word. Get a dog if you need someone to talk to."

Bubba's sciatica was flaring. His discs and joints felt like tectonic plates firing off seismic jolts. "I know you wonder why I need you to scratch me till I bleed, Romy. Maybe you think I need pain so I don't go numb from booze. But it's not about feeling. Every time you scratch me I hope those scratches scar, that they don't fade, even though they always do. You're the closest my life's had to a constant. We're lucky we've had twenty-five years, but this friendship'll get fucked up in the end. Everything does. I'd just like a permanent mark of what you've meant to me, something I can carry, after one of us inevitably fails the other."

He shot both Jack Daniel's and rose.

"I'm gonna take a leak, then drive you home." He leaned over and stroked Romy's cheek. "As for the story, I don't believe half of it myself."

Outside, crossing ten feet of asphalt to the bathrooms, Bubba adjusted the pillow still belted to his back. He entered a stall without latching the door and stopped two careful feet short of the toilet to clear his head. He was ready when someone followed. An arm wound around his neck. He felt a knife tear into the pillow, but it couldn't penetrate the foam to more than nick his spine. He bent forward then launched backward, slamming his assailant into the stall pilaster, just like he'd imagined doing all night. He twisted and grabbed the man's knife hand. His other arm went across the attacker's throat, pressing his nape into the steel partition. He bent his knees until the man's neck rode the pilaster to the metal strike that stopped the stall door from swinging outward. Rising and sinking on the balls of his feet, Bubba sawed the base of the man's skull against the sharp protrusion. The skin ripped and blood splashed to the tile. The man screamed but was too stunned to fight. One punch and Bubba knocked him out.

"Get him out of here."

Tiny Meisel, all bald head and leather, stood in the doorway. Two Mexicans in overalls dragged Iv'ry Cole to an idling Audi A7.

When Bubba stepped outside Tiny slapped him to the ground.

"You told that bitch about me and the Sinaloa boys!"

"I just told her a story . . . I had to tell her something to get her out to these bars!"

"You tell her she's fine. You tell her you got money enough to treat her right. You tell her you gonna fuck her like no other man ever done. You *don't* tell her Tiny Meisel's taking over Iv'ry Cole's territory!"

"I—I made the story so ridiculous that Romy doesn't believe any of it . . . I could never say that *ooh, baby* shit to her! She'd never talk to me again . . ."

"'*Ta repedo*," one of the Mexicans said. Tiny agreed.

"My friend believes you're drunk. Drunk as a fart, he actually just said. I believe that in your intoxicated state you told that woman about Otis to make your own sorry ass look good."

Bubba trembled. "I told you that if he hid that tracker anywhere it'd be at her studio. I did what you made me do. I brought Romy to their bars. I used her as bait to smoke out Otis and Iv'ry."

"Honestly, I never would'a thought Dr. Otis Owen had it in him to turn double agent. Like your woman said, he seems squishy as putty. So we thank you, bartender, for smoking them out for us."

Tiny yanked Bubba to his feet and motioned for the Mexicans to pop the Audi's trunk. Two bodies lay inside, their gashed throats leaking red smiles.

"This one," Tiny said, pointing at Otis Owen, "however Iv'ry convinced him to steal back that cocaine and bury it wherever he did—maybe money, maybe a threat—Otis should'a known better. But look at it this way, Bubba: I done you a favor. You don't have to compete with Otis anymore for that woman's attention."

"You never said," Bubba gasped, "you never said . . ."

"Now this one," Tiny pointed at the body of Marcella Meisel, "I didn't mind her screwing Otis. I just wished she hadn't enjoyed it so much."

Bubba's legs went weak.

"You know what part of your story I liked best, bartender? That last bit, about the fake leg. That was over the top! Farfetched! Well, guess what?" Tiny whipped out a Glock with a silencer and fired three bullets into Iv'ry Cole's kneecap. "Now that part of the story's true! This boy gonna need a new leg!"

The bullets brought Iv'ry roaring back to consciousness. He bolted upright and grabbed his spurting leg. What was left of his knee looked like spaghetti. As Iv'ry opened his mouth to scream Tiny shot him between the eyes. His dreadlocks fluttered as the bullet blew out the back of his head.

"Now give me that goddamn tracker," Tiny said.

Bubba dug his hands into his empty pockets. Sobriety came over him like an instant eclipse. He remembered the rolls of quarters he'd heaved into the woods.

"I—I didn't find it . . . I looked at Romy's place, but the tracker wasn't there."

"What?" Tiny hurled Bubba against the Audi and pressed

the silencer to his temple. "We heard you say, *Got it!*" He yanked the pen from Bubba's placket. Hidden inside was a microphone and transmitter. "We heard every word you said tonight! We even heard you hold the bug up to your speaker, smart ass, trying to blast us out of our socks! Don't lie: at the woman's studio you said, *Got it!*"

"I said it, but you misheard . . . you misunderstood . . . Romy said she'd only come out for drinks if I didn't hit on her, if I kept things platonic, and I said, *Got it* . . ."

The Mexicans began trading agitated whispers.

Tiny staggered back and leaned against a hickory tree. "You just let me kill the only ones who know where that cocaine's buried . . ." He stiffened suddenly and aimed the Glock at Bubba, ordering him facedown.

"Do it," the bartender begged. "Do me that favor."

Tiny Meisel did something worse than shoot Bubba. With a knife he cut away the pillow strapped to his back. Then Tiny jumped up and down on Bubba's lumbar region, a half dozen times.

"Three hours," Tiny said as the bartender curled in agony. "If that GPS tracker's not in my hand, three hours, you and I and probably these gentlemen, too, gonna sit that masseuse down, and she's gonna hear a true story. She's gonna hear why you *ain't* the best friend she's ever had, and why five dead bodies, not three, ended up in this trunk."

After the Mexicans heaped Iv'ry's body onto the other two and the Audi peeled away, Bubba limped like a hunchback across the highway, each step a detonation in his spine. At the woods' edge he lurched onto all fours and threw his hands into the brush where he thought the quarters should've landed. If he could find one roll, just one roll, the tracker couldn't be far.

The more frantically he searched, the more impossible finding the device seemed, until finally Bubba wasn't searching at all. He was hobbling as fast as he could with his sciatica blazing, telling himself he wouldn't stop until he reached an ocean, a different country, another world. Instead he quickly reached the woods' end, where he tripped over a tree root and tumbled down a small hill, rolling upright in a subdivision of new McMansions. It wasn't the same cul-de-sac he'd driven Romy through, but each yard was decorated with the same message: *Let Us Do Your Dirty Work.*

Romy was still at their table when a muddied Bubba lumbered into the BBQ House, one arm behind his back.

"I was starting to think you found another frien—"

"I need your help," he told her. "I lost something. Probably won't change the outcome even if we find it, but I'm apologizing in advance if we don't. I brought you flowers."

He handed her a bouquet of landscaper flags.

CUSTOM MEATS

BY WENDY REED

West Jefferson County

*Love bade me welcome . . . You must sit down, says Love, and
taste my meat: So I did sit and eat.* —George Herbert

Even over the deer's intestines, Jimbo could smell her:
green apple shampoo and Juicy Fruit. He felt himself
harden. All those careful habits formed over the years
like flossing every morning, keeping his knives on the magnet
when not in use, washing with bleach between each kill, and
doubling his condoms were suddenly in danger. Cassie DeBardelaiwin, he sensed, was that kind of girl.

Jimbo did, however, manage to decline her order. Some
things could not be compromised. It didn't matter if she
wanted the Christmas sausage for her family's millworkers or
the queen of England, Jimbo Sutt did not process any animal
that hadn't been immediately field dressed and properly iced.
No matter the season, Alabama heat advantages the maggots.
Besides, Jimbo rarely took wild hogs because pork could be
bought by the pound down at the Piggly Wiggly.

DeBardelaiwins weren't used to hearing no, but Jimbo
held firm.

"You see that sign out front? It says *Custom Meats*. Not
spoiled. Not cheap. *Custom*. I don't give customers anything I
wouldn't eat myself."

Satisfied he'd made himself clear, he went back to finish

the buck that had just been brought in. It was a beast of a specimen. Even with most of the blood drained out, it still felt warm to the touch. Large bucks required extra care around the neck, otherwise you could wind up having to quilt the hide together on the mount. Nothing ruined a trophy like patched trim. As a processor, he'd developed a reputation for the care he took, a trait seldom cultivated in an area now forced to survive through the short-sighted methods of strip-mining. Lately, though, Jimbo was achieving some renown for his white-tail testicle blend he sold in Mason jars that was said to be as potent as those little blue pills.

In the shop, Jimbo dressed and bled deer on a large slab of stainless steel surrounded by a drain his brother called The Moat and built right into the concrete floor. His new knife—the Jackal, according to the catalog from Zac Brown's metal shop—had cost a small fortune, and the verdict was still out whether it was worth it. Before long it would feel like an old friend, but now, as he wrapped his fingers around the carved handle, it felt stiff and more than a little strange. Having a girl standing around in the shop also felt strange, but oddly tolerable, as long as she didn't start up about the sausage again.

The scale read 212 pounds. This was what he called a jackpot buck because it would yield a twelve-point trophy plus a freezer full of quality venison. The girl gave no sign of leaving, so he steadied himself and tugged at the incision to widen it.

"You really set on giving out Christmas sausage?" he asked, tossing the question over his shoulder, wondering for the first time if she was jailbait.

She shrugged.

"Then I suggest Conecuh. It makes pretty good eating."

"That so?" Cassie said.

Jimbo was imagining what she wore under her skirt. It was made of denim—the same color as her eyes—and had a zipper down the front. He didn't respond to her question, if that's what it was, nor did he notice the way her lips curled or how she strutted right up to him until she stopped with her crotch at his face.

"So what do you eat," she asked, "besides meat?"

Jimbo pretended not to hear. He pretended to be engrossed in his work. He pretended not to wonder if her pubic hair also smelled like green apples. He pretended not to feel the jolt of electricity heating him up. Was she still trying to get him to take the hogs or was this something else? Was it some kind of game? Jimbo didn't know chess but he'd played poker. He lifted the buck's tail, revealing a thick stripe of white with a puckered hole of purplish skin in the center. He held the tail out of the way and suspended the Jackal's serrated blade just above the anus. He let the overhead light bounce off the metal and reflect onto Cassie's face. "It's made from old sawmill blades."

This was her chance to leave if she wanted to, before things got messy.

Cassie did not move.

Jimbo plunged the steel teeth about an inch deep and cut a circle around the anus. This was the point when most people left, or at least looked away. Cassie took a step back, but it was to get a better view. Jimbo pulled the rectum out a couple inches and closed it off with a rubber band. He reached into the belly—carefully, but firmly, so as not to puncture or damage anything—and pulled out the entrails with the intact rectum, like a magician with a scarf. Bowel leakage, like maggots, always ruins meat. With two fingers on either side of the blade, Jimbo reached inside, toward the deer's throat, and threaded the lungs out from between the ribs, reading the bones like braille as he went. Even a single bump could signal TB. And with one case already reported this season by Fish and Wildlife, you couldn't be too careful.

Cassie'd begun to breathe hard, but her color looked good. If she hadn't fainted yet, he guessed she wasn't going to.

"What's next?" she asked.

Jimbo stood up and a couple strands of blood or something stuck to his forearm. Color bloomed across her cheeks—not the blush of embarrassment but the flush that comes from standing close to a fire. In heels, she'd be taller than him.

"Ice. Go roll that cooler over here," he said. "It's full."

When she reached the Igloo, she hesitated and made sure he was watching, then she straddled the handle, slowly lifting it up until it disappeared beneath her skirt. Jimbo wasn't sure whether to keep watching. She locked eyes and stared squarely at him, like she was lining up invisible crosshairs. It was impossible, at that moment, to tell who had whom in their sights. That her panties dropped to the floor without being touched or tugged didn't strike Jimbo as anything other than good fortune.

"Maybe I need to cool off," she said, and tossed her panties into the ice chest.

Her grin beat all he'd ever seen. And he'd seen his share of women. Having to raise his brother took certain sacrifices but it hadn't turned him into a monk. Rather than wasting a whole evening on the rigamarole of dating, he preferred to buy off a menu, always glad they charged by the hour and not by the pound.

Cassie gave her hips a slow, final swivel, before she rolled the chest over to Jimbo. As she opened the lid, she bent over farther than Jimbo thought humanly possible and spread her legs. At that moment, it was Jimbo who was in danger of fainting. If Cassie'd asked him to reconsider making sausage for DeBardelaiwin Steel right then, he might have said yes.

The Jackal still lay beside the entrails. Not only did he neglect to put it up, he also didn't wash his hands before he handled the ice. Contamination was the last thing on his mind, fear having vanished from his regular radar. In one seemingly fluid motion, Jimbo crammed the cavity full of ice and was done. It was the fastest he'd ever packed a deer, and probably the only time in the history of West Jefferson County that lingerie and ice had been thusly juxtaposed.

Jimbo hadn't expected to see Cassie again. The DeBardelaiwins lived over the mountain. They did not associate with the likes of the Sutts. So when she kept coming back, he chalked it up to one of several flukes in a fluke-filled season: the albino doe with horns that Jimbo spotted on the way back from Medical West, where his brother Darrell took his regular treatments; the two-headed fawn found behind the sheriff's woodpile; and Darrell graduating to the group home.

Cassie came around for about a month and a half and then without a word stopped. Jimbo wondered what he'd done but he hadn't asked any questions while she was there, so he left it at that. He'd been half expecting not to see her again, every time she'd left, which he told himself was fine, for the best really, because Sutts didn't do commitment. He'd heard the tales of his grandfather and bore the scars from his own father. He knew most men didn't like playing house anyway. They just did it because.

The following autumn arrived like a bobcat in heat—hot and

bothered, foretelling storms that would level a high school and suck up the steeple from Mud Creek Baptist, spitting it out over at the Black Diamond, right on top of the tipple. Cassie, Jimbo'd heard, had gone off up north, where the De-Bardelaiwins were from. To discourage thinking about her, he kept a piece of bamboo in his pocket that he rammed under a fingernail when his thoughts got out of hand.

One evening, Darrell was in the shop listening to something he called music, while Jimbo sharpened his favorite blades. *Having Darrell move back in might offer more distraction.*

Even over the boom box, the long whine of a car horn out front was loud. It was Cassie. Her windows were down, and her eyes looked wild. A smear of blood on her cheek made visible by her dashboard light.

"I didn't see it. Suddenly it was just there, right in front of the car. And then it was staring right at me. It didn't move. Oh God, it was awful. Just awful." Her voice broke but she didn't slow down. "What was I supposed to do? I didn't know what to do. What else could I do? I put it in my trunk." She lowered her head but raised her eyes. "I couldn't think."

The trunk was up.

A doe. Probably a yearling. What a pity. It looked like it'd been healthy, but now it was mostly dead, its legs nothing but a tangled mess. Clearly, the doe was suffering.

Jimbo tried to feel sorry for it, but all he could think about was Cassie. It'd been how many months—six or seven? He'd lost count on purpose and still, his first reflex was to snatch her out of the car and bend her over the hood. He wanted to bury himself inside her so she could never leave again. He wanted to tell her everything he'd imagined doing to her during those long nights he spent waiting, wondering if he'd ever see her again.

But Darrell was there.

Probably best anyway.

"How long ago?" he asked, trying to sound matter-of-fact, trying to hide his real question: *Where were you when you hit it?*

Cassie belonged in a different world and could never stay in his. He knew it, but he didn't have to like it.

Jimbo looked from the doe to Darrell and mouthed, *Let's get it inside.* He grabbed the front legs, motioned for Darrell to get the back legs, and whispered, "On three." As they lifted, Jimbo called from behind the car, "Happens all the time."

Too wounded to struggle, the doe's eyes rolled back in fear. *How far did Cassie drive to bring me this deer? Was she already out this way? How long has she been back in Birmingham? Did she come to see me?* The doe felt more awkward than heavy, and though nothing about Cassie should've surprised him, Jimbo couldn't help being impressed that she'd wrangled the wounded doe into the trunk all by herself. Everything in Jimbo strained toward the driver's side of the car. What harm could one whiff do? But he pushed Darrell and the doe in the opposite direction. "We've got it from here," he said, adding, "It's on the house," so she wouldn't come inside and try to pay.

If he was lucky, Cassie would drive off, out of his life for good. But luck wasn't what he craved.

Too weak to put up much of a struggle, the doe merely twitched her ears when placed on the slab; Darrell, Jimbo noticed, had begun trembling.

"Why don't you go close the trunk?" Jimbo said. "Tell her she can leave."

Despite all Darrell's medical treatment, he was still at risk of going berserk if he got upset. Their father had called him an *idiot*. The doctors couldn't seem to decide what to call him and had created what Jimbo called the Darrell Alphabet inside a folder more than two inches thick, starting with autism and ending with a syndrome that sounded like zucchini. But Jimbo had always just thought of Darrell as different, as he always would.

It occurred to him that something about the doe was different too. When he sliced into the jugular, the fat layer felt thick. *She's pregnant.* He wondered where Cassie had touched the doe. Maybe it still smelled like her. *Does she still even use green apple shampoo?* As he leaned down to sniff, he heard a car door close. If Cassie came in now, Darrell would follow her in and see the doe's throat. He wouldn't understand why Jimbo had cut it. *Better take Darrell on back to the group home now. Let the doe bleed in the meantime.*

But Darrell was not outside, and Cassie's car was gone. *Damn electric cars.* Their silence gave Jimbo the creeps. Maybe Darrell went on into the house after Cassie left, but he checked and it was empty. Darrell wouldn't have gone with Cassie, would he? He steered clear of strangers. Even ones with long blond hair. Maybe she'd won him over with Juicy Fruit, the only gum Jimbo had been able to get Darrell to chew.

Jimbo walked back to the shop. Ordinarily, he hung yearlings so their narrow bellies stretched before dressing, but on the off chance that this one was pregnant, he decided not to move it from the slab. As soon as he inserted the knife, there was a tiny burst of fluid and then a hoof popped out. Another followed. Of all the deer he'd processed, not a single one had ever been pregnant. Maybe he'd cut her throat too quickly. *Too late now.* He sliced through the skin and, for the first time in all the years, felt like he was trespassing. Half of him was appalled at what he was doing, but the other half was too curious to stop.

Out came a fawn that looked coated with plastic, like

it'd been vacuum-packed for freshness. Two dark-pink balloon-looking things glistened with wetness. *The placentomes.* A hoof moved. It was alive.

Jimbo tried to think what to do next. He grabbed some shop towels, wet them, and began rubbing the fawn. How hard should he rub? He slid the fawn away from the doe and alternated between light and hard strokes. He'd had to pound hard on Darrell that time with the hot dog. When it finally popped out, it had been Jimbo who cried. Darrell had toddled off as if nothing had happened.

Jimbo tried not to think about those early days with Darrell.

"This is your brother—Darrell Sutt," his father had said, like Jimbo might not remember his own last name. It was the first time Jimbo had seen his father that year, and as usual, James Sutt Sr. was drunk. Soon as he started sobering up, he was gone again. Jimbo'd practically raised himself and now he was saddled with raising someone else too. He'd tried to find out who Darrell's mother was but hadn't gotten far. If nothing else, Darrell'd been a good excuse to quit school. Most things, he learned the hard way. But they'd survived and because the woods were so full, not once had they gone hungry. Or taken charity, because Jimbo discovered hunters would pay good money for him to process their kill—enough for Darrell to get treatment at the hospital and eventually be admitted into the special school.

Maybe the fawn would turn out normal. With its blunt little button nose, tiny white hooves that hadn't yet blacked, it looked so perfect. Tufts of hair and white spots scattered down the spine like pearls. It was startlingly beautiful and radiated a kind of luminescence that encircled the body like a halo. Could the fawn breathe? Did Jimbo need to peel the shiny stuff off?

Despite knowing just about everything there was to know about killing and processing deer, he knew nothing about their birthing. With Darrell and the Sutt track record, the last thing Jimbo needed was to become a father. Nothing about Darrell had ever been normal. He hadn't even come with a birthday. Jimbo'd made that up too.

Images flashed through his mind: Darrell screaming in that makeshift pen. Darrell covered in red bumps. Darrell slamming his head on the floor. Darrell turning blue. Darrell falling into the fire. Darrell's chest not moving for such a long time. But he was about to turn nineteen; they'd both survived.

Beginning with the nose, Jimbo worked at the spider weblike covering, and was making his way toward the tail when he sensed someone watching. He hadn't heard anyone drive up. *Damn electric cars.* In his peripheral vision stood a woman who looked like Cassie except she was too round.

"Darrell asked me to take him back, so I did. It was the least I could do." Her voice sounded flat and sleepy, but it was the most beautiful music in the world.

He couldn't take his eyes away from her swollen belly. It looked liked she'd swallowed a basketball. Cassie was staring at the fawn. "It was pregnant too?"

Pregnant.

"Here, let me help." She knelt down and took a towel. "Your brother is sweet. I've always heard he was crazy but he seems nothing but nice." She wiped at the fawn's eyes and nose.

Realizing she was pregnant had paused Jimbo's brain.

He couldn't think. There were things he needed to say, but breathing was about all he could manage. The noise inside his ears grew into a roar. Talking hadn't exactly been their thing, yet over the weeks they'd spent together, he'd confided a couple things about Darrell and their father. She hadn't said much about her own father but Jimbo gathered that Josiah DeBardelaiwin kept Cassie in a gilded cage.

Jimbo grabbed her by the wrist.

"Let me go," she said, pulling away and trying to stand, but he squeezed until she gave up. She dropped the towel.

"Is it mine?" He wasn't sure which answer he wanted—for it to be his or someone else's.

Instead of getting up, she lifted the fawn's head between her hands. "It's none of your business."

"You saying it ain't mine?" He suddenly knew which answer he wanted.

She blew into the fawn's nose. "I'm saying it's none of your business." She took a deep breath and blew again. The fawn's face twitched. "Did you see that? It moved. Now what do we do?"

"Then whose is it?" he said. "Tell me."

She slipped off her sweater and wrapped it around the fawn. "Is there milk in the mother?"

"Who else'd you fuck?" Jimbo spat, and palmed her belly like he might steal it, might take the ball and run down the court. "It's a girl, isn't it?"

Cassie sat back on her heels and pulled the fawn to her, as if that was her answer.

"I sensed it. Some things you just know in your bones."

"I didn't say it was a girl."

"You didn't have to. Your face said it."

"You had a 50/50 chance."

"I knew it, same as I know it's mine."

Cassie kept stroking the fawn. It blinked but didn't move. "Aren't they born walking?" she asked. "Maybe I should put it down."

He wanted to hear Cassie say it was his. Even if he had to make her, he wanted her to say it. It was beginning to dawn on him that their two worlds were no longer separate. *We have something in common, something that's ours.*

Cassie swallowed hard. "Here," she said, guiding his hand. "Feel that?"

How could he not? Her belly heaved beneath her shirt. He could see it and feel it. But he wanted to see more. He lifted her shirt and with his eyes traced the veins that spread beneath the translucence. A fragrance rose to his nose—not fruity, not apple—just clean. *Soap.* He expected to be sorry, to be angry that he hadn't used condoms with her. But the only thing he felt was aroused.

"Look. The fawn's trying to walk," Cassie said. "We've got to do something."

"When's it due?"

"Next week."

"What day? Darrell's birthday's the first."

"The second."

The fawn struggled to steady itself.

Her belly button stuck out like a turtle. Jimbo kissed it. "Why didn't you tell me?"

Her belly heaved again. "They're called Braxton Hicks contractions. They're not the real ones," she said, after slowly exhaling. "My father wouldn't let me."

Josiah DeBardelaiwin was a rich prick who thought he owned the entire state. He probably hated the idea that his blood had mixed with a Sutt.

"Say it. I want to hear it. Say it's mine."

"Look! It's up." The fawn was standing, each stick-thin leg quivering. As it wobbled, Cassie's smile spread like a brush fire. Jimbo could drown in that smile; he'd die happy. *That wild tongue. Those sharp teeth. Those pink lips.* He wanted to put his tongue between her lips so badly that he grabbed her and pressed his mouth on hers so hard that her teeth cut his lip. When he tasted blood, he thought his heart had exploded.

"I love you," he said. He opened his eyes.

She was still looking at the fawn.

"I'll take care of the baby, I promise. I'll be a good father. You'll be surprised. Are you listening?" He'd do anything for his baby. He reached out and pulled the fawn to them. It weighed nothing, felt like grabbing air.

"How do hunters shoot anything with such wondrous eyes?" she said.

It was true about the eyes. Jimbo had learned not to look into them.

"I hope our daughter has your eyes," he said, pressing lightly on the fawn's back until it folded onto Cassie's outstretched legs. It rested its nose on her belly. Jimbo stood and with a boot pushed the doe toward the drain. As he did, the incision tore, and he saw several ribs; one was covered with the telltale white bubbles of TB. If the doe was infected, so was her fawn.

So that Cassie could lean back, he rolled his work cart behind her and locked the wheels.

"Do you know how much I've thought about you? Do you have any idea? Don't sit there and pretend like you didn't think about me. You enjoyed it as much as I did."

He remembered those weeks like they were yesterday. He could picture her coming through the overhead door, half-dressed, and wanting to play, like a little kid. One time she was buck naked. Several times she wore layers and, using antlers like a pole, she'd remove each layer in a striptease. If he was too busy to play, she'd pull up a stool and watch, the sound and smell of her breath driving him so crazy that he could hardly stand it. Most of what they did was her idea. Instead of hide-and-seek, she insisted they play hide-and-hunt, using an unloaded gun and a bow with sponge-tipped arrows. "Even vegetarians have to eat what they kill," she'd said. Until Cassie, Jimbo had thought vegetarians, like zombies, were made up.

Cassie rubbed the fawn's neck and cradled it in her arms. She closed her eyes.

"Damnit, Cassie. Do you hear what I'm saying? Look at me, goddamnit. I'll marry you." There. He'd said it. The first Sutt in no telling how many generations.

"Are you nuts?" Cassie kept her eyes closed and lowered her voice to a half squeak, half whisper. "My father would disown me."

"He'll come around. You'll see. What does he know anyway? What did you tell him about us?"

"He thinks you raped me . . . said he would kill you. The sheriff talked him out of it."

"Talked him out of it? What'd Turner say?" For years Jimbo and Sheriff Turner'd had an unspoken agreement about jurisdiction. Fish and Wildlife were from Washington and didn't understand the way things worked around here.

Cassie opened her eyes and stared at her belly. "He said you'd been nothing but decent out here, quietly processing your deer and raising your brother alone. Said there wasn't anybody to take care of Darrell if something happened to you. I let him feel the baby kick. Did you know the sheriff and I are the same age?" With a thumb, she began tracing the shiny purple veins and closed her eyes again.

"Darrell felt the baby? Or do you mean Sheriff Turner?"

"Getting the car fixed is going to be expensive. Daddy's going to be pissed. He stays furious with me since I didn't get an abortion. He said, *Sired by a Sutt, there's no telling what you'll give birth to.*" She pulled herself up against the table leg, her midriff bare and round, and leaned back. "I'd forgotten how things feel out here. All this death makes a body feel more alive." She shifted the fawn in her lap and tucked the hem of her shirt under her arm to hold it in place. Through the thin cotton of her bra, Jimbo saw the complete outline of her nipple. Its roundness appeared to be straining against the material. "I feel free out here. I can let everything go." She rubbed the fawn's nose around her nipple and closed her eyes. As she arched her back, the center hardened to a point. She smiled. "I'll have milk soon."

Weak as it was, the fawn made a perfect rag doll. She lifted her breast over the top of the bra and rubbed it against the fawn's nose. When she pushed her nipple into the fawn's mouth, she started humming some song that sounded familiar.

"The fawn's sick, Cassie. It has TB. Not your fault but it can't live." The smile disappeared from her face. "We'll name our baby Fawna, though. It's perfect, isn't it?" he whispered, as he spread her legs and began rubbing the inside of her thighs. Now his brain spun; no longer paused—fast forward, rewind—it was playing and recording simultaneously, it was running at different speeds. Wasn't he being gentle as he laid her on her side? Wasn't he being careful as he pressed the fawn between them? If he could've, he would've crawled all the way inside Cassie to his baby, where he could touch and hold and kiss her, his perfect, perfect daughter, his Fawna. *His.*

What would she smell like? He would stay there, inside, and be born with her. A perfect daughter deserved a perfect father, didn't she? The kind always there to protect. He could not wait. He would never let Fawna out of his sight. Such warmth. Such softness. With the fawn still between them, he unzipped his pants. The warmth turned to heat.

Maybe when someone loses their mind, it's like floating in space. Maybe there's no gravity or weight. Or maybe it feels heavy, an anchoring secured by weight. Maybe it feels like finally finding home. Maybe it's not crazy to discover for the first time as middle age nears what it's like for something to belong inexplicably to you. Or maybe Jimbo Sutt didn't lose or find a thing. Maybe he simply fell in love.

Maybe love is where things unravel.

He'd told her he'd talk to her father, hadn't he? Had she heard? Or had she been listening to the fawn? Did she think death was silent? She'd seen how messy it was in the shop and liked it. That sound was just the lungs struggling. The fawn would quiet soon. He would bury it. He would not feed it to the dogs. He promised. He would do whatever she liked, whatever she wanted. They were going to be a real family. He was going to be a real father. DeBardelaiwin was a fine name. He didn't care about names. Fawna Sutt or Fawna De-Bardelaiwin. Blood was what mattered—his blood, his baby. Had Cassie started crying? Why? Why was she looking at him that way? Could she see how beautiful Fawna would be? God, how he'd missed her. Every night he'd dreamed of making love again. He'd never imagined her with his baby inside while they did it. Fawna was going to be perfect. Josiah would see what a perfect baby Jimbo made. Not like Darrell. Not like the fawn. Cassie didn't need to listen to her father. It was Jimbo's turn to make the decisions. He wanted to rock back and forth while Cassie sang all the lullabies in the world. Faster. Faster. He didn't want slow. He didn't want to wait. Was that Cassie singing? Was that the Jackal? Was it him? *Hold still and shut up for one lousy goddamn moment. Fawna needs me. We need each other. You'll see. Please God no. Not blood. Please no. I just want to hold her.*

Jimbo replays it over and over in his mind, always rewinding, always fast-forwarding. Some things change, but the end is always the same: The knife is sharp. The blood is thick. And Jimbo's left there, all alone.

When Jimbo visits Darrell at Medical West, he usually parks out front and takes the main elevator. Today, he takes the hospital stairs and walks the four flights to Darrell's floor. "He's asleep," a nurse whispers behind Jimbo, as if he's too stupid to notice. "Why don't you come back later?" Jimbo knows it's not a question.

Darrell looks grown, peaceful, so different than the little boy who haunts Jimbo's memory. He would unmake every mistake if he could. He will not make the mistake now of waking him. Outside Darrell's room, the maze of halls makes Jimbo feel like a rat. He knows what the people here think of Darrell, of him. He won't ask for directions. The ones in the white coats are the worst—pity written all over their faces, thinking they're better than the Sutts because they have education and big words. Jimbo'll be damned before he asks them anything. *This is where Cassie would've been taken to stop the bleeding. These are the people who would've taken Fawna.*

At the end of the hall, Jimbo sees the automatic door to the parking deck and a sign he can't read until he gets closer: *NICU.*

Alphabet code for everything. Just before the door is an alcove and another door with a large window. A pair of colored scrubs hurries down the hall, into a bathroom. There's a metal cart by the door like the one Jimbo uses in the shop. This one has a plastic bin on top and is filled with pink-striped blankets. Everything around it smells sweet and clean. A sound rises that resonates somewhere deep in his bones. Jimbo reaches into the cart, scoops up the bundle, and walks through the automatic door.

PART II

YOUR CHEATIN' HEART

THE PRICE OF INDULGENCE

BY CAROLYN HAINES

Downtown Mobile

The fishy smell of Mobile Bay came through the open car window. Jackie watched the sun come up, casting gold shimmers on the light chop. She drummed her fingers on the steering wheel of the old blue Plymouth Fury, listening to the radio and waiting. The local AM country station was filled with static and aggravation, but soon the *Salvation Radio Hour* would be on. Brother Fred March preached the fiery word of the Lord and offered to save sinners who bought his prayer cloths or blessed water. Stupid suckers.

Jackie sank deeper into the bench seat, shifting to avoid a spring. She lit a cigarette and let the smoke roll out of her mouth. She'd never learned to make smoke rings.

"Hey, you alive?"

She sat up taller and caught the image of the big man in her side mirror. Merle Boykin, one of her best customers.

"More alive than you want to mess with." She opened the car door and got out.

"You a feisty thing." Merle looked her up and down, lazy and deliberately offensive. "Like those cutoff jeans."

"If you had gunpowder for brains, you couldn't even blow your nose." She brushed past him and opened the trunk. "There it is. You carry it inside if you want it. I'm not your pack mule."

"Girl, your good looks take you only so far. Push a little harder and see what you get."

Jackie grinned. "Try your luck, asshole."

Merle turned his attention to the gallon glass jugs in the trunk. He lifted one and looked through the clear liquid. "You ain't got your daddy's manners but you inherited his touch with a still. Never knew a girl could cook mash like you."

"You want it, haul it out of my trunk *after* I have the money."

Merle counted out the bills in twenties. He handed her the cash and then lifted the moonshine out of the trunk. He made eight trips to the ramshackle building that sold bait, fishing gear, rented boats, and also offered white lightning to trusted customers. Jackie leaned against the side of the car and watched him work.

"Your daddy always helped carry it in," Merle said as he hefted two more gallons.

"My daddy was a good man. He died about thirty yards from where I'm standing. Being good didn't matter a bit to the man who shot him."

Merle shook his head. "That eats at you long enough, you're gonna be shittin' in a bag."

"Thanks for the medical advice." She slammed the trunk. The rear of the car still sank low to the white shells of the parking lot.

"Jackie, there's no undoing what happened to your daddy. I don't know who shot him, and fact is, I wouldn't tell you if I knew. You gone get yourself hurt. There're mean and powerful people out there. They'll shoot you too."

"If I thought you knew, I'd see that you told me."

Merle slammed the trunk hard. "See you in a week."

"My date with destiny." She got behind the wheel, closed the door, and spun out onto the two lanes of the causeway that connected Mobile and Baldwin counties. The bay ruffled on her left, and the marshlands and rivers on her right. In ten minutes, she was cutting under the Mobile River via Bankhead Tunnel, a span of roadway that made her feel like she was in the belly of a snake. When she shot up into the light and sun again, she was in downtown Mobile.

She snapped the radio back on.

"God offers sinners the perfect miracle, absolute redemption. Even those who have died and are moldering in the ground, awaiting Judgment Day, can be helped. God wants to love and forgive. I can intercede with God on behalf of those you love, those awaiting final judgment, those who will live eternally in the fiery lake of hell if you don't take action. Cash, check, or money order will do. Don't let the flames of damnation lick the flesh of those you love. Send twenty-five dollars right now and the name of the person I need to pray for. God hears me, and He listens. Let me save the ones you love from eternal hellfire."

The city had begun to awaken as she drove past the businesses and houses, many sporting evidence of the long occupation of the city by the French and Spanish. Wrought-iron balconies, stucco, windows that opened wide and were used as doors, the patio entrances that led back to what had once been stables and elegant bricked courtyards. This was Mobile, all shaded by the monster live oaks she loved.

When she passed the small, cinder-block AM radio station, WRED, she pulled to the curb and stopped. Brother Fred March was inside, doing his live radio show. She recognized his brand-new black Cadillac parked right at the front door. The morning deejay who ran the station was playing a gospel song, "Jesus Is Coming Soon" by the Oakridge Boys.

For the next half hour, she watched the squirrels run up the live oak trees and listened to Brother Fred.

"The Lord Jesus carries your sins every day. He can wash you clean and intercede for those who have gone before you. Here's that address again. Cash, check, or money order and the name of the person I should pray for."

The show always ended with "Will the Circle Be Unbroken." Before the song had even finished, the door of the radio station opened and Brother Fred stepped into the October sunlight. Tall with wide shoulders, he was a handsome man with his pomaded black hair. Before the ministry, he'd been a dock worker. Ten years of hard labor had given him a physical presence. Greed had given him the golden ticket of fleecing the desperate.

March lit a cigarette and a big diamond on his finger glinted. He didn't even glance at the old Plymouth across the street.

Brother Fred wasn't a very perceptive man, but to be on the safe side, Jackie had put on sunglasses and a scarf to hide her white-blond hair. She watched the radio evangelist pull hard on his cigarette and then flick the butt into the grass. He walked around the car and she took note of his fancy suit and cowboy boots. They were made of ostrich and cost a pretty penny, but God wanted him to have them. Brother Fred said so on the radio, and his flock had ponied up the bucks to buy them.

The evangelist left the radio station in a spray of gravel. Jackie waited a minute, then fell in behind him, heading west. The minister's Cadillac cut through the October morning like God's black missile. Brother Fred paid no heed to speed limits, which forced Jackie to do the same. When he turned into a new subdivision of brick ranch-style homes on the outskirts of

Mobile, she passed the entrance, then returned, cruising until she found his car parked halfway behind a redbrick house with gray shutters. She brought the camera with a telephoto lens from the backseat just as March got out of the Caddy and knocked on the front door.

The woman who opened it wore a flimsy white negligee and a big red smile. March swept her into his arms and hurried inside, but not before Jackie had half a dozen photos.

The newsroom of the *Mobile Register* was already filled with cigarette smoke when she clanked out of the decrepit old elevator and went to her desk in State News. She was little more than a cub reporter. She typed up the columns from far-flung community correspondents, wrote obits, helped the back shop proofread legal notices and the classified ads. When none of the male reporters were available, she sometimes got to pursue a crime story. Her boss said she had a flair for sniffing out stories.

At her corner desk she began to type Octavia Fairley's community column and four obituaries. At least she didn't have to write weddings. Her boss came out of a meeting.

"I'm done with my work. Can I go to the darkroom?" She pushed her rolling chair away from her desk and stood.

Clint assessed her for a moment. "Somebody dug up a grave over in Wilmer. You want to check it out, Hepburn?"

Clint was a big fan of old movies and Katherine Hepburn was a favorite. She already had her car keys in hand and her purse on her shoulder. "Address?"

She'd grown up on the west side of Mobile County and she knew every back road. The cemetery wasn't that far from where she lived. "I'll be back after lunch."

"Jackie, were you out on the causeway this morning?"

She stopped in the doorway, debating whether to lie or not. Bootlegging wasn't an approved hobby for newspaper employees. "Yeah, I was."

Clint sat down at his desk. "I know your father's death eats at you, but you need to let it go. If you don't, you'll end up bitter and unhappy."

A smart-aleck retort came to her, but she stopped. "Thanks, Clint. I am trying." She walked through the newsroom, ignoring the elevator, and took the stairs down to the lobby and out into the sunshine.

A solitary sheriff's deputy stood over the open grave in the middle of a small church cemetery. The body had been buried only two days before. Now the coffin had been opened and the body taken. Latter-day grave robbers.

"Who was she, Sandy?" There was no headstone. The grave was too raw.

"Cornelia Swanson, high school senior. Auto accident. It's killing her folks." Deputy Sandy Stewart backed away from the grave and stopped in the shade of a big live oak. It was the only bit of beauty in the sad little cemetery.

"You thinking vandals or someone personally connected with the dead girl?"

"More likely revenge," the deputy said. "Jet Swanson has some serious detractors. Some say he had a beef with your daddy."

"My daddy didn't rise out of the grave to steal a dead girl's body. Not unless you know something I don't." Anger made Jackie's words hot.

"You got a short fuse where your daddy's concerned."

"Do you have a suspect or not?"

"Not. Wouldn't tell you even if I did."

Sandy Stewart was normally easygoing. Jackie had brought out his obnoxious streak. "I'm going over to the Quik Mart there to get a Coke. You want one?"

"Sure." He took the peace offering.

She got the cold drinks and walked back, handing him the icy can. They popped the tops and drank. The day was hot for October. "Did you know the girl?"

"In passing. She was shy. She'd just taken a job at the Quik Mart after school. Said she was saving to go to college."

"What caused the wreck?" Jackie asked.

"Drunk driver. He wasn't hurt. Not even a serious scratch. She was dead at the scene. She was Jet's only child."

"That couldn't have been planned." She thought a minute. "Could it?"

Stewart shrugged. "Facts don't matter to Jet. Now they've gone and stolen his girl's body. Going to be hell to pay. You keep your head down and don't try talking to Jet. I'm warning you, he's not above hurtin' you because he's hurtin'."

"I can take care of myself, but thanks."

Stewart only lifted his eyebrows. "Your daddy said the same thing."

Jackie froze. "You know who hurt my daddy?" She had suspected all along that the sheriff knew who'd shot Jackson Muldoon. He just chose not to do anything about it. Jackson was a bootlegger and because of his profession had given up any claims to justice.

Stewart leveled a gaze at her across the red clay wound of the earth. "Your daddy sold hooch, but he paid off the sheriff and he traded honest as far as I ever heard."

"If it wasn't the law or his customers, then it had to be his competition. Was Jet a competitor?" Her daddy had never talked business with her. She'd accumulated his old customers because he had a name for quality and a reputation he was proud of. Quality moonshine was a family tradition.

"Steer clear of Jet." The deputy frowned. "Not that you'll take my advice. Girl, you got a streak of self-destruct a mile wide."

Jackie had heard that before. "You got any idea who dug this girl up?"

"Nope. I'm just hoping we can find the body before it shows up someplace that's going to make the national news." He gestured toward the empty grave. "She was one of those Angels in White. Did the singing on the radio. You know, they pledge to be pure and sing at the revivals for that Brother March."

She looked down into the hole where the coffin had been opened. The pink silk lining was smudged with dirt. The body had simply been pulled out and taken. "Did this girl have a boyfriend? Someone who might be . . . strongly attached?"

"Now that's some sick stuff you're sayin'."

"Hey, I'm not the one riding around with a dead body in my car."

"No, you're ridin' around with a ghost, Jackie. That can be just as dangerous."

"Thanks, Sandy. I'll quote you in the paper. Give you some fame."

"Keep it. Fame never leads anywhere good in Mobile."

Jackie finished her story and waited while Clint read it. The photograph of the empty coffin in the grave was haunting and disturbing. She didn't know if the paper would run it or not. She honestly was torn herself. The prospect of taking a hard dig at Jet Swanson, who she suspected was involved in her father's death, and the grief the photograph would give Mrs.

Swanson, were conflicting impulses. Clint gave her a nod of approval and dismissal.

Dusk was falling quickly, and she'd been up since four a.m. She left her car parked in the newspaper lot and walked up Government to Royal Street. Work-a-day employees were headed out of the city to Midtown or the apartments along Airport Boulevard near the mall. The day people abandoned the streets to the sizzling neon signs, rock music coming out of bars, and the men who came into the port city from around the world to sow their wild oats.

Two blocks over she pushed into the Port of Call. The bar was so dimly lit that she had to stop to let her eyes adjust. Euclid Adams was behind the bar; Martha Lowell, aka Candy, was on the stage. She wore a pink-and-white-striped baby-doll outfit that emphasized her cleavage and long legs. She was a good dancer. Not all of the stars at Port of Call were. Some had all the right moves in other athletic pursuits.

Jackie settled at the bar. Euclid put a Diet Coke in front of her. "When the streets are clear, I'll pull around back."

"How long you gonna cook mash, Jackie?"

"Haven't decided." She'd known Euclid since she was twelve and started riding with her dad when he made his deliveries.

"Your stories in the paper are good. Folks say you got a set of *huevos*. They also say you gone end up dead, just like your daddy."

Jackie sipped her cola through a straw. "Could be."

Euclid leaned down on the bar so he could look her eye-to-eye. "Girl, you need to stop whatever plan is churning in that brain of yours. I see clear as day you're about to get yourself caught in a gill net. That kind of ending isn't pretty."

"Where's Lyda?" She finished her soda with a loud slurp.

"In the back. You should leave her alone. She's not feeling good."

"I need to ask her something."

"Don't let Johnny catch you back there. He says you make the girls unhappy by telling them things they don't need to hear."

"Yeah, like in five years they're gonna be strung out, diseased, and living in a homeless shelter?"

"Yeah, stuff like that."

Jackie nodded. "I won't be but a few minutes."

"If Johnny comes back, I'll play Frijid Pink on the jukebox."

Jackie ducked behind the curtain that separated a long, narrow hallway with doors on either side from the rest of the bar. As she passed a door, she heard a man laughing. Some of the girls were already at work.

She knocked on the third door to the left and opened it. "Lyda?"

The young woman was stretched out on a sofa, her gaze unfocused. A half-finished vodka on the rocks was sweating on the bedside table. "Go away."

"Lyda." Jackie sat on the floor beside the bed. "I'll get some coffee for you."

The woman shook her head. "Let me ride this high a little longer. You don't know what it's like to be free."

Jackie shifted to her knees and brushed the hair back from Lyda's forehead. Lyda March was only a few years older than Jackie, and she had once been beautiful. She'd danced in New Orleans in the finest gentlemen's clubs. Now she was back home, performing as Lyda Monarch to avoid soiling her family's name.

Jackie got coffee from the bar. She had to get Lyda on her feet. Johnny Zenata didn't put up with dancers who were too loaded to work. "Lyda, do you know a girl named Cornelia Swanson?"

Lyda looked down. "Sweet Cornelia."

"Lyda, she's dead. Did you know that?"

Lyda nodded. "Newspaper. Car wreck."

Jackie heaved a sigh of relief. Lyda wasn't as far gone as she seemed. "Did you know any other of those girls? The White Angels?"

"I know things my daddy did that you'd like to know." Lyda pushed past her and went behind a screen to dress. She was done talking.

Twenty minutes later, a shaky Lyda was in her cowgirl costume and standing upright. Jackie ushered her to the stage just as Johnny Z. came in the back door. He scowled and started to push Lyda, but Jackie stepped into his hand.

"Don't."

He grinned. "What's Lyda to you?"

"A human being." Jackie's fists were clenched.

"If you say so. I don't care if she's a one-legged pig as long as she dances and the men buy drinks." He waved around the bar, which had begun to fill up with shadowy men who sought out the dark booths around the edge of the room. In a far corner, pool balls clacked. Johnny started to turn away but Jackie grabbed his arm.

"I want to take Lyda home to her father. She needs to dry out and get clean."

Johnny's eyes narrowed. "Her daddy doesn't want her. What do you have between your ears, mashed potatoes? He don't want a junkie stripper whore showing up on his doorstep. Lyda has enough sense to know that even if you don't."

"He'll take her in." He would too, or she'd print the photos of Brother Fred and his negligee-clad mistress and glue

them to the doors of his church. The things he'd done . . .
nice people didn't talk about those things and no one would
believe Lyda now. It wasn't the same, but at least Jackie had
the goods on him with his mistress.

Johnny eyed her. "You involved in digging that girl up? I
knew you were crazy, but that takes it. You're trying to play
in the grown-ups' sandbox, Jackie. You're gonna get hurt. Jet
Swanson will cut out your gizzard and feed it to you."

The ringing phone woke Jackie and she knew the newspaper had run the photos of the empty coffin—with her photo
credit.

"Hello." She turned on the burner for hot water.

"Stay away from that still." The line went dead.

The caller was male. She walked to the end of her driveway in her T-shirt and panties. There were no other houses
around. She picked up the paper and opened it to State News.
There was the photo of the coffin and a much more suitable
shot of tombstones shaded by the big oak tree in the cemetery.
It looked haunted and sad. The empty grave seemed . . . de-
praved. She sighed. It was going to be a long, long day.

She showered and built up the wood for cooking. The two
Taggart boys would be by to keep the fire burning.

It was only six o'clock when she got to the paper, so she
went into the darkroom and processed the film she'd taken of
Brother March. She printed up ten big glossies of March with
his mistress in his arms. Both faces were clearly visible. She
went to her desk and tucked them into a manila envelope and
put them in her purse.

From the cross-reference directory she looked up the address of the house Brother March was partial to visiting and
got the name of the woman who lived there. *Charlotte Rush.*

She addressed an envelope to her, slid in a photo, and put it in her purse to take to the post office.

She wrote six more obituaries. The afternoon deadline came and went.

Clint came out of his office. "Jackie, the sheriff called. They have a lead on that missing body. The sheriff asked for you. Specifically." Clint stared at her, giving her the chance to explain.

"Where is it?"

"They left her sitting on the front porch of a house, 125 Walton Street, in the Golden Heights subdivision on the west side of town."

She felt the flush rise to the roots of her hair. It was the same address on the envelope she was getting ready to mail.

"Does that mean something to you?"

She shook her head.

"What's going on with you?"

She felt the weight of what she knew pressing on the back of her throat, but she swallowed it down. "That's just such a gruesome thing to do. Leaving a dead girl's body on someone's porch."

"Put her in a rocking chair by a geranium. Run out there and get some photos and interview Charlotte Rush. Find out how she's connected to all this."

"Yes sir." She grabbed her purse with the photos in it and her camera.

"If folks were upset with an empty coffin this morning, they're going to be choking on their toast over this. Do your best to be tasteful."

"Right. Tasteful." And she was out the door.

She went to the post office and sent the photo to Charlotte

Rush. Dead girl on her porch. Blackmail photos. Tomorrow would be an interesting day in Fred March's life. And it was just the first drop in the bucket.

She parked behind a patrol car, glad that by the time she got there the body was covered with a sheet. It sat bolt upright in a chair, the position of the body telling her that rigor mortis had already set in. She had to wonder how the grave robber had gotten the body to bend into a sitting position. It was downright creepy.

She set to work under the watchful eye of a deputy. The sheriff pulled up and stopped in the drive to talk with some of the other law officers. Jackie ducked inside to find Charlotte Rush sitting at the kitchen table with a cup of coffee untouched in front of her.

"Get out," Charlotte said. "I don't want the newspaper here."

"Did you know the Swanson girl?" Jackie asked. "Cornelia was such a good girl. She was an Angel in White in the church right down the road."

Charlotte stood up. "What are you talking about?"

"Cornelia Swanson. The dead girl on your front porch."

Charlotte leaned against the sink she was laughing so hard. "You fool. That's not a dead girl. It's a mannequin. Someone dressed up a mannequin and left it on my porch. Those fool deputies called it in that it was that dead girl that was stolen from her grave."

Jackie felt the sweat slip down her back and into the waistband of the jeans that hung on her hips. Mannequin. Someone had left a mannequin in a rocking chair. She went outside and pulled the sheet off the body. Someone had gone to a lot of trouble to paint the mannequin's face and dress her in a red, sheer nighty that looked like it came from Frederick's of Hollywood.

She took the photos, capturing the glassy-eyed stare of the plastic woman. When she looked down the driveway, Sheriff Hilbun and all the deputies were clustered, watching her.

"I heard you thought it was the body of that girl someone dug up," Hilbun said.

"Yeah, that was the call that came in to the paper."

"Must have been old home week with Charlotte Rush for you," Hilbun said.

Jackie sensed the ground had shifted. "Why should it?"

"Your daddy was sweet on Charlotte. He never mentioned that, did he?"

Jackie rubbed the back of her neck beneath her long blond hair. "No, he didn't. I guess he figured his love life was none of my affair. He'd be right about that." She picked up her equipment and left the men standing in the driveway.

Jackie sat on her own front porch with a glass of whiskey on the rocks. She sipped her drink and smoked a cigarette. She thought back on the evenings her daddy came home late, smelling of perfume and drink. She'd never asked him. She'd never wanted to think of him with anyone other than her mother, who'd died when she was thirteen. Cancer. A long, ugly death that stole everything from Tilda. First her health, then her looks, then her joy in living, until she'd finally had enough.

Jackson had seen her through it all, feeding, washing, cleaning, bathing, loving. Jackie had never begrudged her dad the solace of another woman after Tilda was gone. But she didn't want to know the details or the woman. But Charlotte Rush?

She threw her cigarette butt into the dying flower bed and went inside to sleep.

She was up early the next morning, long before dawn. As she headed downtown, she watched the colors of the sky shift from indigo to peachy shades of gold and finally the blue-white of fair weather.

She parked in the newspaper lot and locked her car. When Jet Swanson appeared from behind the corner of a building, she couldn't stop herself from reacting. She uttered a cry and stepped back.

"You shouldn't have made that picture of my daughter's grave." His eyes were flat but alert.

"I get an assignment from my boss and I do what I'm told to do."

"Somehow I don't believe that, Jackie. I know you."

She'd recovered her balance. "And I know you. Why do you think I'd do something like that?"

"That's what I've come to ask. Why? And to tell you I want my daughter's body back. I want her back in the ground and left alone. Now, you've got till midnight tomorrow to put her right back in that coffin. You call me when it's done and I'll send some boys around to fill in the dirt."

"You're making a lot of assumptions."

"Folks said you're smarter than your daddy. Prove it. This is your get-out-of-jail-free card, Jackie. Put her back. That'll be the end of it."

"And if I don't—assuming I have a dead body hidden somewhere?"

"I can put you in that coffin and cover you up. One way or the other, I'm telling my wife that a dead girl is in the cemetery. You get me?"

"Why would I take your girl like that? What have you done that makes you think I'd even attempt it?"

"You're smart, but you aren't right, Jackie. Obsessed with

vengeance. That's the word. It's no secret you think I killed your daddy."

"I do. Are you denying it?" Her body was trembling.

"You're not such a fool that you think I'd admit it even if I had done it." He leaned in and tucked a stray curl behind her ear. "Midnight tomorrow. I'll be waiting at the cemetery."

He brushed past her and walked away, disappearing down the gray street in the pale light of dawn, leaving her to face a long day of questions and anxiety.

Jackie woke from a troubled sleep to the sound of gunshots. Just as she sat up in bed, the window of her room shattered. Glass blew in toward her, and she ducked and rolled. Two bullets smacked into the bedroom wall.

When her breathing finally settled back to normal, she crawled up and got a rifle from her father's closet. She went to the back door and slipped into the night. She couldn't see, but neither could they.

A milky film of fog covered the stars and moon, dripping steadily from the trees onto the dying leaves. She knew the woods and moved through the trees without hesitation, making her way to the narrow road. When she saw the sandy lane, she found a place tucked near a fallen scrub oak and set up the rifle, braced on the tree. A hoot owl cried into the night, and she was glad for the company. Whoever had taken a shot at her house was gone. The wild creatures told her that much.

She went back to her house and examined the damage. It was more warning than threat. Not worth involving the law, who'd been eager for an invite onto her property since Jackson had died. She'd handle this herself.

Her phone rang, startling her to the point that she almost dropped the rifle. She put it away, convinced the danger had passed. For the moment. She answered the phone, expecting to hear Jet Swanson's voice. Instead, there was only the sound of breathing, and in the background, a sweet chorus of young women singing "Softly and Tenderly." She realized it was a recording. A train whistle shrilled in the distance, but she couldn't tell if it was on the recording or from the location of the caller.

"Who is this?" She waited. "Who is this?" She was hanging up when she heard what she thought was a sob. The line went dead.

Jackie held the phone for a long moment before she put it back in the cradle. She pulled on her clothes, grabbed the rifle, and headed to the still. Long before she got there, she saw the fire. Someone had torched her still. The blaze danced above the treetops. An explosion that literally rocked the car told her there was nothing to salvage.

She swung the car so the headlights illuminated the path through the woods and stopped. A white dress had been draped over a set of shrubs. The Empire waist and longer skirt told her exactly what kind of dress it was. She slammed on the brakes and froze. "Angels in White." She whispered the words aloud before she leaped out of the car and snatched the white dress. She completed her U-turn and headed away from the still, going as fast as she dared.

There was nothing she could do to save the operation. Someone had put her out of business. Destroyed the thing her father took pride in. And left her a message. Angels in White.

Her certainty that Jet Swanson was the man responsible for her father's death was shaken. Jet would kill a man, no doubt about it. He would kill a woman. But he would not dig up his daughter or use her church clothes to make a threat.

Fire trucks passed on the main road. She gave the police another fifteen minutes to get to the scene, then grabbed her camera and drove to the still. Taking photos for the newspaper gave her a reason to be at the scene. An empty gas can had been left fifty feet back from the still. Hardly necessary with that much alcohol right at hand.

To her surprise, Deputy Stewart was the man in charge. "Any clues as to what happened?" she asked.

He scoffed. "I thought you might be able to tell *me*."

"I was home, asleep. Heard the sirens." The flames had died down considerably, and the volunteer firemen were spraying the surrounding trees to prevent sparks from jumping.

"Who would want to put you out of business, Jackie?" The deputy gently grasped her shoulder when she started to turn away. "You've been poking into someone's business. This is a message. If you don't heed it, they're going to seriously hurt you. Just like they did Jackson."

"Who killed my daddy?" She kept her tone flat.

"Knowing won't bring Jackson back and it could get you killed."

She thought about showing Sandy the dress. It was the best evidence and she'd plucked it from the scene. Angels in White. Dead Cornelia Swanson. An empty grave.

She drove straight to the newspaper and turned in her film of the fire. She wrote her story and left it on Clint's desk.

She made her last delivery at the Forest Grill, a bar on old Highway 45. Freddie McGee was a favorite customer. He was older with bad knees so she unloaded the moonshine. She put the jugs behind the counter. The building was half general store and half bar, with a short-order cook to boot. Dolly

Mason could whip up a grilled cheese in under three minutes. Jackie didn't even have to order. Dolly put the sandwich and a cup of coffee in front of her at the bar.

"I heard about the fire."

Jackie felt the pressure of emotion yet again. She blinked back her tears. "I'm done, Dolly. I'm thinking about moving into town. Maybe buy one of those little cottages on Mohawk or Japonica. Not too close in." She was surprised at how much she revealed and how these thoughts had come, unbidden, to her mind.

"You don't need to be out in those woods alone. Moving into town is a good idea, hon. Maybe find you someone to date." Dolly picked up a strand of Jackie's hair. "You could be pretty if you let yourself. Eat your sandwich."

Jackie sipped her coffee. She had to get back to the newspaper. Clint would be looking for her. She took a big bite of the sandwich and peered at the wall behind the bar. The place was old and not all that clean. Her eye caught a photo of three very young men at the pool table, holding sticks and grinning at the camera. Two small girls sat on the edge of the table. One had white-blond hair.

Dolly followed her gaze. "That's your daddy." She took the picture down and gave it to Jackie. "He was a handsome man. When he was young, all the women had a crush on him. He was also a bootlegger, which made him dangerous. Like a pirate." She laughed. "When he married your mama, we were all heartbroken. I don't think he ever looked at another woman after he said his vows. The same can't be said for the other two. They were tomcats in heat."

Jackie knew her father, but not the other two men. They were so young. "Who is that?"

"You don't recognize Sheriff Hilbun?" Dolly pointed to

the man on the left. "And that one there is Mobile's most famous radio minister, Fred March."

"And that is Lyda."

"She used to go everywhere with Fred. Places she shouldn't have gone."

Jackie ran a finger over the glass that protected the photo. "So that's my dad, the sheriff, and a television minister. That's quite a trio. They were friends?"

"Once upon a time Lloyd Hilbun and Fred March were stevedores at the dock. That's where the sheriff got his base of support to run for office, and Fred went in the other direction. He learned the power of persuasive talk as a union organizer."

"Was Jackson a stevedore too?"

Dolly laughed again. "Not on your life. You father never worked for anybody but himself. He cooked mash alongside his daddy, who learned from *his* daddy. That's why all your daddy's clients kept buying from you. That's generations of trust and quality. They kicked about buying from a girl—I heard them—but in the end, the ties were too strong." She patted Jackie's arm. "What are you going to do now?"

"I'm still deciding."

"Your daddy wanted you to go to college. Get an education. He said legal liquor would push the bootleggers out if the law didn't."

Jackie didn't say anything.

"I'm not your mama so I don't have a right to offer guidance, but your paw and I talked sometimes. He was so proud of you, Jackie. He said you could be anything you wanted."

Jackie stood up and put the picture back behind the bar. She had to get to the paper before Clint blew his stack, but she had one stop to make. She turned back at the door. "Who killed my daddy?"

"Even if I knew, I wouldn't tell you. No one here would. That information won't do anything but hurt you."

The white dress she'd found in the woods was still in the backseat of her car. Angels in White. How long had that eaten at Lyda?

She parked behind the strip club and went in the back door. Euclid saw her and filled a glass with crushed ice and Diet Coke. He put it on the counter. "Sorry about your still."

"End of a family tradition."

"What are you aimin' to do?" Euclid leaned on the bar.

She shrugged. "Freedom's just another word for nothin' left to lose, right?"

Euclid came around the bar. "Johnny's on his way. Lyda's been sick and missed her performance. He's goin' to pin that on you."

She slurped the last of her Diet Coke. "I have to see Lyda. I got something of hers I need to return."

"What would that be?"

"A white dress. She left it at my place."

"I don't know if she's awake. She's in bad shape."

"What kind of shape are you in, Euclid?" She picked up one of his hands and examined his nails.

"What are you doin'?"

"Looking for graveyard dirt. Lyda didn't dig up that dead girl by herself. Johnny Z. is crazier than a shithouse rat, but he didn't do that. Had to be you."

Euclid snatched his hand away. "You can't prove it."

"I don't want to. Where's the body?"

"It'll show up. When the time is right."

Jackie tapped the bar lightly with a finger. "I know what Fred March did to Lyda. But what about that dead girl's mama?"

Euclid looked down at the bar, wiping at imaginary spots with his shirtsleeve. "Folks get hurt in the fallout. You should know that, what with your daddy getting shot and all."

"Who shot my father?" She caught his wrist and dug in with her fingernails.

"Stop." He shook her off. "You need to get out. Johnny said he'd hurt you if he caught you here again."

She left him and walked through the curtain and into the long hallway that smelled of beer and piss. She opened Lyda's room without knocking. Her friend was on the sofa, her eyes closed, her face pallid and waxy.

"Go away, Jackie. We aren't friends." Her lips barely moved.

"Why'd you torch my still?"

"I set you free."

"Why'd you do that?"

Lyda pushed herself up so that she was leaning against the arm of the sofa. "I'm dying."

Jackie shut off her emotions, refusing to feel anything. "That's not my fault."

"No, but it's your daddy's. And the sheriff's. Everybody knew what Fred was doing to me. No one stopped him. No one lifted a hand. Not Jackson. Not the high sheriff. Even when I was working in New Orleans, Fred would show up. It wasn't until I got sick that he stopped. Then he had the Angels in White to fill in the dark places in his soul. He didn't touch those girls, though. He preserved their innocence. Because he had too much at stake. But me, he ruined me for anyone else. For love or having a family. And no one stopped him. Not even your daddy, who set such a store by you."

"You left that white dress so I'd know you set the still on fire."

"I did. You deserve to know. You're the only one who tried to help. And I did set you free. You'd'a run that still until you dropped dead in the woods because it was your precious daddy's. Now you can move on."

Lyda knew her better than she knew herself. The taste of freedom in the back of Jackie's throat was bittersweet.

"Lyda, have you seen a doctor?"

"Liver's gone. Hepatitis." She shrugged. "Shit happens."

"Where's Cornelia Swanson's body?"

Lyda grinned, the skin pulling over her skeletal features. She'd gone far downhill in the few days since Jackie had last seen her. "In the trunk of my daddy's car. He's been driving his dead princess around for days. Imagine that."

Lyda forced herself off the sofa, stumbling as she went to a dresser in a corner of her room. She opened the top drawer and brought out a tape recorder. "This is all you'll need, Jackie. The whole story. Even the part about who killed Jackson."

"It was Fred, wasn't it?"

She nodded. "My dear daddy wanted to make an issue out of bootlegging and warned Jackson it was coming down. Jackson threatened him about Charlotte Rush, and about his visits to me in New Orleans. Next thing I knew, Jackson was dead."

"The law won't be able to make charges stick about digging up that dead girl. Fred'll get out of it."

"Maybe. But I left another recording with the body. One he won't get out of so easily."

"How do you know he won't remove that before he calls the sheriff?"

Lyda inhaled and flinched. She put a hand on her side. "That's the real reason I burned the still. They'll be investigating."

"You're framing a man for something he didn't do."

"Because the things he did do, he'll never be punished

for." She sank back onto the sofa and turned away. Her chest rapidly moved up and down and Jackie thought of two cocks she'd seen fighting in a farmyard. The fierce fluttering of a desire to maim and mutilate. She knew it too well.

"Let me get you some help, Lyda. Have you even seen a doctor?"

"I don't want help. I want revenge, and then release."

"But—"

"Just let me go. That's the kindest thing you can do. Let me go."

Jackie believed her. Lyda had loosened the tethers long ago. Fred March had set her on that path. He'd stolen her will to live, her innocence, and her best friend's father.

"I'll call the sheriff for you. And I'll do what I can to protect Euclid."

Lyda nodded. "I'll tell your daddy hello for you." Her expression held a hint of the old Lyda. "And Jackie, I don't want to be buried. I want to be cremated and my ashes spread in the Mississippi River. I want to wash right on out to the gulf and the Caribbean islands I always dreamed of visiting. Let me go, okay?"

"You're going whether I let you or not."

"We're alike that way. If you write a story, use a picture of me dancing in my cowgirl outfit. Back from the first, when I looked good. Now get out of here."

Jackie walked out and closed the door. Lyda would be dead within weeks. If her plan to frame Fred March failed, she still had her exit.

Johnny Z. was coming down the hall, a scowl on his face. Lyda had escaped him too.

Jackie nodded at Euclid as she crossed through the bar. She couldn't help her friend, but she would see that Fred

March was held accountable. Brother Fred was about to discover that the wages of sin were high, though nothing compared to the price of indulgence.

COME LIKE A THIEF

BY ANTHONY GROOMS

South Titusville, Birmingham

> *But the day of the Lord will come like a thief, and then the heav-
> ens will pass away with a roar, and the heavenly bodies will be
> burned up and dissolved, and the earth and the works that are
> done on it will be exposed.*
> —2 Peter 3:10 English Standard Version

D
r. Blackwood taught literature at Miles College, but
I knew him from St. Paul's Lutheran, where Daddy
had started to take us after we left the Presbyterians.
Dr. Blackwood was a thin man, not much taller than five feet,
a dapper dresser, with bulging eyes and a thin line of mustache, like it had been drawn with a fountain pen across the
ridge of his lip. I loved to hear him speak. His voice was soft
and crisp and he used words that I didn't know the meaning
of. I doubt if anyone who sat on the porch watch on that fall
night understood half of what he said.

"Prof," Mr. Snodgrass (we called him "Snotty") said,
"that's a mighty good speech! Good 'nough to deliver from
the pulpit at Sixth Avenue. You could drive ole Wilson right
on outta there. He puts the dead to sleep. God up in heaven
be snoring through his sermons. The Lord's head be falling
down and rolling around His neck like a ball on a billiard table." Mr. Snodgrass spat tobacco in the bean can he kept with
him. "'Cept nobody in hell know what you be talking about."

Mr. Snodgrass was a bulky man, whose size should have been intimidating, except his body slouched, making itself look soft. He walked with a stoop as well. He worked in the warehouse at the Golden Flake plant. "You never knew tater chips could be so heavy," he often said.

I could see Dr. Blackwood's lips twitching in the silver light that shone through the front-door window onto the porch. "I am too often amused by your flights of imagination, Snodgrass, but to make a spectacle of the Divine is defamation beyond redemption." The whites of his eyes caught the light. My father, who made up the north-facing point of their triangle, shifted toward me, a sly grin, siding with neither man. The shadow of the Remington 11-48, a shotgun he had managed to keep from his time in the service, moved along the porch railing as it lay across his lap, pointing out into Center Street. I ducked behind the curtain, lest he saw me and sent me to bed.

Like in practically every other household in South Titusville, my parents were teachers. My father worked at Lawson State, a vocational college where he taught painting. The test of a good painter was that he could carry a loaded paintbrush across a room, like a debutante balancing a book on her head, without spilling a drop. Papa had studied at Tuskegee Institute, living among the black airmen who would make up the 332 Fighter Group, and the syphilitic farmers who unwittingly became the guinea pigs of the US Public Health Service. He occasioned, too, to meet the humble, effeminate, and by then very frail inventor George Washington Carver. This touch with greatness, he said, always inspired him to do right by people. Mommy taught second grade for Birmingham Public Schools, where in addition to buying school supplies with her salary, half that of white teachers, she would buy shoes, toothbrushes, clothes, and lunch for the poorer of her students.

Early that week, Williams's Store, a mom-and-pop sundry shop, which Sister and I frequented after our trips to the library, had been dynamited. We loved to buy the hard candy from the store, not so much for its taste, but because of its price: two for a penny. A nickel could keep us in candy for days.

Why the store was bombed was a mystery. Bombings— dynamite, Molotovs—were common in Birmingham's black neighborhoods, especially those that were encroaching into whites-only zoned areas. But South Titusville was not one of those communities. It was self-contained, mostly content, mostly complacent, or so it seemed on the surface. It was a neighborhood where nice colored folks minded their business, went to work, to church, to school, and prettified the front yards of their quaint brick and clapboard ranches. But beneath the surface, as in every black neighborhood, bubbled the slow boil of discontent, whispered in the churches beneath the call and response, or over the fence between neighbors, or on playgrounds among children tossing a softball. The city had closed all the parks that year in resistance to integrating them. The next spring would see thousands of children, some as young as six, march in protest, bitten by police dogs and bowled over by jets of pressurized water. I would be among them. That night, though, no one knew by whom or why Williams's Store had been shaken off its foundation and gutted by fire from two sticks of dynamite tied to a brick thrown through the window. But for the week since the bombing, on nearly every street corner in Titusville, both North and South, sat men with guns on porch watch, waiting, as Mr. Snodgrass summed up, "to blow open any Klan sonofabit' stupid enough to drive down Center Street."

"The white man," Dr. Blackwood said as he rolled the knuckles of one boney hand within the palm of the other, "has but one reason to oppress the Negro"—he lowered, shook his head, and recited—"*Black as the night is black, / Black like the depths of my Africa.*"

"Yass," Mr. Snodgrass drawled. My father nodded in agreement.

"They deem to assert a hideous hegemony over us for their parasitic profit. But the Klansman is a white man who has no reason, none other than to brutalize. I am put in mind of Mr. Justice. The pitiable soul."

Mr. Snodgrass folded his arms across his chest. As he was the south-facing point of the triangle, the pistol he held, also a take-home from war service, pointed briefly in my direction. "Reginald, it was."

"Roland, if memory serves me well."

"I knew his Daddy from when I worked over at TCI." Mr. Snodgrass leaned toward Dr. Blackwood, but kept his arms folded around himself. TCI was a blast furnace, one of several which, though diminished, still sooted the skyline. "It was *Reginald*. He wasn't doing nothing. Just walking down the road."

"*Black as the night is black.*"

"Just minding his own business," my father said, and let out a long sigh.

"And what they did to him, I didn't see in Korea. And I saw a lot I won't even tell 'bout. But they sliced him like a pig farmer take a razor to a shoat. Clean off. Then stuck 'em down his throat. What the purpose of that? Boy nearly choked to death and would have too." For a long moment all that could be heard were the grinding screeches of the last of the cicadas.

I turned away from the window, an ache from my navel to my knee, remembering the story of Ronald Justice and questioning my future as darkness swelled in me.

It was several minutes before the conversation picked up again, as if they were all lost in contemplation. I, too, was full of worried thoughts. I was twelve and beginning to feel the sap of manhood springing in my limbs, and with it, not so much a greening, but a blackening of expectations. What had happened to Ronald could happen to any black boy. I would have gone to bed at that point, but Mr. Snodgrass asked, "Whatever happened to Reginald? Did he go up north or something?"

"I never heard. Not even that," Dr. Blackwood said.

I moved back to my peephole behind the curtain and saw that the men seemed to have drawn closer together, forming a conspiratorial circle cut across by the rectangle of light that came through the door. I put my ear closer to the window screen.

"There was that so-called reporter, an investigatory journalist from one of the Northern papers, he said. Philadelphia, he said."

"Oh, yass. I do remember that fellow. Nosier than a six-toed mole. Come snooping around the yard at TCI asking about the boy. It was the end of late shift and that probably was the reason he snuck by the gate. He asking about Justice. By then they was gone. Where, I don't know. Up north, I guess. But he come asking and nobody, and I mean nobody, would speak a word to him. You never seen so many shoulder-shrugging Step'n Fetchits shuffling through the smoke and shadows. *No suh, boss, I don' know nuffin' 'bout what choo talking 'bout.* Flares were going off and throwing that red light on them, and they looked like they just raised from the grave. The cub come round to me. First I act like he wasn't even there. But then I said to myself that I wasn't fixin' to play no bug-eyed Sambo. I looked him right in the face, his eyes in shadow but somehow still sparking when those flares goes off. *Do you know where the hell you is? Asking 'bout that boy? Do you even know where the hell you is?* His mouth opened wider than a cow with a cattle prod up her ass. Too flabbergasted to get out more than a whoosh. He was a young fellow, Irish by the looks of him."

"Yes. Yes. But of course, I recall him well. A scarlet-haired, freckled-face youth. A so-called all-American visage. His name was O'Brien. Thomas O'Brien."

"O'Brien is right—nah!—*Brown*. Timmy—Timothy Brown it was. I know 'cause he followed me home. I was living round Avenue A in Fairfield then, not a quarter-mile from the furnace. Air in the house got so smoky you couldn't sleep some days and for the clanking and clunking too. But not a minute after I got home I heard the dogs barking and growling and come a knock at the door. Sun not even up yet. Cracked the door and there he was standing in the slit of light and looking like a chicken. Hair standing up like a rooster. Asked if the dogs gone bite. *What choo want?* I said it just like that. I didn't cotton to no white man. *Them ain't my dogs anyway.* He mumbled out something 'bout the *Inquisitor*. 'Bout then, one of the dogs took a snap at him and I pulled him on in. Don't need no white man bit up in my yard. *What choo want?*

"The fellow still looked shaken to me. Had that look like he got surprised one day and his face never went back. He wanted to ask me questions about that boy, and was it a better place here than at the plant.

"*Ain't no one damn place better than the other. You can get killed any damn place.*

"He sat down like a fat man with broke legs. Heard my

kitchen chair squeak. Wife gone to work, though. Day work over the mountain. She had left me a pot of greens, cornbread, and a little fried meat. I always ate my supper in the morning. So I offered the man some to be polite, never expecting he would say yes. So I fixed it up the best I could and served it to him. And he ate too. Right slow at first, like he had to smell it, and then a little piece and a little piece more. Then he was smiling and shoving it on in, chewing and grinning, ring pinkie in the air, like he always ate this way. *Ain't this one hell of a strange thing to see?* I was thinking. *A white man, sitting and eating at my table, eating greens and cornbread for breakfast.* I had to shake my head.

"Then he took a pencil and a little pad of paper out of the breast pocket of his jacket and set them down on the table beside his plate. He looked up and smiled, but his eyes darted around like he was nervous too. *You know Reginald Justice?* he asked me.

"*Naw,* I said, *I didn't know the boy. Seen him once or twice, but can't say I know him. I worked with his daddy, though.*

"*Well, tell me about his daddy.* I told him what little I knew, but it wasn't enough to get a story out of. Then he say, *Did the daddy ever mention that the boy had been seeing anybody? A girlfriend?*

"*If he did, I don't remember. I guess the boy was normal and that would have been a normal thing.*

"*A white girl. Girl the name of Ella Grimes.*

"Damn! Bread dropped out of my mouth it hit me so hard. Grimes. That Grimes gal. I started to say I didn't know a thing he was talking about—and truth be told, I didn't. But I did know that Grimes gal, 'cause her daddy worked the snort valve just a way 'cross from where I was on the slag pot. Won't let no colored work the valve. Thought we wasn't smart enough. We shovel the coke and sinter. Pour off the slag. The gritty work. Controlling the valve was hot work too, but that was a white man's job only. He had to be right up next to them air heaters. Likely, it would cook him if he wasn't careful. But Grimes, as far as I knew, was a decent white fellow. He never said a word to me, but he never said a word against me, either. But you don't know what a man will do if you mess with his daughter.

"When I got my tongue back I ask how he knew this. He said he had been investigating over in Hueytown. Talk was the boy and the gal had been seen together outside the plant gate. More than once. She would bring her daddy some lunch. But that would have been about midnight. What kind of gal be hanging around a plant yard at midnight?"

The glider squeaked as Mr. Snodgrass leaned over the arm to pick up his bean can. Dr. Blackwood cleared his throat, apparently to interject, but Mr. Snodgrass held up an index finger with the hand that still held the revolver. "I asked him how he knew. Who he talking to? I was hoping against hope it wasn't Grimes. But no, it was some of them rough boys, three or four of them, over at Hueytown High School.

"He looked kind of nervous when he said it and run his fingers through that stiff lock of hair on his head. Then he said, and he looked down, *They told me the girl liked the nigger*—then he looked up—*That's their word, sir*—he called me *sir*, but he might as well had kept it at nigger. *No offense. I don't talk like that.* Then he stared at me, that surprised look on his face. I could have slapped him into next week.

"But I bit down hard and said, *And then what?*

"*The girl said that she liked the boy.*

"I snorted I was so mad. *But they didn't do nothing to the girl. They just cut up the boy?*

"*Well, one of them said that the girl was* his *girl and he was glad somebody taught the, uh . . . well . . . the, uh, Negro a lesson he won't forget.*

"*But the boy you talk to, he didn't do it?*

"The cub shook his head. Said the rumor was the Ku Klux Klan of the Confederacy. He said it like that was funny. I just grunted. I knew who they was. Those gray-sheet-wearing sonofabit'. Don't wear white like the regular Klan and the meanest sonofabit' there is. They the ones beat up Nat King Cole. Beat Shuttlesworth and his girls too.

"Then he wanted to know if I could confirm the relationship. *What relationship? A colored boy don't have no relationship with a white girl. A white girl is death to a colored boy and any colored boy with a grain of sense know that, so unless Reginald had himself a death wish—*" Mr. Snodgrass was shouting, realized it and quieted. "But had I ever seen the boy with the girl? he wanted to know. And what if I had? Seeing them together don't mean they was together. Lots of people wait by the plant gate if they know somebody that work up in there. And then, I noticed he hadn't wrote a word on that tablet. Not one scratch. *Something don't smell right here,* I thought. *What paper you say you work for?* He said again something about the *Inquisitor.* Something close to that. I said, *And you ain't gone use my name?*

"*Confidential,* he said.

"*Well, confidential or confounded,* I told him just like that, *I'm done.*

"*But did you see the two of the together?*

"*You need to leave.*

"*Just answer the question.*

"*You need to leave, right now.*

"*But what about the dogs?*

"*I got a dog,* I told him. *It'll bark over here and bite over yonder. Now get!* I stood up and made like I was reaching for my pocket. He got my meaning and soon went on out. I watched him from the door as he was sidestepping the mud like a sneak dragging his shadow behind him." Mr. Snodgrass spat a big plug of tobacco into the bean can.

A car accelerated on a nearby street, its engine rising to a whine nearly as loud as the cicadas. The men sat up, looking out from our hilltop porch into the darkness where neither streetlights nor moonlight shone, to TV-lighted windows and the rooftops of Titusville. After a moment they relaxed, the sound of the car muted by distance.

Dr. Blackwood let out a curt sigh and reached into his jacket's side pocket and took out a shiny flask. "I believe that deserves an ameliorative."

"And a drink too," Mr. Snodgrass said. The men passed the flask among them sipping and coughing. Out of the same pocket, Dr. Blackwood took a matching cigarette case, triggered a switch that popped it open, and offered it to the other men. Neither of them took a cigarette and he asked if they were "quite certain," and picked a thin hand-rolled cigarette out of the case and placed it at the corner of his mouth. He snapped open a shiny lighter which flared blue, casting momentary light on his bony face. He blew out smoke through his nostrils.

"Snodgrass," he said to my father, "is a highly imaginative narrator. I doubt if any fact in his tale is accurate. Ah yes, *To make a poet black, and bid him sing!* Snodgrass sings like a whip-poor-will." Dr. Blackwood's lips twitched. My father broke into a broad smile. Mr. Snodgrass spat into the bean can. "Yours was not the only encounter with that intrepid investigator. He ventured onto the campus and somehow found directions to my office in the basement of Ramsay Hall. It's a close, windowless room, so damp at times that the covers of my books curl. But it is the garret from which I launch like Daedalus. Yes. Yes. *I know why the caged bird beats his wing / Till its blood is red on the cruel bars.* Barely did he knock before poking that scarlet pompadour into my sanctuary. My goodness, I rarely let my dear students in, and here he is, a white man, broadcasting imperium with a swagger as if he were the primogeniture of Czar Nicolas and Cleopatra. I can't say I wasn't startled, but I restrained from outburst and continued to jot down the rhyme which he had nearly joggled out of my head. I made him stand for a minute, before I looked up.

"*May I help you?* I inquired.

"He dragged my bergère, my good reading chair, from its place in the corner to the front of my desk. He made some hasty, excited introductions, and I was to believe that he was an investigative journalist from Philadelphia. The *Inquirer*, he said. But something was distinctly off about him, and every hair on my head prickled. *Fill-er-delf-ia*, he said. Not *Fila-dail-fia* or *FIL-de-fia*, as natives might say.

"*The* Inquirer? *Oh, how prestigious*, I said. I put my pen in the stand, and turned the pages of my cahier against the blotter. *So kind of you to visit.* He spoke rapidly enough for a Philadelphian, but there was a lilt that placed him farther south. Maryland, Virginia, perhaps. So I *inquired, How does it go in the City of Brotherly Love?*

"*Just great!* he said.

"*I suppose they must be, this time of year, the weather so pleasant in the spring. And the Swann Fountain at Logan Square as lovely as Trevi, but much more restrained. It's called Swann Fountain, you know, but there isn't a swan to be found. Not a one. It's only named for a family called Swann, not the fowl.*

"His eyebrows arched, or at least one of them did—and he took on that look Snodgrass described. He suspected I was testing him. *You've been to Fill-er-delf-ia?*

"*Oh yes,* I said. *Mind if I smoke?* I offered him one and he took it. I lit it for him, then my own. A minute passed as we took in our smoke, and not an iota of recognition from him of the trap. You see," Dr. Blackwood turned to Mr. Snodgrass, "The *Inquirer* building is located near Logan Square where there's quite a famous fountain, which is called Swann after the family and, incidentally, features many small figures of the bird, as well. But people get it the other way around, thinking the fountain is named for the birds. This urchin was an impostor."

"I thought he was a rascal!" Mr. Snodgrass said.

"And to close the trap, I asked if he would like a cup of tea, or a glass of water. Except, I didn't said *wa-tah* as a Southerner might, but *wood-er* as a Philadelphian would. And I observed him closely, and yes—not recognition, not familiarity, but the slightest crinkle of confusion on his brow. What should have sounded familiar to him did not! And so I leaned back in my desk chair, hoping my face did not show the smirk I bore toward him, and inquired as gentlemanly as I could muster, *And how may I help you?*

"*Oh,* he said, and took a pad and stub of a pencil from his pocket. Something he had seen in a movie, no doubt. I wonder if he'd thought to wear a fedora with a placard marked *Press* stuck in the band. He meandered—groping like a man destitute of vision in a room full of knives. Some whites are that way. Afraid to say the obvious, as if to acknowledge that I am a Negro is an insult to me. So I said it for him. And that very same question he asked you, Snodgrass. Did I know the Justice boy? Suspecting his perfidy, I declared that I had never heard of him, or the incident in which the poor lad was injured.

"*You mean he was . . . what! I feigned shock. Eunuchized! Who would do such a thing? And in America too.*

"The coifed clown went on quite awhile, chattering now that the subject was open. He explained as he explained to you, Snodgrass, about his intelligence from the hooligans at Hueytown High and the KKK of the Confederacy emasculating the boy and leaving him for dead. He went on about the girl too, *Emma*, not Ella. Quite the Queen of Sparta. A willowy, smoky-eyed blonde by the way he described her, his eyes bright and a pearl of spittle at the corner of his mouth. He claimed the Justice lad met her at the plant gate every night, by arrangement. She pretending to bring supper to her father, and he—well, it was never clear what rationale he was to give. This he claimed the girl said, though he never talked to her directly, or so he told me. He went on in a loquacious stream that grew more rapids-filled as he went. I learned more and more about the qualities of young Emma, even details about her fetching eyes and her nymphet physique. All the time, I remembered young Roland Justice, one of the few students I let into the office. Tall, he was, sepia, good-haired, and as athletic as a young John Henry. He would have been quite the ladies' man, but he was a dreamer. Though he had more than a few infelicities in his articulation, I enjoyed listening to his dreams. He wanted to be an astronaut, he said. He wanted to fly off to the planets." Dr. Blackwood paused, blew smoke through his nostrils, and added with a snort, "What Negro doesn't? But I encouraged him. To dream, even so quixotically, adds a glimmer to the gloom."

Like many boys back then, I too wanted to fly off to the planets. It was the years of the Mercury program and five men, that is to say *American* men, had gone up into space in the past year and a half. Just two weeks earlier, Wally Schirra had completed six orbits around the earth and the president said we were going to the moon!

"I had no heart to tell the boy of poor Captain Dwight. Why snuff out his flame? The example of Captain Dwight served as sufficient precedent."

My father groaned, a sound of agony and agreement. I learned much later that Captain Dwight had been the first black man to apply to join the astronaut corps, but officials had bullied him away.

"Finally, I'd heard more than enough of the calumny, and was about to ask the white deceiver to leave my office, when he put a finger to the corner of his mouth to wipe away a luscious glob of drool that had collected there and I saw a small, broad ring on his pinkie. A woman's ring. Gold and garnet. And I made out quite clearly the *H-U-E-Y* of Hueytown High inscribed around the stone. I checked my anger. The poem had been written, so to speak. Now only the rhyming couplet remained unfinished.

"*And you believe them to have been lovers?* I asked.

"His face flushed, a flare of anger or embarrassment or both. *No*, he said. *Nothing like that. She wouldn't have been caught dead . . .* He composed himself. *I'm only saying what I heard.*

"*But why would the boy have been so severely punished, if it were not true? If there had been no true romance?*

"*Romance? There ain't no romance.*

"*Romeo and Juliet. O, happy dagger, / This is thy sheath. There rust, and let me die.*

"*What?* He rose from my chair in a near bolt, both fighting and fleeing. *You need to be more respectful.*

"*Indeed*, I said, and as he turned I changed my tone to lure him back, back for the final conceit, *Young man, one question, please.*

"He turned.

"*When is her birthday? Emma Grimes? When is her birthday?*

"*January . . . He looked puzzled. January the fifteenth. Why?*

"*No important reason. Just curious. Always curious, I am.* I thanked him for his visit, and slowly, as if he were struck dumb by my inquisitiveness, he left the office. I sat listening to the clank of his heels on the stairs. For some long moments my mind seemed clear, not a jingle or rhyme in it. Then the image of that poor lad, lying in a ditch in the darkness with his pants soaked with blood. What horrifying thoughts must have filled his mind. Worse than the pain he must have felt, he must also have felt the fetid gloaming of his future pressing down on him. And then my anger flashed. What an insidious pogrom this petulant pareidolia wages against us! *While round us bark the mad and hungry dogs, / Making their mock at our accursèd lot.*"

The men were silent, but all leaning in, while Dr. Blackwood finished his cigarette and crushed the stub with his foot. "The garnet," he said quietly, "is the birthstone of January."

"You don't think he did it?" my father asked.

"No." Dr. Blackwood shook his head. "Not the crime. But he couldn't believe that she hadn't."

"Damn!" my father said, and suddenly stood and brought the butt of the shotgun to his shoulder. The other men stood up too, staring into the distance, over the rooftops. I stood. To the north, far down Center Street, a bright light blossomed, momentarily casting an orange bubble in the blackness. There was no sound of the blast. No whine of the speeding car. No screams of children or shouts of the men who undoubtedly rushed to the flames. No sirens. Only the imperturbable cacophony of the cicadas.

WHAT BRINGS YOU BACK HOME

BY MICHELLE RICHMOND

West Mobile

Wwhat brings you back home? people want to know.
"Work," she replies.

The assumption is that she has returned for a certain kind of work, as innocuous as it is forgettable. She's in marketing, right? Or is it advertising? One or the other. For some big tech company in California. Married to a guy from San Francisco. She doesn't come home much, hasn't since she met the guy. That was probably fifteen, sixteen years ago. She loves it out there, despite the fires and the earthquakes.

Only after she is gone, after the puzzle pieces have fit together, will someone say, "Who knew?"

Well, *she* knew. She's not one to make it up as she goes along.

Driving through West Mobile on her way from the airport, she sees a subdivision where the pecan grove used to be. The subdivision isn't new, but it's new to her. It looks like it sprung up in the early aughts, one of a few dozen such subdivisions that rose from bare ground, each with a name splashed in cursive across a grand entrance. The entrances were usually made of brick, often whitewashed. For some reason, the developers in those decades gravitated toward the word *plantation*, as though it were aspirational rather than shameful, a word without a history. This one is called Plantation Estates. The whitewash has faded, leaving the bricks a muddy shade of gray. Someone has done a nice job with the landscaping, though, a wild tangle of hot-pink azaleas blotting out the first four letters, so that the sign reads, *tation Estates.*

Meditation Estates, she thinks.

Invitation.

Rumination.

Adaptation.

Lamentation Estates.

Ha! That's it. She likes the sound of it: Lamentation Estates.

The subdivisions spread west toward the airport starting in the eighties and on through the nineties and beyond, out across the pecan groves and pastures. The subdivisions were once populated by people who liked their houses clean and new, who thought "previously owned" was a kind of a curse, people who didn't appreciate the charm of the old homes on Dauphin Street, who didn't like what was going on downtown. Now the city is booming, and people from all over move to Mobile without a history, not knowing West Mobile from Dauphin Street, picking houses online, surprised by how cheap they are, *in comparison,* but surprised they're not even cheaper, because, after all, it's Alabama. Not that long ago, four hundred grand would get you a mansion in Mobile. Now it just gets you a pretty nice house.

Like the other subdivisions along this flat stretch of green, the luster has worn off of Plantation Estates. The community pool has gone mossy. The tennis courts are unkempt. The houses weren't built to last, and it shows. People love it here anyway, their own hot, humid slice of the Southern dream. Which is different from the run-of-the-mill American dream, by the way: friendlier, and with more mayonnaise. Besides, who needs a community pool when you have a better one in your backyard?

At the ass end of the seventies, her parents bought ten acres of land where Plantation Estates now stands. Her mother's get-rich-slow scheme involved pecan trees. She and her sisters spent one sweltering summer on what her mother called *the land*, plucking pecans out of the dirt where they landed, collecting the hard brown shells in black garbage bags, which they transported in the family station wagon to a nut-processing facility way out I-65. It took about two hours to fill a garbage bag, and she and her sisters each earned $2.50 per bag. She doesn't know what the real profit margin was—whether her mother pocketed ten cents per bag or ten dollars. She doesn't know if her mother was subsidizing her and her sisters, or if she and her sisters were subsidizing her mother.

She remembers it as a summer of sunburns, raw fingers, and high hopes. At some point the family abruptly stopped going to *the land*. She doesn't know what happened. She doesn't know if they sold it, or if they lost it—her family seemed to always be losing things in those days—or if they never really had it. Maybe they made a down payment on the land, and that was it. Maybe it was done with a wink and a handshake, and the raw deal was so embarrassing in hindsight that her parents never mentioned it. They were, by all accounts, a sweep-it-under-the-rug kind of family.

How perfect is it that her target lives in that subdivision? Not in the biggest house, but in the second-biggest. On a quadruple lot, no neighbors on either side or behind, because he likes the privacy, and he can afford it. He bought the house when his boys were still small, when the subdivision was still going up.

* * *

The five-star hotel downtown is a real five stars. Everything is sparkling clean. The handsome concierge is sporting a rainbow tie, and even though he can't be a day over thirty, he speaks in the gentrified way of old Southern queens, who *owned* gay before it was acceptable in these parts, but often married women anyway, for the sake of their genteel mothers. Maybe Mobile has changed, a little.

A woman in a pastel-blue sundress presents her with a mimosa upon arrival, which is nice, then a second mimosa after she finishes the first, which is exceptional.

She holds her breath when the porter takes her bags, but figures it would arouse suspicion if she tries to take them herself. Anyway, she doesn't want the staff to think she's not a tipper. It's always like this: she doesn't mind tipping, but she hates having someone carry her bags. It makes her feel colonial. When you come from poor, poor is always in your head, and there's a part of you that imagines your own grandfather carrying some guy's bags, calling a stranger "sir." Her grandparents were sharecroppers, traveling from farm to farm in Louisiana and Mississippi, picking whatever needed to be picked, mostly cotton, their pale Irish skin blistering until it peeled. Coming from what was once known, unsympathetically, as "poor white trash," she'll never *not* feel like an impostor at a five-star hotel, although she sure as hell prefers them to the Motel 6.

"Your granddaddy put himself through college washing other boys' laundry," her mother has said a thousand times. She thinks of it every time she takes her clothes to the dry cleaner, and it's her familial guilt that makes her keep her mouth shut every time a silk blouse comes back ruined or a cashmere sweater doesn't come back at all. Every time she feels like complaining to the dry cleaner, she imagines her grandfather hand-washing laundry in the middle of the night, toiling for the future of the family, and that shuts her right up, even though she never met him because he died before she was born, and anyway, her aunt has always disputed that story about the laundry. Her mother has never been the most reliable narrator of their family's history.

In her room, after the porter leaves, she takes off her shoes and jeans and lies on the cool white bed in her T-shirt, enjoying the chemical chill of the air conditioner. After a while she gets up and showers. The bathroom smells like gardenias, and not just because of the soap. There are actual gardenias, fresh-cut, arranged in a mason jar. A nice touch—the mason jar—as if someone at the hotel has been watching Chip and Joanna on TV and wants to bring a touch of casual Southern charm to the five-star experience. She has always loved the sickly sweet scent of gardenias, though the opaque, velvet whiteness of the flowers strikes her as funereal.

It's half past nine in the evening when she gets out of the shower. She slathers on the hotel lotion, dresses in skinny jeans, sneakers, a long, flowy silk blouse, blow-dries her hair, puts on more makeup than usual but less than the mimosa lady. Her husband always joked that "the natural look" took an hour to achieve and looked about as natural as a dog in flip-flops.

She puts the suitcase on the bed and unzips it. She throws aside the piles of socks and T-shirts, opens the zipper compartment, retrieves the Sig Sauer that she picked up at a gun show near the airport—no ID required, no background check, just cash and a big-ass smile. The guy who sold her the gun was wearing a T-shirt with a picture of a robed Jesus holding a machine gun, defending the Statue of Liberty from a burka-clad figure wielding a machete. So much for subtlety. She wonders what her mild-mannered, laundry-washing, turn-the-other-cheek-preaching grandfather would think of this passionate new marriage between guns and Our Lord and Savior.

She slides twelve rounds into the magazine, loads the magazine into the Sig Sauer, flips the slide release, and places the weapon into the small of her back.

Time to go to work.

Let's say you have made a life together. Let's say this took half a lifetime to accomplish. Let's say that, after several years of trial and error, you met *the one*. You quickly disentangled yourself from previous entanglements, because it was obvious: *him*. You forged a bond. You lived together first to test the waters, though it turned out they didn't need testing; the water was fine. It was more than fine. You got married, had a child. Let's say you were blessed with far more than you ever asked for—the good career, the nice house in a small town in California, the vacations to Canada and Oregon and Mexico and, occasionally, Europe. Let's say the child was challenging, on account of her strong will, but she was happy and healthy, and you knew that stubborn nature would do her good, in the long run. You knew she would always stand up for herself. Also, even as a toddler, she had such a strong sense of justice, a kind of explosively righteous anger when she sensed someone—anyone—was being mistreated.

The husband was hardworking and funny and attentive, great in bed, and if you sometimes fought, you always came back together. There was no one you'd rather grow old with—really. Twenty years later, he was still *the one*.

Let's say everything was going according to plan, and better. Let's say you were happy. Genuinely happy. On a razor's edge of happiness, holding your breath, thinking, *How can this last?*

Let's say it didn't.

It's 11:01 p.m. when she pulls into Plantation Estates. She leaves the headlights off, rolls slowly through the azalea-covered entrance. She's charted it all out on Google Maps. She has photos of the house from Zillow. Not just photos but an actual walk-through, a video. How many times did she mute the Muzak and watch that walk-through in slow motion? The entryway, the living room, the open-plan kitchen, up the stairs to the master bedroom, down the stairs to the basement fitness room.

She deactivated the Nest Cam online before she drove into the neighborhood. She did it from the parking lot of a motel on Government Street, connecting as a guest to the motel's free Wi-Fi. The motel's password was easy to figure out—*Guest2018.*

So was the senator's. He's a well-known Bama fan, and he graduated in 1988. *Bama88.*

It doesn't matter how much you tell people about the fragility of their "smart homes," they will continue to choose dumb passwords, passwords they can remember.

His wife isn't home tonight. His two mostly grown sons are away. It's so easy to map a person's home these days, to map a person's life. So many details are public. The wife is the CEO of a telecommunications firm, and she spends a lot of time giving speeches. This week she's in Iowa. It's good for his brand—such a visible, attractive, articulate wife. Well-spoken but soft-spoken, powerful without committing the cardinal sin of losing her feminine charm. A powerhouse in her own right. Why isn't she the senator, instead of him? At press events and rallies and town halls, someone invariably asks, "When's your wife gonna run?" and he invariably smiles and says, "The day she runs is the day I hang up my hat. One politician in the family is enough."

She checked the sons' Instagram and Facebook profiles before she left the hotel, just to be 100 percent certain. The youngest son just posted drunk pictures from a frat party at Vanderbilt, and the eldest is leading an all-night coding session at his start-up in Greensboro, North Carolina. By noon tomorrow, she knows, the wife and sons will be heading home, converging in a cloud of shock and grief, a thousand unanswered questions. She feels bad for the sons, not necessarily for the wife. The wife helped him get where he is. Half a million dollars and counting from the NRA, the organization that would most keenly approve of her back-channel, unlicensed, untraceable purchase of the Sig Sauer.

She knows from interviews that he exercises in his home gym, at night between ten thirty and eleven thirty, while watching TV. He is regimented in his exercise schedule. He claims to only need six hours of sleep per night, and he says doing the elliptical before bed helps him sleep like a baby. He's not shy about his state-of-the-art sound system, or his affection for eighties TV. In an interview for a regional magazine last year, the wife said she had the whole thing soundproofed to save their marriage.

The sliding glass door on the back of the house is easy enough to open. He has never given up his pride at being a regular guy, living in a regular neighborhood, foregoing the security detail.

She finds him in the basement. It looks just like it did in the Zillow walk-through, only without the wallpaper. He is on the elliptical, facing a large wall-mounted television, his gray sweatshirt and blue running shorts streaked with sweat. The TV surround-sound is turned up loud, *Hawaii Five-O*—the original series.

If he were to turn around, he would see a woman who looks like a Girl Scout mom or mabe a new neighbor. She is not a scary person. She waits a moment. Perhaps he will turn around. She wants to tell him why she is doing this. She wants to tell him he is only the first one.

She wants to tell him she is starting at home. She wants to say, *This is the only way to make you people listen.*

Standing four feet behind him, she is not certain she would find the words. She is not certain she would be so articulate, or that she could even go through with it.

He doesn't turn around.

Is it even worth going into the details? The phone call from her sister, saying, "I just saw the news and wanted to make sure you're okay."

She was in the middle of trying to find colored ink cartridges for the printer, because she needed to print some photos for her daughter. She was sitting on the floor of the hallway, going through the cabinets where she thought the extra ink cartridges would be, if they had any.

"What news?" she had asked, holding her breath, but of course she already knew what kind of news it would be, because it was always that kind of news, once every couple of weeks or so. You just hoped it didn't happen in your town. You never thought it *couldn't*—that kind of arrogant assurance, "it doesn't happen *here*," ended at an elementary school in Connecticut—but you hoped it wouldn't. You hoped your town would be spared.

"Are Brian and Dottie at home?" her sister had asked carefully.

She could hardly get out the word "no"—wasn't sure if she said it, or if she just thought it so loudly that her sister heard.

"Where?" she asked.

One beat, two, an eternity. "Burlingame Avenue," her sister said.

"I have to go."

She called her husband, but there was no answer. She got in the car, hands shaking. They had gone out to Walgreens. Dottie had a poster due the next day. She was Star of the Week in her fourth grade class. They needed poster board, foam letters, and photographs, which was why she was searching for ink cartridges.

The last thing Dottie said to her was, "We never have *anything* we need in this house!" The last thing she had said to her daughter was, "I love you." Because that's what you say when you're a parent—no matter how mad your kid is at you, no matter if they won't say it back. You say "I love you" when they walk out the door, *in case.*

Goddamn poster board. Goddamn Star of the Week.

That first month, she kept finding herself parked in front of Walgreens, in a haze, sitting there, about to go in to buy poster board. If she could just get the poster board, none of this would happen.

Here's the thing: you have to start somewhere. A law is a law is a law, until somebody changes it. Death is impersonal until it happens to your family. She knows this, everybody knows this. But she wants people to know it in their guts, the way she does. She wants this man's wife to feel it when she wakes up in the morning, rolls over in bed, and her husband isn't there.

She even wants the sons to feel it: the absence of their father.

They won't know her name tomorrow. It will be years before they know her name, because this is a very long story. Longer than she wants it to be. It starts in Alabama, but who knows where it will end? She's determined to pull the pesky thread until the whole thing unravels.

Advertising? an old friend asks her on Facebook.

Marketing, she clarifies. Like any decent campaign, this one won't mean anything until it goes viral. One dead senator is a story, sure, but what she wants is much bigger. A movement. Something so catchy, the public can't turn away.

For a campaign to really take fire, you can't let the messenger get in the way. It has to be an invisible machine. No one can know who's working the levers.

In order to go viral, a campaign must be visual. Some say it's wrong to show the bodies of the victims. She understands, she gets it. On the other hand, she thinks of Emmett Till, how his grieving mother insisted on a photograph that changed the whole conversation.

Only bodies show the true nature of the violence. Without the bodies, the brutality is whitewashed, a blurred vision with a movie-like sheen. Just another action movie you forget after you leave the theater. All the movies run together; they're putting out so many these days. Her own family's death barely made the news. Only seven people died at Walgreens, after all. Twenty-three had died in a mass shooting on a high school campus the week before, fifty-seven at a concert a few months before that. "The incident" at Walgreens hardly even qualified, to the outside world, as a horror.

* * *

Four months after the senator's death, when the mystery remains unsolved, she takes a flight to Paris, a bus to Belgium. At an Internet café in Brussels, she enters the dark web. She posts three photographs of the senator lying on his living room floor in his own blood. There is a hole in the back of his head. This was not a matter of torture, but of expediency: she wanted to make it quick, and did. From the angle of the photo, you can see the exit wound in his forehead. The phrase *exit wound* sounds tidy; the reality is not.

After he fell she put a hole in his back, another in his right calf, another in his upper arm. Four bullet wounds, just like her nine-year-old daughter. She wanted to show what a body with multiple gunshot wounds looks like. Not under a body bag, but in full color.

Six months before she entered the sliding glass door at Plantation Estates, nine weeks before the murder of her husband and child by a man with a history of mental illness who legally obtained an assault weapon in Nevada and brought it across the state line to California, where such weapons were illegal, the senator had stood on the senate floor and lambasted the parents of dead elementary schoolchildren for "politicizing" a school shooting. He had led the charge against a bill that would prevent people with mental illness from purchasing weapons, and had sponsored a bill making it illegal to publish photographs of the bodies of victims of mass shootings.

There are those who will say that her grief made her crazy, but the fact is, her grief made her rational.

She had expected to feel more. She had expected to hate herself. But as she stands over the senator's body, gazing at the shredded exit wounds, the bits of brain and tissue scattered across the room, amid the rising stench of it, she does not feel guilt. She feels sadness, but not for the dead man on the floor. She is thinking of her daughter at Walgreens, and of her husband, who would have shielded their daughter's small body with his own if he'd had the chance. But he'd been in the next aisle over, and the gunman got to him first. He had been shot in the back, running toward their daughter. Only after the fourth bullet struck him did he collapse, and he was hit with three more after that. Then, one aisle over, the gunman found their daughter, crouching on the floor, trying to hide behind a sheet of neon-green poster board. The whole thing was caught on the store's surveillance camera.

The next day, after the detectives had completed the crime scene investigation and brought her family to the morgue, she insisted on seeing the bodies of her daughter and husband. She was told that she should not see them, but who was she, what kind of wife and what kind of mother, if she could not face the truth of what happened to her husband and child?

The senator had often boasted that he kept more than a dozen guns at home to defend his property and his family. "A gun in every room," he'd say with a wink. "If the bad guys come to my house," he had drawled in a widely televised ad for his latest senatorial run, "they're gonna have a fight on their hands." In the advertisement, which had been, after all, too common and too cliché to go viral, the polished wife and his polished sons were all holding guns of their own.

All along, she had suspected he might use one of them on her, and this thing might all be over before it really began. A failed marketing campaign, like so many other failed marketing campaigns.

So be it, she had thought. If she died, she died. She does not believe in heaven, and yet . . . if, somewhere in the ether, some atom of her dead husband and child exists, perhaps she would find them there. Probably not. And yet.

She walks back out through the sliding glass door into the hot, sticky Alabama night. She is wearing plastic gloves, plastic covers over her shoes. She is waiting for lights and sirens, but they don't come.

She is thinking, *This should have been more difficult.*

Walking through the yard, she feels the crunch of pecans underfoot. She reaches up and touches the leaves of a tree, rubbing them between her fingers. She remembers the last time she was here, thirtysomething years ago, on the land that was briefly in their family, until suddenly it wasn't. She and her sisters had competed to see who could gather the most pecans. In her sweat-drenched shirt, she lugged the heavy bag from tree to tree. Later, after the trip down I-65 to the nut-processing plant, they returned home and her mother had made the first and only pecan pie of her childhood.

"How Southern are you?" her husband once said affectionately. "You don't even like pecan pie." Her mother's pie was burned around the edges, a heap of brown on more brown. The outside of the pie, where the pecans had caramelized, was pleasingly crunchy, the burned taste not unpleasant. Inside, the pie was dense and gooey, the sugar so sharp it hurt her teeth. She and her sisters sat hip to hip on the floor in front of the television, drinking cold milk and eating pie.

She had a strange sense of elation but she felt it couldn't last. She didn't know what or why. She had that fragile feeling of her life existing on a knife's edge, as if the universe itself were a razor-sharp blade that could slip at any moment and slice right through her happiness.

MURDER AT THE GRAND HOTEL

BY WINSTON GROOM

Point Clear

Gordon V. Pumps whacked at the bamboo in the cane-brake as if he were possessed. He saw in each whack of the gleaming machete a death stroke against his nemesis, Horace P. Dumpler, head of the Alabama Department of Revenue, who was trying to put him out of business—or so he was convinced.

Gordon V. Pumps gathered the cane in his arms and threw it into the back of his truck, then headed to his house in Point Clear, not far from the Grand Hotel. The hotel had been a fixture on its great spot of land since 1842, and was considered a queen of Southern resorts.

Gordon had unctuously befriended a desk clerk, knowing firsthand that Dumpler visited the hotel for a week every spring to play golf, at which he was basically no good since he was a hunchback, although he excelled at putting. He played in a foursome with several of his revenue agents. That's how Gordon had encountered him, a year earlier.

For three decades Gordon had offered the public sightseeing trips into the exotic Mobile-Tensaw River Delta, which was the second largest of its kind in the country, and luxuriated in a diverse plethora of flora and fauna. Gordon had fished and hunted the Delta since he was a boy and knew as much, if not more, about it and its various features as anyone. He had a pleasant, folksy manner of speech and some people went on his trips just to hear him talk. He had a few years back taken courses and received a degree in what amounted to swampololgy from a local university, and he considered what he did more than mere sightseeing—it was *educational*.

That was where the rub with Dumpler came in. The previous year, while visiting the Grand Hotel, Dumpler had read a piece in the local newspaper on Gordon and his boat, and on a whim had booked a trip. The price was eighty dollars per passenger, and Dumpler had graciously included his revenue agents–cum–golf foursome in the retinue.

Everyone seemed fascinated as Gordon pointed out eagles' nests, eagles, cormorants, mergansers, herons, pelicans, snipes, wood ducks, ibis, alligators, nutria, wildcats, deer, feral hogs, possums, raccoons, various types of snakes, poisonous and otherwise, and turtles that sunned themselves on logs in the early spring.

The revenue agents asked questions about all this, but Dumpler's mind seemed to be elsewhere. Then, when Gordon cut off the engine to drift up on a flock of white pelicans, Dumpler broke the silence by proclaiming in a stentorian voice, "You must make a good living doing this."

The pelicans, of course, flew off.

Gordon was somewhat taken aback. "Not bad," he replied. "When the weather's good."

"Well, let's see," said Dumpler, "today with us you're making $320. If you have an afternoon trip, that's $640—I'd say that's better than just *not bad*."

"Like I said, there's a lot of days when I'm down because of weather."

Since the pelicans had taken off Gordon cranked up the engine. They'd been out a good two hours so he headed back to the dock. Everybody left seemingly satisfied and Gordon thought no more about these men until Monday morning, bright and early—at seven a.m. in fact—when a woman, wearing a purple pantsuit and a man's felt hat, showed up at the dock as he was preparing the boat for an eight o'clock trip. She said, "My name is Lucille Bratt and I'm from the Alabama Department of Revenue."

Gordon smiled politely and replied, "Pleased to meet you."

Lucille Bratt got right to the point: "Are you paying your Alabama State entertainment tax?"

"The what?"

"The entertainment tax. It was passed by the state legislature six years ago."

"Never heard of it," Gordon said.

"Ten percent of every dollar you take in," said Lucille Bratt.

"Ten percent? What for?"

You are entertaining people and they are paying for it. It's taxable."

"Well, my business is more *educational*," Gordon told her. "There are 346 different birds in this Delta, and I can spot every one of them. From time to time."

Doesn't make any difference," the woman said. "People with these duck-boat tours, and those folks down at the gulf who have the parasailing concession—everybody's got to pay it."

"Well," Gordon said, flustered, "I never heard of it. I've never heard any of the fishing guides mention it."

"They got themselves exempted."

Gordon stood there flabbergasted. Finally he said, "How did you come to be here telling me all this today?"

"My boss brought it up."

"And who would that be?"

"Mr. Horace P. Dumpler, commissioner of revenue for the state of Alabama."

"Dumpler? You mean the guy I took out last Friday?"

"I guess so," Lucille Bratt responded. "He was the one who told me about you. Said to tell you he had a nice time." She fumbled in her large handbag. "I've got these forms for you to fill out and sign. You'll have to pay the tax this year and back taxes for every year from the date the act was made into law."

"I've what?" Gordon exclaimed.

"It's the law," Lucille muttered resignedly.

On the back steps Gordon had taken out his $400 eight-inch Shun Hiro Honesuki butcher knife and was splitting the cane four ways from the top. He had already cut it into a dozen sixteen-inch pieces. He thought of Dumpler and sneered. When he had gone back six years to when the Alabama Entertainment Act was passed, he'd calculated that it would have amounted to approximately $28,000 in back taxes. Cash. That was on top of his federal income tax, his regular state income tax, sales taxes, boat taxes, car taxes, etc., etc.

He didn't have it. He would have to sell his boat. It would be the end of his business. He'd hired a lawyer but nothing could be done. The unfairness of the exemption for the fishing guides rankled him as well. He was providing an educational service. He was seventy-four years old, and he was dispensing all the wealth of knowledge he had accumulated up in this Delta since he was a boy of eight and his father had taken him duck hunting.

All his life he'd tried to be a good citizen—well, maybe in his drinking days he'd strayed from the narrow path, but those were long behind him. He'd always paid his taxes, he'd served honorably in the army in Vietnam, in combat. Served his country and now in his twilight years it was treating him thusly!

A murderous scowl twisted Gordon's face. *That low-life Dumpler!* he thought. *Comes on my trip, accepts my hospitality, then turns on me like a snake.* Now Gordon was sitting on the back steps of his house trailer carefully shaving one end of each of the bamboo pieces. It was large, heavy bamboo, similar to the kind they had encountered in Vietnam. That was what had given him the idea—a punji stake trap for that scumbag Dumpler.

On the golf course no less. It was an intricate plot but rewarding in Gordon's mind. He'd seen a number of punji pits in Vietnam—about three feet square and three feet deep, camouflaged. He could dig that in a night. He would do it about twenty yards from the eleventh hole on the Lakewood course, one of two eighteen-hole courses that the hotel maintained.

The plan was so ingenious that it gave Gordon a warm feeling inside, a premature sense of accomplishment. Number eleven was a short hole and there was a bit of swamp alongside the fairway in which he could hide and watch both the tee and the lie of the ball. His dog Lesly, perhaps the best bird dog in the South (everybody said that about their quail dogs), was intricately involved.

Having shaved each of the punji stakes to a point as fine or finer than the $400 Shun Hiro Honesuki knife, he gathered the pieces and placed them in a preheated 375-degree oven where they would bake all night. In the morning he would plunge them into a bucket of ice water, and when they had dried they would be as razor sharp and strong as the tempered steel in the Shun Hiro. The Viet Cong dug punji pits on trails everywhere Americans patrolled and not a few soldiers were maimed and even died from their wounds. The bamboo stakes were so strong they would actually go through the soles of leather boots until the army wised up and put metal plates in the soles, but that didn't make walking patrol any easier. The worst thing was that the Viet Cong smeared the tips of the stakes with human feces to create horrible and dangerous infections. That would be the finishing touch, Gordon thought, knowing full well where he would obtain the feces for that rat Horace Dumpler. There would be no steel plates in boots here. Only flimsy golf shoes. Gordon rubbed his hands.

While the stakes were baking in the oven, Gordon got into his truck with a shovel and drove to the Lakewood golf course of the Grand Hotel, and trudged to the eleventh hole, Dogwood run, now bathed in the light of a silver three-quarter April moon. He'd already sighted in the spot for his pit and had brought a small wheelbarrow with him to dispose of the excess dirt.

Lesly's role had been well rehearsed. He would hide in the swamp with Gordon until Horace Dumpler and his companions appeared on the eleventh tee. It was a fairly long way off but Gordon would be able to identify Dumpler because as a hunchback he never used a driver or even irons—he always used his putter, even to tee off. That might seem ridiculous but he'd perfected long putts up to fifty yards, and on a short hole he could be on the green in three shots; once there, he was deadly at the cup. Gordon had watched him every day since he'd arrived. At the cup, Horace Dumpler cleaned up.

The trick was to watch and make sure Dumpler was up to drive—or putt, or whatever it was he did—and then, when the ball got down close to the green (and the punji pit), it was Lesly's time to go into action. On Gordon's signal he would rush out and grab the ball and deposit it just on the far side of the punji pit, so that Dumpler would have to address his shot by standing on the pit—then, *voilà!* For the time being Gordon had put a piece of plywood over the hole, covered with leaves to disguise it, but as Dumpler's foursome neared, he would replace it with a light screen, camouflaged with leaves, which would immediately collapse when stood upon.

He could picture Dumpler writhing in agony when he fell into the pit, one or more of the deadly stakes driven into his feet and legs. Infection would begin immediately. Death, hopefully, would follow.

The first of the foursome teed up his ball. He drove a shot that landed square in the fairway, about forty yards from the pit. Gordon held Lesly back by his collar and he struggled to break free.

The others took their turns and then Dumpler addressed the ball with his putter. His first putt was straight down the middle of the fairway, but about a hundred yards distant. Dumpler, in his peculiar crouch, ambled down from the green toward his ball. Apparently it was the practice of the others to let their boss take more shots out of turn in order to catch up.

Dumpler hit his putt, which rolled to a stop within ten yards of the green and about fifteen yards from the punji pit. Gordon released Lesly's collar and he shot out from the edge of the swamp and scooped up Dumpler's ball with one smooth motion, turned, and trotted over to the lip of the pit and dropped it on the ground.

It all happened so fast that no one in Dumpler's party seemed to notice.

That bastard, Gordon thought. *Probably has these clowns playing with him on taxpayer money—hundred-dollar green fee—*

five times a week, plus meals, drinks, rooms, tips. Probably costing the taxpayers five grand. Maybe more. Bastard!

Dumpler approached his ball with a frown on his face. The others were standing around at the edges of the green, waiting. Gordon felt his throat tighten.

Dumpler had carried his putter over his shoulder but now swung it down as he reached the ball. He stood just beyond the leafy spot and scratched his ass, looking from the ball to the green. It seemed to Gordon that he could have used a 9-iron here, even with his hunchback crouch, but he kept to the putter.

Dumpler took a step forward onto the top of the pit. As his foot was still in the air, Gordon caught his breath and grimaced. The foot hit the pit. Nothing happened. The other foot stood on the pit as well, and Dumpler addressed the ball.

"Scheisse!" Gordon hissed, and slapped his forehead. He had forgotten to remove the plywood and insert the screen. Dumpler made his putt, which rolled right up the slope and onto the green. He then hunched over the ball and knocked it right into the cup. The others began to nod and clap. Dumpler smiled. The golfing party moved on.

Gordon sat at his kitchen table, steaming. It had been one of the dumbest mistakes he'd ever made, but he was determined to make up for it.

Later that afternoon he sidled up to one of the bellmen at the Grand Hotel and inquired what room Mr. Horace Dumpler was in. "I have a gift for him," Gordon told the man nicely.

All through the cocktail hour and dinner Gordon secretly watched the Dumpler party. After dinner (in the most expensive restaurant in the hotel—steaks and champagne all around) they repaired to Bucky's Birdcage Lounge for nightcaps. The men sat at the bar talking to several women, one of whom was, of all things, a dwarf, apparently on holiday. Gordon shook his head. He watched as long as he could, then snuck out and got his old golf bag, which he had left with the parking valet. Inside was a large, heavy, finely sharpened ax, a length of rope, an eyebolt, a small collapsible ladder, a measuring stick, a stud detector, a metal rod, a portable drill, and some light string.

He hid in the bushes waiting for Dumpler and his friends to go by; it was close to midnight when he heard them coming. It was too dark to see but they were headed back to their building, which was on the harbor where the boats were docked. Fourth floor. They had adjoining rooms.

Gordon gave it an hour and then went into action. He entered the building in the parking garage and took the elevator to the fourth floor. When he got to Dumpler's room he put his ear to the door. Dead to the world inside.

He worked quickly, taking out the ladder, the drill, and the eyebolt. In the ceiling Gordon made a small hole in a stud that was, fortuitously, directly in line with Dumpler's door. He used the metal rod to screw the eyebolt into the wood.

Bastard! he thought. *Probably wasted a thousand bucks more of the taxpayers' money tonight, and he wants to put me, an honest working man, out of business.*

Gordon used the measuring stick to cut the rope so that it would put the ax exactly five feet and four inches high in the doorway. That's how tall he figured Dumpler was. He tied the rope securely around the end of the ax handle and ran the rope through the eyebolt, winching the ax tightly against the ceiling; then he affixed the light string to the end of the rope and put the ladder and the drill away.

Gently, on tiptoes, Gordon tied the end of the string to the doorknob of Dumpler's room. He moved the golf bag around a corner, then marched up to Dumpler's door and banged on it five times with his fist. In a crack beneath the door he could see a light come on, and then he heard a voice complain.

Gordon stepped back into the shadows to watch the fun. The door opened and, as planned, that broke the string. This set the ax free in a huge swing toward the center of the door, and whoever stood there—namely Horace P. Dumpler—would get the blade right in the center of his face.

There was a muffled sound of locks being turned and then the door sprang open. Simultaneously the heavy ax, its razor-honed blade gleaming in the hallway ceiling lights, swung down toward the door. Gordon waited intently for the grisly *thud.*

But this did not happen. Instead the ax swung back, and then back and forth several times, before dangling to a rest in the middle of the hallway beneath the eyebolt. Puzzled, Gordon stepped out of the shadows, and there in the doorway was—the dwarf! Dumpler had apparently picked her up in the bar and brought her back to his room! The ax had swung a good foot and a half above her head.

Scheisse! Gordon thought. *How could I have known?*

Gordon followed Dumpler all that day and the next, trying to find an angle. He noted that at precisely five p.m. Dumpler visited the indoor swimming pool. He liked to dive, it turned out, and was fond of doing flips on the diving board. There was no lifeguard and few other people visited that particular pool, as there were several outdoor heated pools they could go to.

On the third day Gordon waited for Dumpler, hiding in some plants by the indoor pool. The revenue chief arrived exactly on time. The dwarf was with him—that could be a snag. She sat down in one of the lounge chairs beside the pool but Dumpler took off his robe to reveal only a bathing suit. His hump gleamed like a polished dromedary's dome in the ceiling lights.

Gordon slipped out into the hall and went to the reception desk. "Could you page a Mr. Horace Dumpler?" he asked innocently. The receptionist obliged, and Gordon sidled back toward the hallway where he saw Dumpler striding importantly through the doors leading to the reception desk.

They passed quickly in the hall; Gordon deliberately stared at the wall hoping Dumpler wouldn't recognize him. He didn't, though Dumpler did find something vaguely familiar about the encounter.

Gordon walked quickly into the pool area and stripped off his shoes, pants, and shirt. Underneath he had on a bathing suit. He went straight to the diving board clutching in his hand a bottle of Johnson's baby oil. He stepped out on the diving board and there squeezed the contents as discreetly as possible onto the very end of the plank. Then he bounced once, held his nose, and went feetfirst into the warm, heated water.

This ought to break his crooked neck, Gordon thought as he got out of the pool. Then he went over and engaged the dwarf in conversation.

Dumpler returned looking puzzled, muttering something about strange things happening in the hotel. Seeing that the dwarf was engaged in conversation, he went immediately to the deep end of the pool, stepped up, and addressed the diving board. Measuring distance like a football placekicker, Dumpler backed all the way up and then ran forward.

When he reached the end of the board, he hit the baby

oil and took off in the air, sort of like Rocket Man. But instead of doing a half flip as Gordon had envisioned, landing on his head on the springing board, Dumpler did a complete flip and a half, landing on his ass on the end of the board, which then propelled him—*sproing!*—straight up in the air once more for two additional flips before he hit the water in a kind of modified swan dive.

Both Gordon and the dwarf, whose name was Lorraine, watched this spectacle speechlessly. Dumpler's head soon emerged from the water and he cried out, "By God! Did you see *that!*"

Lorraine began to clap and shout. Dumpler staggered up the steps and out of the pool, into the waiting arms of his lover. They both jumped for joy.

"I was twenty years in the circus and I ain't never seen anything to match it!" Lorraine exclaimed.

Dumpler, noticing Gordon, said, "Say, haven't I seen you someplace before?"

Gordon stood for a moment twisting his hands. "Well, yes, you have. I have the boat that takes people up in the Delta."

"Oh, yes. Of course." Dumpler extended his hand to Gordon, who shook it lightly. "Say, I'd like to take that trip again. I'm here till the end of the week. How about it?"

"Well . . ." Gordon replied. He was thinking, thinking, thinking . . .

"My golf buddies have to go back on Friday . . . so it would just be me. I hope that's all right."

"Ah, yes, yes, certainly," Gordon told him.

"You know what I liked about that last time?" Dumpler enthused. "The alligators. I liked the way they come out in the springtime—especially that big fellow. How big did you say he was?"

"Seventeen feet. Maybe a little longer. Nobody's been exactly able to measure him."

"My, my," said Dumpler, "a man-eater. My, my."

"Yes," Gordon responded, serenely now. "Just meet me at the dock at eight a.m—or should we make it nine?"

"Eight," Dumpler said. "That last trip—don't know when I've enjoyed myself more! Just you and me!"

"Yes," Gordon smiled. "Just you and me . . ."

SWEET BABY

BY ACE ATKINS

Gu-Win

S he'd been so damn cute once, not even six years old, with big false eyelashes and a curly blond wig. People would travel for thousands of miles just to look at her on that shopping mall tour of '08, get her to autograph her signature porcelain doll, or hear her sing her hit YouTube song, "Sweet, Sweet Baby." Onstage, they'd dress her up as a rodeo chick, a genie, a pirate, and even a Vegas showgirl. Feather headdress, tall plastic heels, fishnet stockings, and attitude to spare. Her momma took a lot of heat for the showgirl costume, thousands of letters and e-mails to the cable channel asking why in the world a mother would want her child to look like a gosh-darn streetwalker. But her mother, Big Nadine, would look right in that camera, a Virginia Slim tucked between her fingers, nails long and red as blood, and say there wasn't nothing wrong with the costume, only with twisted, sick minds.

"Did it all start with pageants?" the man asked. He drove the black van in shadow, a hulking shape over the wheel speeding east along Corridor X toward Birmingham. Speaking with no accent, sounding like some kind of Yankee.

"At first," Cassie Lyn said. "After I won runner-up in Little Miss Lower Alabama, that's when I got noticed by Rick. He was the talent scout up in Birmingham. Mainly he worked with rodeo dogs and race car drivers. But he told Momma he saw something in me. They took a video at that pageant in Wetumpka and that's how I got on that show."

"You sure looked good on TV," the man said, following the highway blasted straight through hills of rock and stone, winding its way through the darkness from her hometown of Gu-Win. "You were so photogenic. So sassy. Such a cute little mouth on you. Blue eyes as big as marbles."

"Is that why you come for me?" she said. "Now I'm nearly eighteen."

The man didn't answer as they shot past a Love's Travel Stop and Cracker Barrel settled down in a valley below the interstate, Cassie Lyn hungry as hell, not eating since her evening shift at the video trailer. *Cassie Lyn TV.* She wondered if he'd feed her before he got to wherever it was they were going. He was a white man, maybe thirty or forty, with thin black hair and a mustache. He wore thick glasses and one of those shiny black windbreakers her granddaddy still wore. Members Only. The man didn't give his name. And she didn't ask.

She turned around toward the backseat of his car and saw a large section of rope, zip ties, and some silver duct tape. A shiny revolver, probably just a .22, showed from his jacket pocket.

"You didn't need that gun."

"Would you have come anyway?"

"I would've hopped in the car with the devil himself," she said. "To get free of that place. Is that who you are? Mr. Satan himself come up to Alabama to find Miss Cassie Lyn, former pageant baby all growed up?"

The man didn't answer, a long strange silence between them as they passed Cherry Road, and headed onto I-65 South that ran from Birmingham down to Mobile. His face flickering in and out of darkness from the tall lights along the guardrail.

"I wanted to hear you sing," he said. "It's sad you don't sing anymore, Cassie Lyn. It makes me so very sad."

"What do you want me to sing?"

"Come on," he said. "You know. Everybody on this planet knows your song."

"'Lady Marmalade,'" she said. "Shaking my little tail in that French maid outfit? Like when I was a kid, on the show."

"Exactly like the show. I even brought you that very same outfit. I bought it on eBay for a hundred dollars."

"That all you want from me?" she said. "For me to shake my tail? Or are you wanting a whole lot more?"

"I don't know. I guess I want everything."

Cassie Lyn could never remember a time she wasn't famous. Big Nadine said she'd been born wanting to perform, strutting right out of the womb and giving a big dazzling smile to the doctor. *Ta-da, I'm here*, covered in placenta and blood. When she was an infant, her mother sewed custom outfits for her, satin and rhinestones, denim and sequins, little cowboy hats, berets, and big straw sun hats. She learned to dance at ten months, got her ears pierced before she was one. Cassie Lyn not recalling what life was like without blush and lipstick. Big Nadine saying that God had given her a gift, a pinkish light shining across the sky the night she was born, never mentioning her no-count daddy who she'd only met twice. Their life nothing but pageants, from Baby Miss to Petite Miss all the way up to Little Miss. The plan—to hear Big Nadine tell it as they crisscrossed Alabama from one high school gym, church rec center, or livestock arena to the next—was work your way up to the big show. Miss Alabama. Miss America. Or Miss

USA if that didn't work out. On the cable show, Cassie Lyn got famous for saying she was all about the money. *Money, honey. Where my money at, Big Daddy?* Twitching that little behind and shaking her index finger.

Those were the good times, the high times, when she and Big Nadine split their time between Gu-Win and their condo in Orlando, Florida, shooting their reality show. Her new stepdaddy with the boat in Tampa. The money had been good, real good, almost enough to make her forget what it had been like when her momma didn't have a car that would run or having to sleep in some crummy old trailer. They went to Universal Studios and Disney World for free. Pictures with Minnie and Goofy. A princess makeover at Cinderella's castle.

Momma said she was proud. So very proud.

Folks comped them rooms at hotels in Las Vegas and over in Branson, Missouri, her big blue-eyed face with big red lips on T-shirts, coffee mugs, and her own line of gentle hand soaps. Momma said the design had been inspired by something called the Shroud of Turin.

But then there was that breakdown at Legoland, caught on a thousand different iPhones for the whole world to see. Cassie Lyn taking her little fists to that sculpture made in her image, the damn thing fat and blocky and seeming to mock her—index finger raised. Big Nadine said that's what killed them. And that woman never forgot, telling Cassie Lyn that was the reason things turned out the way they did, how their whole damn life crumbled and turned to Shit City, making them both broke and unimportant and worse yet, a sideshow treasure back in Gu-Win. Snickers behind their back at the Piggly Wiggly. Folks wanting to lay hands on them at the Shell station, praying for their future. More little kids—cuter and brighter, shaking their asses even harder at Big Nadine's classes at the Baptist church and finally that metal prison where they kept all those cameras. *Cassie Lyn TV.*

Watching "Sweet, Sweet Baby" twenty-four hours a day on the Internet . . . Rick, the agent's idea. It had something, a *revenue stream* is what Rick called it. Kept them fed and clothed. But Cassie Lyn knew that wasn't even a proper way to keep a dog.

She worked that goddamn trailer day and night, nothing to do but eat ice cream, stare at those six eyes watching her everywhere but the toilet, while she watched real TV or exercised in her underwear. All you had to do was sit there and take requests from subscribers. A man once offered her a thousand dollars to eat a banana real slow. Most wanted her to get nekkid but that wasn't part of the deal. Her mother called *Cassie Lyn TV* wholesome online entertainment. The video trailer was just another step in reality entertainment is what Rick said. This would be just a stepping stone back to the cable network.

But when that man, *BIGDADDY88*, offered her a way to escape, she didn't give it a second thought. *How the hell could it be worse?*

"What are you thinking about?" the man asked.

"That trailer," she said. "*Cassie Lyn TV.* Big Nadine never did tell me how much money we made."

"It was a subscription service," he said, heading toward the bright lights of Birmingham. Cassie Lyn hoping she was getting kidnapped back to Florida. Florida sure would be something. Palm trees, sand, warm breezes across her bare legs. "It cost nineteen dollars for the first month and then thirty-five after that. If you paid up front for a year, it was an even two hundred. That was really the best deal."

"Is that what you did?"

"Well, that didn't include the tokens," he said. "You probably made most of your money on token sales."

"I know all about the tokens. They make a jingle sound every time they slip into the virtual piggy bank."

The van smelled like hamburgers, burned meat, and onions. There were fast-food wrappers and empty cups down at Cassie Lyn's feet. The man fumbled with the radio, finding a local Christian contemporary station playing that song "Only Jesus" by the Casting Crowns. Big Nadine sure loved their music, saying she'd first heard them on Mike Huckabee's radio show, being real impressed they'd been one of the only American bands to perform in North Korea.

"You can make real good money on the Internet," Cassie Lyn said. "I just wish I knew how much. Big Nadine told me that I didn't need to mess with all that business."

"What your mother did to you wasn't right."

"Momma says she did her best."

"She used you," he said. "You should be a star on the Disney Channel right now like that Selena Gomez or Demi Lovato. That tall pasty girl from *Bunk'd*, Peyton List? You're a hundred times prettier than that skinny Peyton List."

"That was the plan."

"What happened?" the man asked. "How could Big Nadine screw it up so bad?"

"Guess you didn't see what happened at Legoland?"

The man snorted, the engine revving them up past seventy miles per hour, passing signs advertising VISIT MOBILE, "America's First Mardi Gras" and billboards proclaiming HELL IS REAL, the front of the van all black and slick, reflecting light along the darkened interstate. "That's not what did it," he said. "What happened is your stupid mother devalued the

Cassie Lyn brand. She took it too far, too fast. It didn't bother me when they first started selling your dolls on QVC, but when y'all did the skin-care line, shampoo, and costume jewelry, it made me sick. Even before the spinoff show and the meltdown, you'd already become overexposed."

"Overexposed?" she said. "That's why we went back home."

"To Guin."

"We live in Gu-Win."

"That's not what the sign said."

"Gu-Win is between Guin and Winfield," she said. "Wasn't a bad little town before they built the interstate and made us a drive-by community. We've still got a Walmart and a drive-in movie theater called the Blue Moon. My momma ran a vegetable stand right off the highway for nearly fifty years selling tomatoes, corn, cantaloupes, and hot-boiled peanuts. Fifty years, can you imagine?"

"I hate to say it, but your mother treats you like a trained monkey. I think she went back home because she couldn't cut it. Back to a forsaken state like Alabama? Does Big Nadine drink? She looks like a drinker, with her face all big and pink. Someone who'd down three or four lemondrop martinis a night."

"Momma's a Baptist," Cassie Lyn said, her little hands folded in her lap, bubblegum nail polish starting to chip. "Sometimes she'll slip and have one margarita at Los Amigos over in Hamilton. We like that place lots better than La Casa Fiesta. Big Nadine says they make the best taco salad in the whole state."

The man didn't answer, just drove with his mouth shut. Cassie Lyn grew quiet too, as they took a wide turn on the overpass right through Birmingham, headed toward the tall hills, and she looked over the city to see if she could spot the Vulcan statue. If the eyes were red, that would tell Cassie Lyn something, a sign from Jesus that she needed to go ahead with what she'd planned. She knew what she was doing walking out of that trailer with her pink backpack slung across her shoulder, seeing that black van parked out by the roadside. Everything she owned in the world in the backpack: two changes of clothes, her special teddy bear Reuben, sixty-two dollars, and her MacBook Pro.

"Can I at least ask your name?"

The man didn't answer.

"Can I call you Daryl?" she said.

"Why?"

"'Cause first minute I laid eyes on you, when you hopped out of that van, I said to myself, *That looks like a Daryl*. Also, you had what Momma called crazy eyes. I could see it when you took off your sunglasses, playing that loud music from your car stereo. What was that song anyway?"

"'I Want to Know What Love Is.'"

"That some kind of praise music?"

"It's Foreigner."

"Hmm," said Cassie Lyn. "Sounded like they were speaking English to me."

The man reached down, knocked an old tape into the radio, the praise music going away, a heavy guitar chord vibrating the insides of the car. "How about this?" he said. "Journey. You like to rock, sweet baby? I'll play you some real music from back in my day."

"Where the hell we goin', Daryl?"

"I can't say."

"Why not?"

"You might run off."

"Run off?" Cassie Lyn said. "Why on earth would I do that? This is the best goddamn day of my life."

"Me kidnapping you?'

"Yes sir," she said. "But you better stop off for a six-pack and Marlboros soon. I don't travel on no fumes."

"Don't you see what I brought?" Daryl said, wiping his eyes, nearly in tears. "Look in the back. I brought duct tape for your pretty little mouth. Ropes to bind your sweet, delicate limbs. And you know what? If you'd fought me, I even brought a gun. Doesn't that scare you? Doesn't that just chill you down to the bone, thinking on what I might do?"

"There's an exit coming up," she said. "I think they got a Stuckey's. You mind getting me a pecan log? Sweet baby's getting hungry."

⚜

PICTURE UP, B ROLL OF TODDLER CONTESTANTS TAKE THE STAGE . . . BIG SMILES. SPARKLY DRESSES. BLING PERSONIFIED.

CUT TO:
INT: EMBASSY SUITES, NASHVILLE.

Big Nadine rushes around the motel room in a frenzy. Her assistant, Rosalita, runs into the bathroom and closes the door to the camera crew, sobbing.

BIG NADINE: The hair didn't curl, we was running late on time, my dumb-ass boyfriend didn't find the right ho-tel. We are standing around at the lobby, waiting for him to show up with Cassie Lyn's wardrobe. I don't think any of this could go anywhere. This is the big time. This isn't just any competition. This is gosh-darn Little Miss Sassy Nashville. This is the damn Daytona 500 and the Super Bowl rolled into one. My people have messed up. And Cassie Lyn knows it. Look at her in tears, that little girl. I hate to disappoint her. This is all about her. All about her.

Close: Cassie Lyn in full makeup and pajamas, playing with an iPhone, looking up at Bugs Bunny on the motel television.

BIG NADINE: If that little girl ain't happy, Momma ain't happy. I think we better just pull this thing. Stop it. I can't put my little girl onstage like this. It just tears the guts out of me to send her on not pampered and prepared. How in the world could Rosalita be so almighty stupid as to mess up that wig? There ain't nothing to it. It's just some basic bouncy curls, made stiff with rollers and some hair spray. I swear to Jesus Christ Himself that woman didn't have but one job to do. I'm gonna send her on back with my boyfriend. That dumb bastard got himself drunk last night at an Applebee's in Chattanooga calling me like I'm supposed to come get him and make things right. He has all Cassie Lyn's things. How damn hard is that to remember?

INT: EMBASSY SUITES LOBBY.

Cassie Lyn, six, in a blue-velvet tracksuit, hair and makeup done, as they wait for a ride to the convention center.

INTERVIEWER: Are you nervous?

CASSIE LYN: Nope.

INTERVIEWER: Do you hope you'll win?

CASSIE LYN: I guess so. I hadn't really given it much thought. I'm really hungry. After the competition, Momma says she'll buy me some Popeyes fried chicken. I haven't eaten since breakfast yesterday. My stomach is making weird sounds like it's mad at me.

INT: HOTEL VAN—DAY.

Big Nadine stares out the window, hand touching her temple, crying.

BIG NADINE: Well, it's all about her and for her. If Cassie Lyn ain't happy, I'm not happy. This is all about her. All about her.

☙

Daryl looked tired, rolling into the Stuckey's off the Hope Hull exit at nearly three o'clock in the morning, only to see it was closed down for the night. Cassie Lyn turned to him, giving him that real pouty look with her bottom lip poked out. "Sure had my heart set on a pecan log, Big Daddy."

"Pecan log?" Daryl said. "I thought you had to pee-pee. Damn it. Just get on back in the van and we'll go across to that Love's. I need to get some gas anyway."

"Why won't you tell me where we're going?"

"It's a surprise."

"You said somewhere real special and real warm," she said. "Is that true?"

"Maybe."

"Are you gonna kill me?"

Daryl didn't answer, stroking his mustache, knocking the black van back in gear, driving slow and careful, blinker flashing to make a right turn. His face still half-covered in shadow.

"You sure are funny," she said, trying to brighten the mood. "Where is that little outfit, anyway?"

"The French maid?"

"Yes sir," she said. "You've got the song? 'Lady Marmalade'?"

"I have the *Moulin Rouge* soundtrack on cassette," he said. "I taped it off HBO last year. Between us, I think you outdid Pink and Lil' Kim. And that Christina Aguilera. They don't have a thing on sassy little Miss Cassie Lyn."

"I'm not so little anymore," she said. "My ass is as big as a steer."

"Don't you say that," he shot back, pounding the wheel. "Don't you ever say that. Those people making comments online don't have a soul. You're as pretty as you've always been. Who am I to complain about a few extra pounds? I'm fat and bald. I lost my job selling TVs at Sears. My good years left the station about fifteen years ago. You look great, sweet baby. You look so damn great."

"Do you love me?"

"Of course I do," he said. "What do you think this story is all about?"

It was morning by the time they got to Gulf Shores, Daryl nearly nodding off at the wheel as he pulled into the Red Roof Inn parking lot. Cassie Lyn finishing up her third warm beer, eating a package of little donuts from the gas station, powdered sugar scattered across her little chunky legs. Looked to be nothing around them but miniature golf centers and water parks. Across the street, she saw a sign for a place called The Track that offered go-cart racing and an arcade for the kiddos.

"Don't you even think about running."

"How many times I got to tell you, Daryl? I'm not scared. Not one damn bit. I'm excited. Excited about where we're going. Excited about our future together."

"Not even a *little bit* scared?" Daryl said. "You do know I'm going to have to tie you to the bed while I get some sleep. And if you try to run or scream, I'll have to put that duct tape across your pretty little mouth. You'll have to take in all your air from that pert little nose."

"I won't run," she said. "I won't scream. But if you tie me up and tape up my mouth, just how am I gonna sing 'Lady Marmalade' for you?"

Daryl shifted behind the wheel, like his insides had suddenly seized up, pain somewhere deep in his tight blue jeans. In the early morning light, she noticed his thick glasses were dirty and smudged. White powdered sugar on his mustache as he looked out at the motel lobby, thinking on the best way to play things.

"You'd do that for me?" he said. "Why would you do that?"

"Because you gave me a ride," she said. "You're my hero."

"I'm not gonna drop you off like some kind of hitchhiker, Cassie Lyn. You're coming back with me to my special home. I spent the last two months getting the basement all nice and ready for you."

"Like a pet," she said, smiling, twinkle in her eye. "Right?"

"Don't say that. Don't you ever say that. You're not a pet. You're my special princess. My sweet, sweet baby. My cutie patootie."

"Go get us the key, Daryl," Cassie Lyn said, touching his bony knee under the wheel. "I'm not going anywhere."

Cassie Lyn watched Daryl run across the parking lot toward the office, reaching down and unzipping her backpack. The laptop was charged and ready, the gun strapped to her meaty little thigh. In the early morning dawn, Cassie Lyn let down the passenger window and breathed in that Gulf Coast air, smelling just like summertime. *Ah.*

Wouldn't be long now.

The French maid outfit was a little snug, Daryl obviously not aware Cassie Lyn had put on ten more pounds over the holidays. There had been boxes of holiday cookies, Conecuh sausage, and dozens of little candy canes she sucked on in that elf costume. Every day was so damn boring in that little airless trailer, nothing to do but watch television, mostly the Hallmark Channel, and flip through trashy magazines Big Nadine bought for her at the Piggly Wiggly. *National Enquirer, US Weekly, Cosmopolitan,* and when she really felt generous, those big deluxe magazines that cost fourteen dollars about Jesus or the Civil War. Since Cassie Lyn had dropped out of school at eleven, Big Nadine figured buying her reading material was part of her education.

She stared at herself in the mirror, smudging on the eye shadow and combing through her lashes with mascara. She'd normally have stuck on some falsies, added some blue or pink extensions into her hair. But Daryl, or whatever his name was, would have barely noticed. The man's hand shaking as he lowered himself into a chair by the window of the Red Roof Inn, Cassie Lyn telling him to be patient, she'd be right back.

Cassie Lyn had set up her MacBook on the dresser, telling

Daryl that she needed it to play her signature song. Daryl had offered to play his scratchy tape from his busted-ass boom box, but Cassie Lyn said it'd be more special, more like the show, if she handled it herself. She'd set the screen with a nice view of the room and then left to get ready.

"My God," he said. "You've grown up. You're all grown up."

"You don't like that?"

"No," Daryl said. "It's just different."

"Good different or bad different?"

"You've gotten boobies," he said. "Big fat boobies."

"Sit on the bed, Daryl, and shut your mouth."

Daryl adjusted the thick dirty glasses on his face and did as he was told. The carpet was blue, the bedspread was gold and stained. Cassie Lyn reached for the coils of rope and threaded it through the headboard. She could hear the trucks and cars zooming past on the highway, morning light shining through the curtains, the yells and screams from the kids at the go-cart track. She bound his wrists nice and tight like she'd learned from Big Nadine's third husband, the sailboat captain. Just as Daryl was about to protest, she ripped off a nice thick strip of duct tape and covered his mouth. "Sit tight," she said.

She removed his dirty glasses, his eyes looking like they were going to pop from his head. Daryl just getting the idea.

She walked over to the dresser, pressing the space bar to illuminate the screen. *Cassie Lyn TV* was live and streaming. She already had 562 folks watching, more following every second. When she got to two thousand, she'd start taking requests.

Cassie Lyn pressed play on iTunes and "Lady Marmalade" started pumping from the tiny speakers, sounding tinny and hollow as she began to shake, bend over, and smack her butt.

Looking between her legs, she could see more and more and more followers coming online. Request after request before even asking.

When she'd realized that BIGDADDY88 was finally coming for her, she'd changed the settings on the Cassie Lyn site, sending money into her own personal account, something she'd had for three years but Big Nadine never knew about.

Cassie Lyn set her foot at the edge of the dresser and unstrapped the gun from her chunky little leg.

Daryl's eyes got real big as she posed in front of the camera, Daryl being able to see himself as clear as a reflection in the mirror. Cassie Lyn brought the little barrel up to her lips and blew on it as if it were hot. More and more and more requests. More cutesy poses. *Shoot him! Kill him! Right in the nuts!* People online were like this. So damn bloodthirsty behind the keyboard. They wanted to see some real fun, reality-based action.

Cassie Lyn bent over the keyboard and simply typed: *HOW MUCH?*

Before even pressing send, TOKYOJOE09 presented an offer even larger than she'd imagined. It was what Cassie Lyn had decided was her "getting with the program" amount.

"So sorry, Daryl," she said, aiming the pistol at him strapped to the bed. "Ain't nothing personal about it."

He was screaming down deep behind the tape, thrashing in the bed from side to side. Snot coming out of his nose. Cassie Lyn aimed the pistol, turning back for a moment to see how high her tokens had gone. Spinning and spinning, coins pinging and pinging that piggy bank.

It was enough. It would get her far. She turned back to Daryl with a big ol' pageant smile. *Make 'em love you!*

"It was never about you, sweet baby," she said. "It's all about the money, honey. Good night, Big Daddy."

The man closed his eyes and began to weep.

PART III

I'M SO LONESOME I COULD CRY

THE GOOD THIEF

BY RAVI HOWARD

Escambia County

F or his final meal, all Thomas Elijah Raymond asked for was the cake, the one he remembered from Rachel's Luncheonette in Phenix City. Prison rules would not allow food brought in from the outside. Safety concerns. So if Rachel Walker said yes, she would have to come to Holman on the day of the execution and make it there. How to feel about such a thing. Reluctant but somehow compelled. When the day arrived, the warden's assistant greeted Rachel and escorted her to the kitchen. She could now match a face to the familiar voice she'd heard so many times over the phone in the few weeks before.

"Mrs. Walker, the warden will be here in just a minute. Can I get you anything in the meantime?" Francine asked.

"No thank you. I believe I'm fine." Rachel wanted to sound more certain, and to dismiss any worry on her behalf. She wanted to manage that on her own.

As Francine disappeared out the swinging metal doors, Rachel watched her through round windows. The secretary walked past the corrections officer stationed outside and made her way down the corridor. The sound of her heels on the concrete was muted by the thick steel doors that had by then stopped swinging. Rachel was alone now, in the newly constructed wing of Holman Prison. It was the biggest kitchen she had ever seen.

The smell of her restaurant kitchen had always given her comfort. It was not the smell of any particular dish, but instead, the slow, thin layers built up over the years. There was always cinnamon near, even if it wasn't needed for a recipe. Bowls of it curled like scrolls used to write down histories. She wished she had brought some with her. This place smelled of bleach and ammonia. It whispered nothing.

Stainless steel shelves lined the freshly painted walls. Ceiling lamps spread a dull glaze across the metal fixtures. Fluorescent bulbs gave a uniform pale, except for a single lamp that flickered, blinking rays the color newspaper turns. A dozen parallel steel islands rose from the white tile floor, wrapped in thick blue plastic pulled taut over narrow shelves and secured around the edges of the counters. Two adjacent counters had been uncovered and arranged for her use.

Francine said that the new wing had been finished just a few weeks ago. The men would arrive soon, and from this kitchen they would be fed. In the meantime, the warden had arranged for her to work here. According to Francine, the warden thought the space would be ideal. Out of the way. Clean.

Rachel had dressed for a warm autumn evening. She was not prepared for the cold confines of the prison kitchen. It seemed the temperature was set for a space full of toiling and heat, so the cold air, unchecked, was too much. The place wasn't walk-in cold, but damn near, with air washing over her feet in waves, snaking around her ankles, and running along the floor. She placed her purse on the counter and removed a black apron, *Rachel's Luncheonette: 35 Years in the Baking* in silver lettering. The silver blouse beneath her black suit matched the silver in her hair. This was how she dressed for the events she catered. Yet she had taken pause when readying for this occasion. There was no proper dress for preparing a last meal.

She'd made the three-hour drive alone. Told her family she was driving to Atmore for the weekend. Her daughter and son-in-law were busy running the kitchen, had been for years. A few days a week, she would walk the dining room and the lunch counter, speaking to the first-timers who had her cookbooks, had seen her on television here and there, and she greeted her regulars as well, trying to dole out the same welcome to any and all. She could come and go, be there without being there—her face on the menus, and the sides of buses, and the coffee bags and cookie tins they sold in the gift shop. So when she told her family she had a small job in Escambia County, a repast for an old acquaintance, she'd saved herself the strain of a lie she may have to remember later. The truth itself was troublesome enough.

The prison kitchen was empty except for the ingredients. Francine had requested them a week before. Shortening, sugar, molasses, salt, baking soda, and flour had been lined up in a perfect row, labels turned outward. Someone had seen fit. Perhaps an eye for detail, but certainly a nod toward normalcy in a place where there was little.

On a nearby table sat an antique mixer. In the kitchen of a prison, the comforts of home seemed strangely out of place. She flipped the power switch on the mixer, and the familiar hum rang out.

She remembered having a similar one years before. Its heavy body and thick insulation produced a hum unlike the rattling of the new ones that cost more than they should.

Chrome, as beautiful as it could be, was hard to keep clean. Working folk had no time to worry about fingerprints and smudges. The matte metal about the kitchen reflected indistinguishable masses of light and dark, but in the chrome she could see herself.

She examined her reflection in the mixer's oblong body, getting closer to it until the moisture of her sigh obscured her image. With one of the neatly folded dish towels, she wiped the chrome clean.

"It was my mother's."

She had barely grown comfortable in the silence when his voice rang out.

"I'm sorry. I didn't mean to frighten you, Mrs. Walker. I'm Lionel Peters. The warden here. I'm sorry I haven't had a chance to meet you previously."

He walked over to greet her but waited for Rachel to extend her hand first. An old-fashioned stance that she hoped would fade; indeed, Lionel Peters looked a few years her junior. Set in his ways, she was sure. But he carried himself a little older than he was, and his clothes didn't help. His suit surely had the right cut and hang before the years settled into it. He was conscious of his posture, but the slouch in his jacket remained.

"Did Francine offer you anything when you came in? Excuse me if she didn't. We can forget our manners working in here. Can I get you anything, coffee or something?"

"She offered, but I didn't need anything."

"Well, everything you asked for is right there on the counter. Your perishables are in the refrigerator over there. The ovens are behind you. Officer Earle will be right outside. Holler if you need anything. He can escort you to the facilities if you need to use them. I apologize we didn't build a ladies' room on this end. You sure I can't get you anything, coffee or something?"

She shook her head.

"What else?" the warden said while flipping through a deck of papers on the clipboard he tapped against the counter. "I feel like I'm forgetting something. Oh yes, the list. I want to make sure we got everything. Shortening, eggs, sugar, cocoa, flour . . ."

"There is one thing. I realized much too late that I left something off the list: my vanilla syrup. We make our own to sell in the gift shop, so I'm just so used to having it around and not buying it. Coming down here's out of the ordinary, to say the least, so clarity has been a little challenging."

She knew they had rules about bringing things in, but she prayed they could look the other way. The warden was killing a man, and he had made a show of this little bit of kindness, so certainly he could see fit to say yes. She took from her bag a bottle and set it down gingerly, almost like a beg-your-pardon for it being there against the rules.

The bottle rested between them, and the warden walked a bit closer and turned it so the label faced outward like the rest of the ingredients. He smiled a bit then, looking from the label to her, the pattern in the design the same as the embroidery on the apron she carried. Good branding. Her smile in the photograph was clockwork, perfected after years of showing her teeth because she had to, and then because her enterprise made it worthwhile.

"I understand. I got no qualms with it, considering."

He was decent enough, but Rachel could tell the warden wanted no part of this. The letter in two places said he would understand if she said no. She could just send a recipe, and they'd honor his wishes. But if she'd said no, she would still know Thomas Elijah Raymond's execution date, and she would probably look at the clock well aware of the hour. She would have wandered there in her mind even if she had said no to making this drive.

"We pick a fine time to pay attention, don't we," she said. Rachel was looking away, but the edge to her voice was unmistakable.

The warden said nothing.

She paused before she spoke again. "Nobody looking after him for years, and he's got all kinds of eyes on him now. More this evening, I suspect. Spectators."

"Witnesses. The family of the victim." He pressed the clipboard flat against his waist, a stance that seemed automatic. "He doesn't deny what he did."

"I'm thinking about what *we're* about to do. Me and you both. Trying to wake up and go about my business tomorrow and thinking back on this here."

A hand on the counter then, like candor needed a different sort of balance before the words came freely. "You'll probably feel worse about this tomorrow than you do today. I always do."

"Why do it then?" she said.

And there they were on the other side of the nicety. She saw in the warden a decent man, but maybe that was part of the problem. What decent folks were willing to go along with. He was quiet for a minute, and he breathed in and out with too much intention. He glanced away in a room with no windows, and he seemed too accustomed to conjuring some good memory, a little daylight stored away for days such as this one. The ease in his face said as much.

"My wife reminded me this morning that we ate at your place awhile back. We were on our way to see some of her people in Tuskegee. Enjoyed it immensely—just a good meal on a good afternoon. I didn't mention it to Raymond, because it's rude to reminisce on things. Get casual with the outside world. Do you remember him?"

She shook her head. "So many kids over the years, it's impossible to say."

"Well, in any case, you're appreciated."

"Please tell your wife I said thank you. To you as well. Like you said, it doesn't sit easy, so—well, thank you."

It was quiet for a while again, except for the lights and the freezers, and the sound of Lionel's wedding band against the countertop, a little sonar to bring him back to whatever was next on his clipboard.

"You sure I can't get you some coffee or something?"

"No thank you. You've done just fine with the mixer."

The warden excused himself then, and as he made his way down the corridor, the metal doors swung to silence. Rachel was alone again, her mind holding vigil. She had lied to the warden about Raymond. How could she not remember?

The boy couldn't have been more than six or so, because she remembered him sitting at the table with what looked like his grandparents, coloring the children's menu with the Crayolas she passed out in sardine cans. His family was on the way to Huntsville, the space center they said, and he had lined up the salt and pepper shakers, the Louisiana Hot, and the Heinz bottle as rocket ships taking off from the tabletop. To get dessert, he had to promise to finish the green beans, alone on the plate where the chicken had been, the wing and drumstick reduced to gristle and bone. He chewed with purpose but not enjoyment, like he was practicing handwriting with his jaws. But the booth they chose was across from the cake display, so he did a bit of window-shopping while he finished the last of the beans. Rachel was on the other side of the glass loading the shelf of red velvets. She remembered him studying his options. He didn't like the green beans one bit, but he'd kept his word and intended to make the most of it.

He asked for the molasses cake, while his grandparents had red velvet and buttermilk pie. They thanked Rachel as they left, and then she looked away and didn't see the boy fall to the ground. A child on the floor raised no alarm at first. Kids were prone to go from dillydallying straight to sprinting and stumbling. And the tantrums. But something was wrong because when Rachel finally noticed the boy on the floor, his eyes were widening as he struggled to breathe.

In the commotion, his people thought he was choking, but there didn't seem to be any obstruction in his throat. He held his mouth open wide, still searching for air. Rachel got to the boy first, the allergy syrup from the first aid kit in hand. He coughed up the first dose, but she gave him more while his grandmother rocked him, his grandfather fanning with a napkin. By then the boy was breathing easier, and the gentle wheeze faded a bit.

After taking several deep, full breaths, the boy cried some and peered around. He hadn't lost consciousness, but his eyes looked beyond them, apparently seeing nothing. Then he finally recognized them—Rachel, his grandparents—and it seemed he had to lock eyes on everyone gathered around him to fully return to the world. And then it was over, the scare behind them.

Rachel was always careful about nuts and other common allergies. But the boy's reaction to molasses was a rare occurrence. People like to sue over such things, but these folks sent her a letter of thanks. She would find out later that the grandparents were guardians, new to his care, and they hadn't known about his condition. She wondered then about his parents, what tragedy or rift had brought him to the care of his elders.

It was a blessing to discover his condition in caring company.

Beneath the cursive of the grown-up handwriting, the boy had signed his name: *JoJo*.

In what she read about him during his trial, she discovered that his grandparents had died. He had made his money as a day laborer, and Thomas had killed a man who refused to pay him. He had gone through the victim's pockets for the money he was owed. Murder in the commission of a robbery.

There would be no clemency. As part of the death decree, the state of Alabama would use three chemicals for his lethal injection. After the first drug, he would lose consciousness. The second would shut down his muscles. The third would stop his heart.

What Rachel carried in her bottle would do the same, answering the young man's request for a final and private mercy. All he asked for was the cake like the one that showed him what his body could not take, what in the right dose might knock him unconscious or even kill him. Molasses had stopped his breathing once, but he'd been a boy then. She knew it wouldn't be enough for a man, so she had turned to her garden.

She had years ago planted a small plot of cassava in her greenhouse and used it for her baking. The lined skin of the cassava felt as rugged as cypress knees, but the flesh, handled carefully, was a wonder to be fried or roasted or used in her baking. She took the time to learn how to prepare it safely. Cassava carried its poison in the coarse skin and the leaves, the parts exposed to the world. And perhaps that was how it should be, a shield to survive in a certain kind of world— to thrive even. To carry out JoJo's request, Rachel had saved what was meant to be discarded, the cyanide in the pot liquor, thickened with the starch of the root.

During his trial, Thomas Elijah Raymond had been shuttled back and forth from the new county jail to the new courthouse. Depending on the road they took, he may have passed the hillside where Russell County did their lynching, out on a hill they named Golgotha. The name had confused Rachel when she heard those stories as a child. The killers had tried to sanctify their work, but it was nothing more than blasphemy. She knew that hilltop from the Easter hymns, New Testament scriptures, and the Sunday school books. Three crosses. The Bad Thief cursed it all, and the Good Thief asked for grace and mercy.

Thomas had asked her for the same, and she'd brought his grace and his mercy, and it floated there in the thick sweetness of her bottle, a dose large enough to claim his body. He would die that evening, but she wouldn't let them make a carnival of him. The spectators would have nothing to witness, because he could do his dying, make his peace, in private.

She turned the dial on the oven to 350 degrees. The perishables, she retrieved from the refrigerator. The other ingredients, she opened, poured, and measured. The pans, greased and floured, lay waiting for the batter. When the time came, she turned on the mixer and listened to its baritone hum as it folded the necessary elements, one into the other.

HER JOB

BY TOM FRANKLIN
Clarke County

Three months to the day—it was past time, she told herself—she drove to her son's house to pack his things, get the place ready to sell. She hadn't been back since cleaning up the mess in the bathroom, where he'd done it and given her five hours of hard work, so much bleach it burned her eyes and, perhaps permanently, irritated her throat. She'd avoided going inside the house since and left it locked, driving out here once or twice a week to make sure no one was vandalizing it, paying a black boy to cut the grass and collect the mail.

Now she stood at the door, finding the key among other keys and fitting it in.

Inside it smelled. She'd emptied the garbage before leaving three months ago so it wasn't that; the fridge was empty too, and the deep freeze. She walked by the cellar door and stopped. That's where it was coming from, something sour, a dead rat maybe. She'd never been down there, in all these years, just in the living room where they'd sit, her chattering and him grunting when he had to.

The cellar door was padlocked. Her last time here the slow-lidded deputy hadn't even bothered to go down there he was so ready to get out. She'd tried the keys then and none had fit and none fit now either. It was why she'd brought a crowbar.

She went to the recliner where she'd left it by her purse and was sweating by the time she pried the hinge off.

The door swung in and she stepped back, the stench so awful she covered her mouth and nose. She was suddenly frightened, thinking how secluded this house was, the nearest neighbor a quarter-mile away. Her son used to say that was the one thing he liked about Clarke County being so isolated. He said he could be himself and not give a bleep what anybody else thought. She hadn't wasted much time worrying about what he meant by *being himself*. Who else could he be? The truth was she had no idea why he'd done what he did in the bathroom. He'd always been a private boy, guarded, gone at seventeen, she never learned where. And he'd been back, here, in this house, a year before she even found out. Gone for a whole year and then back for another whole year, with no word! Worse, she'd heard about his return from Lamar Jones, of all people. How delighted Lamar had been to tell her, how everyone knew about the son before the mother, their dirty laundry flapping for the world. She'd come over that day all those years ago and knocked and then pounded, and her son had pretended not to be home. She'd known he was, though. She'd felt him.

She felt him here too, now, as she descended the stairs, tracing her fingers along a rail silky with spiderweb and dust, the crowbar heavy in her other hand.

At the bottom it was cooler, the smell worse, the concrete floor so cold she could feel it through her shoes. She stood among vague shadows, a washing machine maybe, or a giant sink, and swept her hand in the air until she touched a string.

When she pulled it and the light flickered on, everything

became clear, everything, and she knew that she'd always known.

The crowbar clanged by her feet.

It had been him, her son, him all along. That missing girl, from Thomasville, from such a good family . . .

That poor girl, her poor, poor mother . . .

She backed up the stairs pulling at her fingers and at the top began to scream.

But nobody heard, not out here, this far out, not in Clarke County, and soon her voice was gone and her throat sore and she went into the bathroom, panting, thinking she might vomit.

But she didn't. Instead she remembered her last visit, a few days before he did what he did, and she wondered now if the girl had been in the cellar then, if she'd heard them talking, above, through the ceiling, did the girl wonder at the mother's high, empty chitchat? *That's your problem*, her son would say. *Who cares what she thinks?* Sitting in that recliner of his, he would've reminded her of, say, the time that lady at the church said he stole from the collection money and she, his mother, believed the lady over her own son. He would remind her how, later, another boy confessed. One thing nobody told you about being a mother is that they grow up and remember all your mistakes.

But did he remember the croup, the screaming, how she had to sit up all night with him? Did he remember getting expelled from Bible school for biting? From elementary school for exposing himself to a girl? Did he remember all the snotty teachers, nosy neighbors, and ex-husbands? Did he remember ignoring the one who tore herself open to give him the very breath he seemed to resent?

Maybe she would throw up after all. At least the bathroom was clean. When she was done she would rise from her knees and go outside to her car and come back in with her bleach and her brushes and get to work.

Another thing nobody told you about being a mother: you never really stop.

XENIA, QUEEN OF THE DARK

BY THOM GOSSOM JR.

Avondale, Birmingham

The sliver, a lone ray of sunlight, slipped inside the crack of the door, cutting into the pitch-black darkness inside the building, and shined on the thick black curtains she hid behind. Where in the hell was Justin?

She was scared! Pissed and scared. She had told herself she would not be, but . . . She had promised her therapist she would not be, but . . . Her brain raced uncontrollably. She could not slow it down. *What ifs* chased each other in circles. She had to face it. That was part of the agreement with her therapist. But . . . what if it was going to start all over again? What if they were all waiting outside, cameras and microphones? What if it was a joke?

"You leaving?" asked Arnold, the big reliable engineer, her bodyguard, the closest thing she had to a friend other than Justin.

Mentally occupied, she heard him but didn't. She looked right through the massive Arnold, but didn't see him. Would mass hysteria again be a part of her life?

"Yes, waiting on Justin," she finally answered.

"You okay?" Even though Arnold knew the whole story, he pretended he didn't. She pretended she didn't want or need Arnold to be standing there looking after her. Arnold pretended he didn't notice.

Arnold was a Birmingham native, and like many Birmingham natives he was a daily lunch customer at Niki's West on Finley Avenue, a popular buffet restaurant featuring home-style cooking. It was part of his daily itinerary and his three-hundred-pound legend. When he wasn't working, he was eating. When he wasn't eating, he spent many hours in porn chat rooms where women knew him by name but not physical appearance. He used his handsome cousin's photo to entice the older, more mature women he preferred.

Justin and Arnold were Xenia's entourage, confidants, and support system. Arnold, a childhood friend with no family of his own, was a brother to both Justin and Xenia, as well as a part-time bodyguard to Xenia. Justin trusted Arnold with Xenia's life. Arnold saw it as an honorable calling.

Arnold opened the curtains and let in the morning sunshine. It shined brightly in the big window that was blacked out from the outside. Xenia gave him a look.

"I'll just be right here," he reassured her as he stepped into the next room. "Get my phone and call Justin."

Call Justin. That had not occurred to her. *Fear does that*, she thought.

The juxtaposition of the beautiful sunshine and the ugly fear crawling inside of her . . . would have made her laugh if she was not so terrified. Now that she was back, the terror, like last time . . . struck a nerve.

Where was Justin? He was supposed to be here! DAM-NIT, JUSTIN!

Six hours earlier

The hands on the old-fashioned black circular Seth Thomas clock on the faded green wall sat still. No motion. Time literally stood still.

There had been so much anticipation of this night, the

return of Xenia, Queen of the Dark. The Internet world buzzed. Websites and social media platforms crashed around the world. Media of all types descended onto Birmingham, where she had resurfaced to claim her crown.

A nervous twinge tickled her insides.

Slowly . . . but definitely, the big hand on the old clock shifted right, made a loud click, and covered the minute hand, striking midnight. The theme music kicked in.

"Girl on Fire" by Alicia Keys brought the room and the international audience to life. The Queen was back! Arnold grinned at her through missing teeth, from his technical sanctuary in the accompanying booth. The new studio Justin had built for her, in a nondescript office park in Birmingham's Avondale community, was perfect. Xenia had a condo she called home, with underground parking so she wouldn't be seen outside. But she was so excited to be back; she often spent her days at the studio working.

Diana Krall's aptly named "I've Changed My Address" was next.

It was almost as dark inside the building as it was outside. "The Queen of the Dark likes it that way," she said.

She'd inherited her fondness of the dark from her dad, who had been one of the first black deejays in the 1970s to work at a white station in the city of Birmingham, when AM radio dominated the dials. His handle, "Ronnie Dodd up here in the dark," fit his midnight-to-six shift in a downtown high-rise. Because of his tales, Xenia had never considered a daytime gig.

She knew they were all waiting: fans, friends, and newcomers.

Not yet ready to fully engage, and to pace herself for the next six hours, Xenia came back with "Everything Must Change" by Randy Crawford.

The worldwide promotion for her return had been off the charts. The big sponsors, their briefcases full of financial promises, hustled aboard their corporate jets and headed to Birmingham International Airport. They all wanted her: *Good Morning America, The Today Show,* Hollywood, the fashion houses. The same sponsors who'd abandoned her when the trouble arose now wanted back in. They would have to pay! Justin would see to that. He had the whip hand.

"Less is more!" bellowed Justin in one of their backyard sponsorship meetings over spicy Popeyes chicken and beer. "We make Xenia super exclusive!"

It had been shameless, but strategic. Xenia would be everywhere and nowhere at the same time. There would be no appearances—she would not be seen in public (without a disguise). No television interviews. Yet she would be seen all over television, social media, and heard on radio in carefully crafted messages promoting her return.

"Everyone will know Xenia, of the Dark, but no one will know Xenia, Queen of the Dark," Justin bragged.

The strategy fit Xenia. She'd had enough of the spotlight the first time around. Besides . . . everything was changed, different. She didn't need or want that anymore. Fear brings humility.

The show's format would be the same. Xenia would command the midnight-to-dawn hours and she would talk, interact with her worldwide audience, play music, interview celebrities, interview whomever, until six a.m., five nights a week.

Arnold counted her down to the new beginning, their future: "And three . . . two . . . one." He pointed his big stubby finger at her, and she went into full Xenia mode.

"Hey, everybody," Xenia's smooth melodious voice cooed

across the Internet. She breathed seductively into the micro-phone, "I am Xenia, Queen of the Dark."

The Queen was back! If it was possible, the world shook.

She had been born beautiful. Everyone in the hospital agreed. The green eyes set deeply in her mocha-colored skin and wavy, flowing, jet-black hair made her stand out among the other newborns. "What a beautiful baby!" the onlookers all exclaimed. They were Xenia's first audience.

She grew to be more beautiful. Her smile, her full lips, her body cried out for attention. The charisma that flowed from her character, her personality, and her kindness highlighted her physical beauty. Kindness was the most important thing her dad had taught her.

As a teen and young woman, modeling was her founda-tion. It came easy to her. Stand there, put some nasty thought in your head about some boy you know, and pose. She was good at it and it paid her well. As one of the world's most sought-after supermodels, she did promotions, advertising, and runways at all the major fashion stops in Paris, London, and New York. Her mixed ethnicity made her seem exotic and she was accepted all over the world. When asked about her background, Xenia exclaimed, "I am Xenia, I belong to the whole of humanity!" Until . . . she started to feel like a piece of meat.

"When that happens it's time to get out," her parents had warned.

Ronnie Dodd, her dad, had come to Birmingham from Opelika, where he had been hired for the midnight-to-six time slot by the local radio station because no one else wanted it. "Give it to the young black guy," management had rea-soned. Ronnie became Opelika history, the first black guy

. . . *thing.* Ronnie then turned the opportunity and the station into a moneymaker. Within a year he was scooped up by WSGT, the largest and most popular station in Birmingham. WSGT broadcast from a downtown high-rise, which looked out over the city. Ronnie was once again given the midnight-to-six slot. It wasn't long before "Ronnie Dodd up here in the dark" was born.

Within a couple of years of arriving in Birmingham, Ronnie knocked up his girlfriend. It caused a stir.

Mariessa was her own melting pot, Anglo mixed with Greek, Italian, and Latino. In Alabama, if you weren't black you were white. Being white, she wasn't supposed to be Ronnie's girlfriend. Not openly in the 1970s, in Birmingham, Alabama. Hell, it was still illegal for blacks and whites to marry.

Her world was the over-the-mountain upscale neighborhoods and country clubs of Birmingham's suburbs. Her family, without hesitation, barred her from ever bringing Ronnie home again after that first time, after dating him in the shadows for a year. Plus, Ronnie was ten years older and already had a son, eight-year-old Justin, with his high school girlfriend in Opelika.

Mariessa announced her pregnancy to her family on a Sunday after church. Her mother, knowing how headstrong her daughter could be, accused her of intentionally getting pregnant. Had she? Mariessa smiled. Rather than fight it out, she and Ronnie packed up his VW bus, Justin, and the newly born Xenia, and headed to California. They were married on Venice Beach with Justin as his dad's best man and tiny Xenia in her baby carrier, the flower girl. Ronnie worked out a deal for the midnight-to-six job at KPCH in Santa Monica overlooking the Pacific Ocean. He was operating in the dark once again, this time in California.

* * *

Mariessa's mother led the way back.

Marcella, Mariessa's mother, an educator/artist, decided that being in her only child and grandchild's life was worth the friction with her husband John. She didn't confront him about bringing them back to Birmingham, nor did she ask him to visit them in California with her. She instead made the cross-country flight three times a year, rented a small cabin in Santa Monica, painted at a local studio, and enjoyed her family and the Southern California lifestyle. During these visits she came to think of Mariessa's stepson, Justin, as her grandchild as well. She grew as close to him as she was with Xenia.

John's resistance would last another fifteen years.

Working to piece her family together through the grandchildren, Marcella would pay for Justin to go to law school if he agreed to do it in Alabama. Justin consented. He alone moved back with his grandmother. Marcella leased an apartment for him. John insisted Justin stay with them, but in the gardener's cottage behind the house.

After law school, John bragged about his "black grandchild," who had finished atop his class and was recruited by every major law firm in the state. John's firm hired him. Justin was on his way to being a pillar in the New Birmingham.

The Temptations' "My Girl" ended.

"Hey, everybody! It's so good to reconnect. I love you all," Xenia told her fans around the world. Mentions, hashtags, and tweets all echoed their love back to her. "I'm back, stronger than ever. Better than ever," she assured all.

Xenia's voice sounded almost like Sade singing—smooth, soothing, and personal. Her listeners felt she was talking directly to each one of them. And she was.

She got right to the heart of the matter: "Hey, everybody, I want to be perfectly clear . . . I did *not* have an abortion." She dropped that bomb in a firm and even tone.

The rest of her soliloquy to "her people" around the world went smoothly. She went into more detail about her miscarriage than she could have ever imagined. The miscarriage had almost killed her. To then be accused publicly of having an abortion! How could she? *Why* would she? The pregnancy had made her so happy. So excited. Her life had meaning beyond herself. She had started bringing little baby trinkets to the studio.

It had begun with a phone call, "The Voice," and then the firestorm on social media. She was still on the air in Santa Monica, having taken over the midnight shift from her dad, who was semiretired.

"You're going to hell! Hellfire and damnation for you! I know your secret," the creepy voice had threatened. The Voice accused her of killing her baby. "A mixed-breed murderer, a whore," he had called her. He demanded that she reveal to her audience who the dad was and whether she had told him about the abortion. "You're going to hell," he repeated. "You got the devil in you. And *I* will be your judge and jury." When he was ignored he became more threatening, more menacing. *I will be waiting . . . and when you least expect me,* he texted.

There were not enough ways to stop him. Even when his calls to the studio and her cell were blocked, he used burner phones to text and e-mail. He dominated every night's show. Changing her numbers did no good. Somehow, he always found her . . . Every time she blocked his attempts he got angrier. "You will burn in hell!" he spit at her. They were the longest nights of her life.

"Who is this?" she would question him repeatedly. She

had no idea. She had not dated steadily for some time. She was not interested in marriage. Her life would not be traditional.

One memorable night, each word of explanation triggered more e-mails, texts, tears, phone calls, tweets, and hate from the people she had thought were her fans. *How could they be so mean*, she wondered, *when they don't even know the real story?*

She wanted to explain . . . yet the artificial insemination was no one's business but hers. Tabloids splashed their pages with Xenia and her abortion. *Is she a whore, a murderer?* they asked.

Xenia became another fallen celebrity. The pitfalls of fame nearly ruined her. The social media rumors of an abortion and the harassing threats, on top of her miscarriage, sent her into a hole she could not crawl out of.

She stopped trying to explain herself. She fell apart. She refused to work. Refused to eat. Refused counseling. Refused to leave her bedroom. It was her right to grieve and give in to her terror, and she did.

Her doctor declared her physically fit, but still she wouldn't utter a word. She listened to the hip-hop artist snaPz's suicidal song "Dear God" over and over. Then it was Van Morrison's lyrics, *"Just like Greta Garbo, I just want to be alone."* Finally, on their fifth try, Mariessa and Marcella got her in front of the right therapist. Still, Xenia went two more months without speaking. At four months, she started crying, inconsolable weeping. At six months, she announced she wanted to go back to her show. "I have to," she declared.

Justin began the rebuild. He, Marcella, Mariessa, Ronnie, Arnold, and even John brought her back through love and reason. The new show would originate out of Birmingham.

"You're the girl," her mother and grandmother assured her.

* * *

The night rolled on. Three o'clock. Four o'clock. It was as if the Queen had never left. Xenia gave a shout out to her friends in Cumberland, Maryland, and the annual DelFest Music Festival that featured the folk group the Infamous Stringdusters.

Aretha Franklin's "(You Make Me Feel Like) A Natural Woman" . . . caused a sensation with many of the female listeners.

Women tweeted, e-mailed, and called with their own stories. Subjects were dear and personal. Men listened.

Xenia took a couple of calls. A guy flirted with her and then proposed. Xenia laughed it off.

The Internet blew up. Social media numbers set records, then more records. News media trucks roamed around Birmingham broadcasting from the many Xenia parties, receptions, and concerts. Xenia had not sought the attention again, but it felt good.

She soothed the Internet crowd with Dr. John's version of "In a Sentimental Mood."

Then . . . "I know where you live, whore! You can't get away from me. You're the devil." It was him! She knew it instantly. The Voice. She froze. Fear shot through every fiber of her body. The Voice, the one who had started the abortion rumor, the one who had terrorized her. "Yeah, I'm back, whore."

The last time he had stalked and terrorized her, nearly driving her crazy. She became the victim of Internet bullshit and the many people who had nothing else to do around the world but share and forward Internet bullshit.

He had never been caught. Justin and John had tried. They'd worked with police and private cyber hackers. They'd invested in seminars. How to Bait and Catch the Anonymous Person Harassing You; How to Stop Online Stalking; How to Catch a Cyber Stalker. But the Voice was always two steps ahead. After it all became too much, Xenia had dropped off the grid.

Her mind now raced. *What if he's here? In Birmingham? What if . . . ?*

"You think you can move and get away from me?" the Voice threatened. "You think I won't bring the wrath of God Almighty down on you? I'll prove it to you—" The call abruptly cut off before he could finish.

Arnold had activated the security and tracking measures that John, Justin, and a young technology associate at the law firm had installed as they built the new studio. Arnold swiftly blocked another incoming call from the Voice. A call was immediately placed to the Birmingham chief of police, a good friend of Justin's. Arnold switched the phone line to another caller. A different man who expressed his admiration: "Hey, Queen, we love you." But the damage had been done.

Frozen, Xenia's look to Arnold asked if the security measures were working. Were they able to track him? Could they locate him? Turn him over to the police? Finally get rid of him? If only she could be certain . . . she would not be so afraid. *What if he really does try to kill me?*

In the lengthening silence, Arnold cued up "I Can't Quit" by Robert Cray.

She was surprised at how quickly the fear had returned. How quickly and immediately she felt threatened. Would she really be able to move on?

Arnold would not look at her. He nervously fidgeted back and forth between his iPad, cell, and laptop. His hands raced over the keyboard, clicked his mouse, and jumped from one piece of sophisticated equipment to another while red, green, and yellow digital lights flashed. Were the lights signaling that they had caught him? Did they have a line on him?

When Arnold finally made eye contact, she knew. His face loudly spoke his disappointment. The Voice had eluded them again. *Damn!*

Social media messages continued to flow in, all positives, all full of love.

We love you, Queen.

We'll catch him.

The fight for Xenia's soul was being fought over the Internet. Her mother and her grandmother texted, *Be strong. Stay fierce. You're the girl.*

Emboldened and determined, Xenia ended it all with five words: "I have spoken the truth." The simplicity reverberated in the Birmingham communities of Titusville and Woodlawn, in the suburbs of Vestavia, with fishermen in Maine, millennials in Japan, down below in Australia. *#TruthMatters* became the leading hashtag the world over.

The Voice did not return. The Queen relaxed. She reconciled herself to the life she had chosen. Could she handle it?

She played snaPz's "Neva That."

She signed off with, "Love, peace, and happiness to all." With emphasis she promised, "See you again tonight at midnight." Arnold grinned and nodded his approval. The show had been a big hit! She had made it all the way back. The Internet buzzed, people around the world expressing their joy.

Now she stood back, maybe ten feet from the front door. The Voice was all she could hear in her head. *I know where you live.* She wanted to move but couldn't. The uncharacteristic hesitancy upset her. *Deal with it*, she told herself. Was she afraid to go outside? No! Yes! She was. Would they all be waiting? Would *he* be waiting? *Deal with it*, she repeated in her head.

The old framed cover of *Esquire* dated December 1986

grabbed her attention. Ronnie had left it hanging by the door so she would see it when she entered and when she left. The cover title read, *What Are You Doing with the Rest of Your Life?* She smiled. At seventeen, she had asked her dad, "Were you ever afraid of working at night?"

"Most nights," he had answered. "It's some interesting cats out after midnight. Got some threats when I started dating your mom. But that motivated me. *Fuck fear*, I'd tell myself. Once I started spinning the records and talking with the people, it was on."

Her fear dissipated. Each step made her stronger. Arnold walked with her. *You're the girl* echoed within her.

Then she saw him, a dark silhouette in the sunshine. The fear shot through her like a .38-caliber bullet.

Justin! It was Justin! The fear left. The terror subsided. The tenseness exited her body. She relaxed. An uncontrollable smile raced across her face.

Fuck fear, she thought, and stepped out into the bright sunlight.

PART IV

The Angel of Death

LAUGHING BOY, CROOKED GIRL

BY BRAD WATSON

Gulf Shores

Betty dangled the first chicken by a yellowed leg above Russell's head and waited till she saw his prehistoric eyes shift just a fraction up to see it. She'd worked the old wig onto it, poked a bobby pin through, and fastened it to the chicken skin as best she could. She waited only a second, let go, and marveled at how the fat old alligator snatched it out of the air. The wig had been made from Aunt Sip's own hair, cut off when it was long and young, when Aunt Sip had no need for a wig. And now that Aunt Sip was old and sick and her real hair was falling out, she never wore it, go figure, didn't even care if she was nearly bald and ugly as a troll.

The sky was clear and so bright blue you'd never know there was a hurricane coming into the gulf, supposing to hit land smack in the mouth of Mobile Bay. The tourists had already thinned out with the coming of September and the few remaining were packing up to leave before the storm. No one was taking time to visit the souvenir shop and museum, anyway. No one much stopped in anymore at all.

Betty climbed back down the little stepladder she'd set beside the pit. There were two chickens left in the sack. She'd taken them all out to thaw the night before. The butcher at Winn-Dixie saved and sold them to her for next to nothing after their color turned, which mattered not a whit to a gator.

Russell was supposed to get one a day, but she'd held off feeding him the last two days and now was going to give him three at once. She thought he might like it that way better, more like in the wild, where some days he might catch something, and some days he might not.

Into the cavity of the second chicken she had tucked the reading glasses, gold watch, and stinking dental plate with two teeth snaggling down. Into the cavity of the third chicken she stuffed a handful of snot rags, a photo of Aunt Sip on the beach in Key West with maybe the man who was later half eaten by the shark, and a thimble Aunt Sip had stuck to her finger when she fell asleep that afternoon while sewing a patch of disintegrating calico back onto an old quilt. When Betty gently pried off the thimble, Aunt Sip had only murmured something she couldn't understand, something like *Never*, and *Mmm-hmm*, and *Onions, that's what*.

She climbed back up the ladder with the second chicken and held it with both hands, so the things in the cavity wouldn't fall out. She could see Russell's eyes looking up at it, wearing his smug, crooked alligator smile. She dropped it and Russell had it down in a snatch as if it were no more than a little leg or a thigh.

She took up the third chicken and wrapped it in a piece of the nightgown Aunt Sip had told her to throw away on Monday because it was rotten, saying it was rotten because she, Betty, hadn't washed it right, which wasn't true, it was just that Aunt Sip had worn it out and Aunt Sip was so nasty it didn't take any time to soil her clothes. It had been rose-colored but now had barely the tint of any color at all, like the color of a pan of water if you've cut your finger and washed it in there. She tucked the loose ends of the nightgown into the chicken's cavity, climbed back up the ladder, and dropped it in.

She put up the ladder and washed her hands in the tub sink outside and crept back into the apartment in the rear of the museum building, down the dim narrow hallway, past Aunt Sip's bedroom, through the living room, and had the door open to enter the museum when she heard Aunt Sip.

"Betty," Aunt Sip said, her voice a gravelly purr followed by a phlegm-racked cough.

"Yes'm."

"Where the hell you going?" A voice both plaintive and peeved.

"Just down to the beach awhile."

"Did you feed Russell?"

"Yes'm."

"Bring me some warm milk when you come back."

"Yes'm."

All this poised in the doorway with one foot just above the museum floor, frozen midstep and praying she wouldn't have to go back into the room, and when Aunt Sip didn't respond to the third "Yes'm" she quickly stepped through the door and closed it quietly, then moved past the Native American displays and basin racks of shells and starfish and seahorses, rubber toy sharks, snorkel masks, the standing racks of postcards and suntan lotions, then she was out onto the shell parking lot and across the deserted highway, through the little pass in the dunes, and down to the surf. Nobody was out just then at all. She could see the hazy shape of a shrimp boat on the horizon. The breeze flapped her lank black hair around her pale cheeks and thin, wide mouth. She was so thin and runty she looked like a little crooked, stunted sylph on longish skinny legs, her tiny torso twisted with scoliosis, a small face and large ears that stuck out through her hair like a bush baby's, and huge eyes that almost seemed to frighten people. She would stand in the middle of her tiny pantry bedroom looking down at her crooked chest with one healthy breast blossoming like a ripe nectarine and the other nothing but a discolored little prune. The scoliosis bent her to one side and down, so it was always surprising what strength she had in her skinny shoulders and arms. She was all too aware of her appearance, not that anyone ever let her forget. She had attended the high school up in Foley until her sophomore year, and then dropped out, tired of the snickers and jeers and the boys who would imitate her crooked hobble down the halls. Of course, the principal wouldn't let her out of gym, where the other girls barely tried to hide their horrified laughter, their *oh my gods* behind their palms, their cow eyes cutting over to stare. But it was the mimicking that hurt the most. Hearing laughter after she'd passed a group in the hallway and looking back to see Jimmy Teal humping along, face twisted into a grotesque freak's, one arm hanging down nearly to the floor, twisted that way, and loping along in a hobbled gait that, altogether, looking like someone doing Frankenstein's Igor a lot more than someone imitating Betty. It was after one of these incidents that she left school early, caught a ride to the beach in the bed of an orange grower's pickup, and never went back.

Up the shore where the state park pier jutted into the gulf she could see a scattering of people out on the beach. She thought to walk up there and get away for a little while but knew she'd better go back and get Aunt Sip her milk.

She listened to the sand ticking against the front windowpanes, a steady, irregular ticking and spattering when the wind gusted harder. Candlelight dawn crept into the room. She heard Aunt Sip calling in her harsh, crusty voice, "Betty. Betty."

Betty cut her eyes that way but did not move. She couldn't move, not now. Not thinking what she was thinking now. If she moved now she might not be able to think it anymore and she wanted to. She wanted to think it until she knew she could do it.

"Coming," she said. "In a minute."

Je'sus stood at his post in the corner behind the glass diorama case, face and hands the color of smoked ham skin. Leathery lips sewn shut with cat gut. Arms crossed over his chest. He was said to be a Creek Indian, and she liked to imagine how it was he got the wounds in his hands that were the reason they'd named him as they did. A shop joke. Aunt Sip made her pronounce it in the Spanish way so as not to offend any Christian customers. Betty went to the library one day and looked up some traditional Creek names, and decided she would secretly call the mummy Chebona Bula: Laughing Boy. It was why they had stitched his mouth shut, to stop him from laughing, make him shut up.

Aunt Sip coughed.

"Betty."

The cases filled with conch shells, flint arrowheads, little dried dead seahorses, augers, sand dollars, starfish, and sharks' teeth—in such moments the small dried creatures and angular artifacts seemed still alive, trembling in a stasis barely contained within their dried skins, the polished surfaces of their shells, their coiled and chambered passages. Each glassed-in scene—of a Typical Dinner Preparation Among the Creek Indians of the East Gulf Coastal Plain, of ichthyosaurs-eating plesiosaurs, of sea crocs and prehistoric sharks, of Je'sus the Creek mummy, of Typical Wildlife of the East Gulf Coastal Plain and the Gulf Shore—watched her in reverence of the moment when she would either act or not.

She rose from the stool behind the counter and went back to the door to the apartment. She hadn't emptied Aunt Sip's ashtray and maybe that was what Aunt Sip was calling about. Would say, *Betty, be a dear and haul your worthless little hyena ass here to dump that goddamn ashtray.* She practiced not flinching and blinking but she always did, stood there like someone had just brained her with the blunt tomahawk at Je'sus's waist, waiting for Aunt Sip to start laughing in her raspy coughing way, falling back into the bedcovers and trying to reach for a Pall Mall, knocking everything to the floor. She was tired of smelling like Aunt Sip's cigarettes all the time too. She could smell it on her clothes when she'd wear them over her swimsuit down to the beach, where she'd swim if there was no one around. And when she came out of the water and lay down on the sand her towel stank of it, and when she pulled her oversized shirt on over her shoulders again later, the shirt stank of it. It all stank of Aunt Sip.

Her whole life stank of Aunt Sip. The cruelest thing Aunt Sip had ever done was agree to raise her so her mother could go away to Hollywood and be a movie star, then tell her she'd never made it that far, was a prostitute in Las Vegas. She didn't believe that for the longest time. But when you never hear otherwise, well. So maybe she would do the same. Maybe she would take some man's money for whatever nasty he wanted to do, and then she would do the nasty all the way to Las Vegas and one night she would take a man away from some old lady who would turn out to be, once she looked hard through all the makeup, her mother, and she would laugh and maybe spit at her and say, *Well all right now, how does it feel to be left behind, you old whore?*

I don't know you, she would say. *I don't care a thing about you at all. You can just shift for yourself.*

She said these things, whispered them, to her image in the mirror in the bathroom, practiced the tough-looking sneer on her face when she said them.

She straightened one of the embroidered silk pillows Aunt Sip claimed she'd gotten in Shanghai. Said she'd been there buying whores, in the good old days, before the barrier island casinos in Mississippi closed down. Well, she guessed that could be something close to the truth, if you figure Aunt Sip was the head whore. The pillow's material was smooth and almost slippery between her fingers. The pillow itself was very light, as if filled with the finest of down. She balanced it on one palm at arm's length.

"What in the name of holy hell are you doing?"

The voice had gargled up from the covers.

"Nothing but fluffing your Chinese pillow, Aunt Sip."

Aunt Sip's face was a doughy gray, her eyes like old, dry, blackened wounds, punctured slits that somehow imparted derision. Hands atop the covers like large bloated frogs at the ends of her arms atop the tattered comforter.

"Well, would you kindly," Aunt Sip started in, gathering her breath like someone trying to yank a stubborn lawnmower to life, "just light me—a cigarette—and get me a—cup of coffee? And I'm hungry, for god's sake, don't we even eat breakfast in this godforsaken shithole anymore? You might want to starve yourself to death, I wouldn't blame you, but I don't."

Betty stood there, a bit lost in her thoughts, until Aunt Sip noticed and shouted, "DID YOU EVEN HEAR WHAT I SAID?"

Betty flinched. She couldn't help it. But now Aunt Sip lay there purply and gasping. Betty gathered the silk pillow to her chest and walked over beside the bed. The blackened eyes followed her.

"You're up to something." Aunt Sip's cracked lips worked at forming some other cruelty. Betty's fingers tightened on the pillow's silken fringe that brushed the backs of her hands like water.

She knew that, even with her bent-up body, and maybe because of compensating for it, she had the physical strength to do it. She tried to will it into her mind. She pictured herself pressing the silken pillow down hard on the face and holding it there, her knees on the covers on either side of Aunt Sip's arms, pinning them. Aunt Sip like a little dog wriggling under her, playing a game. Then like her rocking horse, bucking, she could just barely remember that, from when she was about three, before her mama brought herself and Betty down here in the first place. She remembered how she loved to hold on tight to the handles beside the horse's head and buck away, the way she wanted to hold on to the pillows and grip Aunt Sip's big flappy ears too, and hold on.

"You always were a strange child," Aunt Sip muttered. But there was something different in her eyes, and for the first time Betty thought there might be a little of the something there that Aunt Sip had always made her feel, in this house. She thought Aunt Sip might be just a little bit afraid.

She went into the kitchen and fried up some chopped on-ions until they were good and soft. She broke three eggs into a bowl and dashed in a little milk, sprinkled in some salt and pepper, and beat it all with a fork. She had a little thought that paused her, and without really carrying the thought to the front of her mind, she opened the cabinet beneath the range and peered into it. There was an old, crumbling box of rat poison back behind the pots and pans, some of it spilled out. She took the box out and sniffed at it. It didn't smell like anything much. She sprinkled a little into the pan with the eggs and onions, stirred it in. Then shook in a good bit more. She put the box back into the cabinet, straightened up, and stirred it all together. The color was a little funny. She poured Worcestershire on them as sometimes Aunt Sip liked her eggs Western style and the sauce would stain the eggs dark brown. She cooked them harder than the way Aunt Sip liked, then took the plate in to her, saying, "Here, Aunt Sip, maybe you can eat these eggs while I try to find your dentures. I thought you might be wanting some onions in there too, so I chopped them good."

Aunt Sip looked up at her from her silk pillow with eyes that reminded her of nothing so much as when Russell's eyes would shift just so slightly up to her and make her blood chill in her veins. Aunt Sip took the plate, set it on her big stomach, and took a little bite, still looking at her.

"I made them Western style, how you like," Betty said.

Aunt Sip sniffed at the plate and stared at Betty a long moment.

"Get your evil little witch's tit out of my bedroom while I eat."

Betty backed her way out of the room, never once taking her eyes from Aunt Sip's, bobbing her head like a bobble toy, her mouth cocked just slightly open in the only way she could hold it to keep herself from smiling, just a little.

The sounds when they came were a little disturbing, so Betty put her hands over her ears and hummed a tuneless song to fill up her head between her blocked-off ears and let her eyes roam swiftly around the museum to distract herself from any one thought, and when that didn't work she hurried out the front door barefoot and ran in a ragged circle around the shell parking lot above which darkening clouds scudded fast to the north, blindly following the bend of her frame, shouting out as loud as she could, "A, B, C, D, E, F, G! H, I, J, K, LMNOP! Q-R-S! T-U-V! DOUBLE-U! EX! WHY AND Z!"

Aunt Sip was heavy, but Betty had been lugging her around for a couple of years now. Lugging her to the bathroom for a bath, lugging her to the jeep to drive her to the doctor. Aunt Sip was too cheap to buy a wheelchair, and her arms had gotten weak from not using her walker, and she'd got heavier from not moving around, so Betty would lug her around with her heels dragging on the floor and through the bleached, crushed shell in the parking lot, where she would lay her down until she could get their old army jeep's door open, hoist her again, and pull her up into the passenger seat. Aunt Sip cussing the whole time.

Now she pulled a pillowcase over Aunt Sip's head, hiding the stricken face, and lugged her, arms hooked under her armpits, down the narrow hallway of the apartment. Out back, the property was enclosed behind a seven-foot wooden privacy fence. The museum's visitors, when there had been any, would wander through the "garden" looking at the wildlife, which in the old days included swamp rabbits, a great blue heron, two bald eagles, an osprey, a spoonbill, six different kinds of poisonous snakes, a sting ray in a big aquarium, a mangy coyote in a chicken cage, Russell, and some parrots imported from the Virgin Islands. There weren't any parrots native to this area, but people liked to think there were. Out of all that, the only thing left now was Russell, who'd gotten so old and fat he could hardly move except to raise his head to snatch, with surprising vigor, his two-week-old yellow pimply chickens or hunks of gray and sheeny beef.

Russell's hide was so dark as to almost be black, and he

was broad as a barrel. She could hardly see his clawlike feet poking out from his fat sides. He lived in a few inches of water in the bottom of his too-small pit, the walls of which were just four feet high and slippery on the inside, though Russell was far too fat to climb out now even if he'd had the opportunity or the inclination. Which he might have had during the past few days, since Betty had avoided feeding him, and the last couple of nights his call had woken her up, a loud bellow and a hissing moan. She hoped Russell would be able to handle Aunt Sip, and that she wouldn't have to cut her up into pieces for him. She didn't think she could do that.

She heaved Aunt Sip's head and shoulders up onto the top of the pit's wall and rested a moment. Russell took no notice except to cut his old slit eyes toward them and stay still. After a little rest, Betty took hold of Aunt Sip by her fleshy hips, like grabbing a giant sack of tough blubber or something, and shoved her a little more over the wall, so that now Aunt Sip's hands touched the dry floor where the pit's water had receded in the heat. Russell blinked. Betty rested again, then took Aunt Sip by her wrinkly, discolored knees and heaved her so that most of her went on over into the pit, then pushed at her old horny feet and fell hard onto her bony bottom from the effort. The silence just after was huge, the scuff of her nervous sneakers on the concrete as loud as the scratch of some great beast at the door. But then there was a thrashing noise from the pit and she looked up to see Aunt Sip twirl rapidly through the air, and heard another little splash, and a crackling, ripping sound, the pit walls getting knocked so hard they might crack and fall over.

Betty backed away from the pit on her bottom so as not to see inside there, until she reached the door, got up, and went inside without looking back. She walked through the apartment and into the museum. She stopped in front of the Je'sus diorama. Looked at the mummy boy standing there, holding his little spear, ever in between whatever had summoned him to stand and what would've come next. A hunt, maybe, or some kind of a dance. "Would you want me, Laughing Boy?" she said aloud. "Would I be a holy woman in your tribe? Or would y'all just sacrifice me to the gators?"

She went out into the shell parking lot and across the still-deserted highway, debris and sand skittering along it from the wind picking up hard from the gulf, the sky full gray and beginning to boil. She made her way to the beach. No one was out, not a soul down toward the public beach or east toward Perdido Pass. The waves white-capped and thrashing, brown, seaweedy, wind whipping her thin, limp hair. Windblown sand stinging her bare legs and face. It was a big storm coming in, maybe the worst she'd ever seen.

TRIPTYCH

BY Daniel Wallace

Shelby County

How to Build a Coffin

B uilding a coffin is a demanding but satisfying project for the ambitious carpenter to undertake, and entails a number of skills, including edging, corner joinery, trim, and finishing. You don't have to be an expert carpenter, but the more experience you have the stronger the coffin will be. The last thing you want is for your coffin to fall apart. Ninety-four pounds may not seem like a lot, but if the corner joinery is weak you can bet on disaster. You can bet on catastrophe. *Better safe than sorry*, as my wife would say.

Choosing the wood. Hardwood veneered plywood is made of thin slices of hardwood, including oak, birch, maple, ash, or cherry, that are factory-glued to a soft, plywood substrate. You can buy this at any lumber store. Depending on the time of year it may have to be special-ordered, so it's a good idea to start the process a week or two before you're actually going to need it. You may find this difficult: building a coffin while its future occupant is still alive presents a number of questions, among them being, *You're not God, how do you know for sure she's going to die?* Well, just look at her. She weighs ninety-four pounds! You think she's going to live? You hope so, sure, but hope was something you gave up last month, so the most productive thing you can do now is to build a coffin.

It's a good—and practical—distraction. Just hope she doesn't hear you hammering.

Corner joinery. I know: I'm a broken record when it comes to corner joinery, but it's by far the most important part of this project. You can use fluted dowels or plug-covered screws. Screws are especially attractive for three reasons: they don't demand special equipment; they act as their own clamps by drawing the sides and ends together; and they are ideal for caskets destined to be shipped long distances, if, for instance, the future occupant insists on being buried in a plot in California, beside her mother and father, even if she moved to North Carolina years before, following her husband, who could find work nowhere else. One thing to take into consideration here is if this decision, this *desire*, to be buried so far, far away was made under duress, or if her mind was muddled by medication, or maybe the chemo. In those instances it should fall to the husband to decide, regardless of what other family members might think. But just in case, use the screws.

Trim and finishing. Moldings make an enormous difference to the look of any do-it-yourself casket. As a general rule, put the largest moldings along the bottom, smaller moldings around the lid. Personalizing your coffin, of course, is one big advantage of the handmade option. Create a design. Carve her initials on the side. You can add custom cushions to the interior, or maybe just wrap a favorite quilt around some bed pillows. Are you really going to keep those pillows anyway? They're covered in hair, her hair, hair as brown as it was the day you met her. What kind of life would that be? Especially if you fulfill her last request, which is to remarry. The new wife can't be expected to sleep with that quilt, those pillows, in that bed—not that you have plans to remarry, but who knows, things might change. Things *will* change. That's the thing about things: change is all they do.

Summary. That about covers it. Following these instructions will ensure your coffin will be the best possible coffin you could build, a box you can be proud of—or a box of which you can be proud, for those of you, like her, whose goal in life it was never to end a sentence with a preposition. I don't mean that. She had other goals, many, among them: to be kind, to love me with all her heart, to live a longer life. But what can you do? Nothing, it turns out. You can't do anything, so you might as well build her a coffin. In a way it's like holding her forever—like that, but *not* that. Nothing is like that. Nothing nothing nothing.

Neighbor

I remember the old man perched in his second-story window, milky behind the wavy glass, glaring at all us kids like we were the mice and he was the hungry hawk. We played in his yard sometimes. I never met him. I thought—in my nightmares—that one day he'd pitch himself through the window and grab one of us, hold us in his arms until we crumbled, sucking our life out through his withered chicken-skinned body and dragging himself back inside, appearing at the window again, waiting for another one of us to drift into his gaze, living forever. He didn't live, though: one day he died. It happened the way it happens when you're young: on a different plane, like clouds. I just remember wearing the coat and tie I never wore, the shoes so tight my toes bled, in a church we never went to, surrounded by the smell of the strange and old. We headed back to his house after, and I went inside for the first time. His ancient wife shivered in a big green chair on an Oriental rug, not even crying: I think she was all dried up. I ate a little sandwich, then I went outside to see if he was still there at the window—and he was. I knew he would be. He waved, all friendly now, and I waved back, I don't know why. My throat felt strangled, my eyes so dry I thought they'd crack. Then he disappeared, fading back into the dark, and I never saw him there again. I didn't tell anybody. How could I? I didn't know what it meant, or could mean, because even that young I knew I didn't believe in anything. I told my wife about it, though, twenty years later. We were in bed in the dark. Just married, our lives ahead of us—so far ahead we couldn't even see them from where we were. I wanted to tell her everything, though, everything about me, and so I did, and part of the everything was this. It had stayed with me all these years. The story scared her, of course, but not the way it had scared me. I asked her what she thought it meant. *It means you'll be a ghost one day*, she said, *and so will I*, and she cried as if this was the first time it had ever occurred to her, because she never wanted to think that even this—all of this, our brand-new world together, the love so big we almost couldn't bear it—wasn't going to last. *It means I won't be with you forever*, she said, and she was right.

The Men in the Woods

The men who live in the woods behind my house have been getting out of hand for some time. They are all in their midfifties, golfers formerly, and meat eaters—jolly men in general—but since their wives sent them away to live in the woods they have become grumpy and discontent. At night they bellow and howl. They want their televisions and ice makers and chairs beside the vents. They live like animals now in badly made straw huts and eat anything that wanders too close to their turf. We know what's happening to our dogs and cats, but there's nothing we can do: some of these men are very powerful; all of them belong to the country club.

Last night from a window I saw them leaving the woods and marching, single file, toward my home. They knocked at the door.

"What is it?" I said, staring at their wretchedness through the peephole. "What do you want?"

"Your telephone," they said. "We'd like to use your telephone."

"That's out of the question," I said. "You can't come in. My wife—"

"Your wife?" one said.

"She won't allow it."

"His wife won't allow it!" said a second man.

"His wife says no," added another.

"She must be wonderful," the first one said. "Really, I bet she is."

"She is," I said. "My wife is wonderful."

"We knew your father," one of the men said. "You're not your father."

Then they went away, grumbling, back into the woods.

Later in the night, in bed, I told my wife what had happened.

"They came *here?*" she said. I nodded. She was appalled. "I want you to go down there and tell them not to do that. Tell them never to come here again."

"Now?" I said. "It's like midnight."

"Now," she said. "For me." She kissed me on the cheek.

I walked down the little trail which led to the woods behind our house. I saw a light, followed it. The men were cooking squirrel around a fire. They were drinking coffee from old tin cups. They bellowed and wailed. But they seemed to be having a pretty good time.

"Hey, fellas," I said, and all the bellowing stopped, and they looked up at me and smiled. "Please don't come around our house anymore. Okay?"

They looked at each other, then into the fire.

"Okay," they said, shrugging their shoulders. "Fine."

It didn't seem to mean that much to them. All they had wanted was the phone.

When I turned to go I could see my house on the hill above me, and watched as one light after another was killed and it was all darkness. It seemed I could even hear the doors shut and lock, as my wife prepared for sleep. My house seemed to disappear into the black sky. I paused.

"Going away so soon?" one of the men said. The fire was bright, warm.

"Yeah," said another. "And just when we were getting to know you."

THE JUNCTION BOYS

BY D. WINSTON BROWN

Ensley, Birmingham

C olesbery Simon had been home three months and
seven days before he decided that the way to get his
life back was to deal with his ex-girlfriend's father.
Years since they'd seen each other, but her story had become
his, no matter how long it had been, or how far away he was
in the world. He and his ex, Chelsea Gradine, first met in
a small side room of the library in their high school, a connected but isolated spot with walls of dusty books and a few
shoulder-high shelves lined up in the middle, which created a
space where Colesbery met Chelsea frequently in the months
that followed. That first day he'd been looking for *The Invisible
Man*, the Wells book, but Chelsea gave him the Ellison one
with its near-identical title. He read the prologue that night
and the next day asked her was she trying to be funny. She
told him no, that her choice had nothing to do with them
being different races, it was only that she had a crush on him
and thought he'd like the book. She'd been like that about
most things, direct, except when it came to her father. That,
Colesbery learned on his own.

He didn't make a plan. Instead, he called Lincoln Fontaine, an old friend who'd always had a knack for knowing
what needed to be known. They were meeting at a pizza place
on Birmingham's Southside, a few blocks from his old high
school. When Colesbery turned off University Avenue onto

20th Street and headed up the hill toward Five Points South, his mind entered a maze of memories, most of which involved Chelsea. A minute or two later he passed the new coffee shops and restaurants, the Storyteller's fountain, the pizza place, and then turned right. The street was narrow, with cars parked on both sides and a canopy of trees that cast everything in shade until near the intersection, and when the reddish brick of the block-long high school finally came into view, Colesbery felt his breath, momentarily, snatched. He found a parking space, and stared through the windshield. The school rose up like a brick horizon, one that had not changed since he graduated five years earlier. In reality, the school both had and hadn't changed. A few buildings had been added on either end, some cosmetic niceties done, but the main building was the same, still with the brick ramp that curved up and in front of the school and spanned much of its length, before curving down and back toward the street.

"Thinkin' of a master plan."

The voice was a smooth baritone and came from behind Colesbery, and he knew who it belonged to without turning around. "'Cause ain't nothin' but sweat inside my hands," Colesbery replied. By the time he finished the lyric, Lincoln Fontaine was standing next to him. Even though they'd seen each other a couple of times since Colesbery came home, they grasped each other's right hand, smiled at each other, then leaned in and embraced.

"What's up, army man?" Lincoln said.

"Like I told you last week, and the week before that, and the week before that, just happy to be home, bro." Somehow Lincoln had found out Colesbery was home two days after he got there. He stopped by the apartment the next day with a slab of ribs from Rib-It-Up and a prepaid cell phone for Colesbery, told him it was for when he needed something. Lincoln had kept his distance since, stopped by once or twice, mainly just called here and there to check, a minute conversation at the most.

"Thanks again for the ribs," Colesbery said, turning back to stare at the high school.

"You don't want to know," Lincoln said.

"You found her?"

"I find everything."

Lincoln was one of those people who could always make money, who could always talk to people, anywhere, and get them to talk to him. He was wearing jeans, an Ensley High School sweatshirt, and a pair of Converse, but he was equally at ease when in a pinstripe suit. He'd started his own computer consulting company out of college while he worked at Alabama Power, but he quit Alabama Power when it took off.

"Tell me," said Colesbery.

"Tell me how you are," said Lincoln.

"I'm good. I already told you that." Colesbery turned toward Lincoln now. He'd heard some rumors about Chelsea having come back, and he wanted to know what Lincoln had found out. "How long since you seen her?"

"How long you gone play games?"

"Bro, relax." Lincoln turned his head toward the high school. "You remember being there and—"

"Of course."

"—how we use to sit in the parking lot after school listening to old-school rap. Remember when we first heard Eric B. and Rakim, drinking Thunderbird and smoking that good Bush Hills bud."

"Of course I remember." Colesbery knew Lincoln wasn't stalling, but rather, trying to figure out if Colesbery really meant to do what he'd told him he was going to do. They'd been friends since they got into a fight on the playground as second graders at Holy Family Elementary. They had already known each other, but fighting made them *respect* each other, especially because neither of them had really won, just sort of knocked each other around and down, then wrestled to a stalemate.

"What do *you* think happened to her?" Lincoln asked.

"You know what happened."

"I don't mean the drugs," Lincoln said. "Something was always off with that girl, always walking around with those feathers in her hair, disappearing for days." He paused. "You dated her for two years. What was really up with her and those mood swings?"

"Just tell me what you found out."

Lincoln turned away, started walking down the hill. "Let's get that pizza first," he said over his shoulder.

Colesbery watched him disappear around the corner. He turned and looked at the redbrick school once more, and began thinking about the library. He'd had girlfriends before Chelsea, but none like her. She wasn't that glow-in-the-dark pretty, but her eyes were open whenever Colesbery asked for something in the library, like she actually *heard* him, like she wanted to help him. She cried right there between the shelves in that back room when Colesbery told her about how he'd walked in on his parents doing drugs so often as a child that when he walked in that last time, he just thought they were asleep. She'd taken his hand in hers, leaned her head on his chest, and cried.

By the time Colesbery entered the restaurant, Lincoln was already in a corner booth with a pizza, a pitcher of beer, and two mugs. He filled them both as Colesbery slid into the booth across from him.

"Thought you might want a beer."

"I didn't come here to drink beer."

Lincoln took a sip from his mug. He bit a slice of pizza. Colesbery stared, not touching either.

"Did you call that number I texted you?"

"I don't need to talk to anybody."

They stared at one another. Colesbery waited, watched Lincoln's face until it fell away, the public one full of pleasantries and vague language, and then Colesbery saw the face of Lincoln that he knew, a brown angular face with a narrowed heaviness in the eyes that only truth could render.

"He's still here," said Lincoln. "He moved out of the house in Ensley Highlands." He plucked a piece of pineapple off the pizza and tossed it in his mouth. "But he still has that tire company down on Avenue F, and yes, he still walks around the block at lunchtime."

The information at first swirled around Colesbery's head, then he felt that twitch in his stomach that always came before a mission. The plan materialized in his brain—how he would do it, when he would do it, where he would do it. He rubbed his eyes and then stretched his fingers wide, balled them tight, stretched them again, and settled back into the moment.

"You sure about this?" Lincoln asked. "You don't have to do this, you know."

Colesbery focused his eyes, picked up a slice of pizza but didn't take a bite. There were too many ingredients, too much going on on the pizza. He put it on the plate. "Yes, I do," he said. He didn't say any more, just looked at Lincoln, his eyes steeling themselves as if seeing beyond his friend to a target.

"Well, I guess that's that." Lincoln refreshed his beer. "You don't drink anymore."

Colesbery took a gulp from his mug. The coolness felt calming on his throat, in his stomach. "How's your business?"

"You don't care about that, but I got a job for you when you're ready." Lincoln motioned for the waitress. "Remember Mrs. Gordon? She passed away last month."

Colesbery knew Lincoln was worried, was trying to get him to back down. But it got to him anyway. Mrs. Gordon had been one of those teachers attracted to strays. And there was no more a stray than Colesbery when he entered her sophomore literature class. Dead parents, a halfway-locked-up alcoholic uncle he lived with, clothes that were ill-fitted and seldom clean—Colesbery became her cause. She lived in Bush Hills too, a few blocks away on the boulevard, and she often gave him rides to school, even invited him over for dinner sometimes. But he didn't respond, didn't accept her attention, until she put a book on his desk one day in class and walked away. He left it on the desk when class was dismissed, but she placed it on his desk again the next day, so he took it. At that time he was a skinny kid who only wanted to avoid attention, and confrontation. *Narrative of the Life of Frederick Douglass* was the first book he ever really read. He read it and reread it, especially the chapter where Douglass fights Mr. Covey.

"What happened to her?" asked Colesbery.

"Old, as far as I know. I just figured you'd want to know." Then he asked, "What did you do with all those books she gave you?"

After he read the Douglass book, Colesbery had put it back on her desk one day before class. She'd asked if he'd read it, he'd answered yes, and that led to her bringing book after book after book. Every time he put one back on her desk, she reached into the top drawer and withdrew another one. He read them all.

"My uncle burned most of them when he set the apartment on fire."

"She was good people."

It was Mrs. Gordon who'd lost her copy of *Invisible Man* and told him to check it out of the library. He'd made the mistake in thinking she'd meant the Wells version (even though he also read it later). Mrs. Gordon had been a stout brownskinned woman, widowed and childless, who always seemed so much taller when she stood in front of the class and peered over her glasses at each student, calling on them, cajoling them, encouraging them, correcting them, explaining things to them day after day through the semester.

"And Mr. Foster finally retired." Lincoln drank from his glass. "Remember when he caught us with that beer behind the school?"

Colesbery was glad not to keep talking about Mrs. Gordon, but he also knew Lincoln was working him, trying to get to the real reason for his plans. Lincoln had always had a knack for getting people comfortable, getting them talking, and then getting them to reveal more than they intended.

"I need to go," Colesbery said.

"Is it happening again?"

Lincoln had stopped by the apartment one day when things weren't going well. There had been a smell, an odor like fried onions mixed with stale mayonnaise, which had triggered something, transported Colesbery, made him see things: jagged faces, torn limbs, trails of blood. Colesbery had heard the knock, yanked open the door to the courtyard, and tried to hit Lincoln, but Lincoln was strong enough to grab and hold Colesbery till he calmed, till he convinced Colesbery that what he thought he was seeing was not real.

"I'm good," Colesbery said. "Thanks for the information."

* * *

That night Colesbery couldn't sleep. His bed always felt too big, too *something*, so he often couldn't sleep there. Around midnight, after staring at the ceiling for an hour, he got up and went into the den. He watched TV for a while, tried to sleep on the couch. No luck. Again he got up, and then went out into the tiny courtyard. He didn't have any chairs, but the courtyard made him feel more secure.

The square footprint of his apartment was evenly divided into four quadrants: the bedroom, the den, the courtyard, and the galley kitchen and bathroom split the last quadrant. Both the den and the bedroom had sliding glass doors that opened up onto the courtyard. The first week, Colesbery sat staring from the bedroom, then from the den, at the outside door in the far corner of the courtyard. He checked the lock five times a night.

Now he just leaned against the outer wall, peering into the apartment, thinking about what Lincoln had told him. He wouldn't find Chelsea. She was strung out, probably dead, but in the wind for certain. She was a year older than him, and light-years ahead in experience. Colesbery knew about cheap wine—Mad Dog, Red Dagger, Boone's Farm—but Chelsea drank vodka, tequila, and she knew about drugs and where to get them. White neighborhoods that Colesbery didn't feel comfortable in sometimes. *Nobody's going to bother us*, she would say as they rode past small one-story sixties and seventies houses, almost all of them with a small beat-up car and a pickup in the driveway. *You think that because you white*, Colesbery would say.

It was six months before she introduced him to her parents. Her father, slim and wiry with stringy black hair on its way to gray, owned a tire wholesale shop in downtown Ensley. They shook hands when Colesbery picked her up to go to Junior Achievement, but Colesbery sensed his displeasure at this black boy there to pick up his daughter. Colesbery picked her up every Tuesday for the meetings, which they did actually attend, but they also left early often, rode around and drank, and found dark, quiet, secluded spots to park. At school, Chelsea had taken to pushing Colesbery back into the side room between the shelves and giving him hand jobs. He'd stand between the two shelves, a hand on each to maintain his steadiness; she would unzip his pants and stroke Colesbery till he finished, and when he did, it was often in the pages of a book, which she would then fold closed and return to a shelf. But when they were in the car, Chelsea always pulled him hard inside of her, often grabbing his bare behind with a force that thrilled him. What always surprised him was her need to look him in the eyes when he came. Sometimes he would lower his head and she would place her hands on his cheeks and lift up his face. The first few times they used protection, but when she told him she was on the pill, that she wanted to feel him inside her, Colesbery complied. Sometimes she would cry afterward, tell Colesbery nothing was wrong, that she was just happy. And he wanted to believe her, even after he found out it wasn't a lie, but wasn't the truth either.

When Junior Achievement ended, Colesbery started working at Rally's, and when he got off at night, he would sometimes bring Chelsea a burger and some fries and a strawberry soda. He always parked on the street at the end of the block and walked up the alley. From there he could slip in through the fence and make his way to her window. It was dark, shaded by trees and a fence, and her parents were usually in the den on the opposite end of the house. But one night they were on the porch when Colesbery got there. The grass was thick and usually soundless, but there were still a good number of leaves on the ground, so he had to be careful, move slower than usual. As he neared Chelsea's window, he heard her parents talking. Before he tapped on the window, her father said his name. Colesbery froze, but no one was coming at him around the front corner of the house. They were discussing him. Her mother, a woman with long and frizzy auburn hair and a penchant for cookbooks, was saying she didn't like it much better than her husband, but she thought it was a phase, that it would pass. Mr. Gradine then said that he just didn't want that nigger coming around his house into the next year, and his friends were starting to talk, saying that she was tainted now. He'd heard the word before, but hadn't expected it here, not after so many months of her parents being civil to him. He wanted to confront them, but just stood frozen, looking into the window of her bedroom. She was on the bed reading, but he couldn't knock, not then.

He'd left, run back to his car, but only drove around. *Fuck that*, he kept telling himself. He was going to have to say something. An hour later, near midnight, he was back. Chelsea's light was still on. When he got to her window, what he saw nearly made him throw up. Chelsea's nightgown was puffed up near her neck and just over the tops of her breasts, but she was naked from the waist down, her face turned toward the window where he stood. He thought she saw him, but her eyes were blank, absent. Her father was on top of her, then pushed himself up till he could turn and sit at the foot of the bed. He reached down and pulled up first his boxers and then a pair of dingy work pants. Colesbery looked from him to her and back to him. Mr. Gradine rose and left. Colesbery didn't knock, his anger from earlier now transformed into something that he didn't know how to handle.

Standing now in his small courtyard, Colesbery replayed those moments in his mind. He could have done something, *should* have done something. But he just turned and ran, from Chelsea, from everything. Didn't tell her what he saw either. When he did see her again, there was distance between them, which became less the sporadic interruption and more the norm. They argued more and more. He began not showing up when he said he would. Once, when he was high and stopped by, her father was on the porch smoking a cigarette. *She ain't here*, he'd said, but kept talking. Colesbery noticed the empty beer cans, the cigarette butts. That night Mr. Gradine had been the first to suggest Colesbery go to the service, and for once something made sense to him. He could remember it now just as clearly as when it happened. He'd wanted to tell the man to fuck himself, that *he* should leave, but getting away sounded like the best option. Getting as far away as possible from Birmingham, from his drunk uncle, from school, from Chelsea.

The next morning, after putting cereal into a Styrofoam bowl, Colesbery took several minutes to pour enough milk to nudge the cereal, the white just visible here and there, peeking out. Still, he couldn't look at the milk, kept seeing faces, boys halfway around the world, dead. He wasn't surprised, the milk thing had been happening since he got home. He left the milk sitting there, got dressed, and left.

His uncle lived in the same run-down apartment. Colesbery knocked, then walked through the unlocked door.

"What the hell you doing back? You must've come back to see 'bout that little white girl who was having your baby when you left." His uncle was sitting in a goldish-brown chair from another era. His hair was nearly gone now on the top, and his arthritis had turned his fingers into twisted roots and knots. "Go to the kitchen and get me a beer."

"Just came to see how you doing, Uncle." Colesbery went to the kitchen and grabbed a can from the refrigerator. "Got to go to the bathroom," he said as he handed it over. He bypassed the kitchen and went to his uncle's bedroom. In the same drawer, in the same box. Colesbery exhaled, surprised his uncle hadn't sold the .38 by now, and relieved at knowing he wouldn't have to find another one. He checked it over, then tucked it into the back of his pants.

"You coming back?" his uncle asked when Colesbery returned to the den and told him he had somewhere to be.

"I'll bring you a twelve-pack, Uncle," he said, and left.

Downtown Ensley hadn't changed. Shortly before noon, Colesbery parked his pickup in a lot near Carter's Barbershop and walked back the two blocks, past Hawkins Park. When he was in high school, he and his friends would sometimes gather there, call themselves the Junction Boys 'cause they had been a couple of times to the Function in the Junction, an annual festival that took place in that park and celebrated the musical history of Ensley. But they didn't know about the history then, just liked to call themselves the Junction Boys because it sounded like it carried weight, like there was something there to be respected. Didn't know it then, but now it seemed to Colesbery that everything in the world came down to respect. It was his uncle who had told him about how Erskine Hawkins had written and recorded that song as a B side, and about how a white dude recorded it later and had made a boatload of money, none of which went to Hawkins. "It's always respect," Colesbery said aloud.

He walked almost to the corner, near where they placed the historical marker on the Belcher-Nixon Building, and waited. He wondered what it was like back when the streetcars used to come through and all the black folks would unload. The housing projects were gone, replaced by some new Hope VI housing. It was clean and newish and modern. *Maybe they got some hope now*, he thought. Yet nothing felt much different, even though he'd driven by the sign of some smiling city councilman touting the changes that were happening.

When Mr. Gradine rounded the corner like he had at lunchtime for as many years as Colesbery could remember, he came face-to-face with Colesbery, almost walked into him, and stopped. He was shorter than Colesbery remembered, and his face was lined with age and his eyes looked tired.

"You remember me?" asked Colesbery.

"I don't know where she is."

"I don't care about her." He had the pistol now in the waistband in the front of his pants, and raised his shirt, then placed his hand on the handle. "I'm here for you."

Mr. Gradine looked around, over Colesbery's shoulder, then to the right toward the KFC. "What does that mean?" he asked.

"Need you to know when you made her get that abortion, the child you—"

"What are you talking—"

"—killed was mine."

Chelsea had tracked Colesbery down and told him. When he told her about what he saw that night outside her bedroom, she said that was the first time her daddy had done that in close to eight months, that she knew she was pregnant before that.

"I didn't kill any child." Mr. Gradine's face scowled into indignation. "Back then I thought you were just a ni—"

The shot was not loud. Mr. Gradine seemed more startled than injured. He put his hands on his chest, then wavered left till the bricks caught him, held him up for a moment. The stain spread down his white shirt from beneath his hands. He slid down the wall, the whole time staring with disbelief at Colesbery.

Colesbery stepped closer, and as he was looking down into Mr. Gradine's eyes, he reached into his pocket and pulled out a playing card. When he first thought of this moment, he envisioned leaving behind his dog tag, a spent cartridge from Afghanistan, and his Airborne shoulder patch, but he'd changed his mind; he would not end his life here. He'd decided this moment, if he got away, would be his beginning. The playing card was white, and it said *JOKER* in black in opposite corners. In the middle of the card hovered a jet-black figure, a dancing joker.

Colesbury pinched the card between his index and middle fingers, then flicked it. The spinning card flew in an arc and landed on Mr. Gradine's chest, just above the growing bloodstain.

"What's that for?" asked Mr. Gradine through the blood and spittle gurgling out of the corner of his mouth.

"I'm playing my race card."

Colesbery waited till death claimed the eyes, then turned and walked away. He heard no sirens, no screams, nothing. Things would be different now, he told himself.

ALL THE DEAD IN OAKWOOD

BY MARLIN BARTON

Montgomery

for Wayne Greenhaw

His name was Hiram. The moment she met him at the songwriters group she knew who he was named after. He'd right away told her no, he did not go by Hank as the man himself had done. If he looked his age, she put him at twenty-nine. When she asked, he nodded. She knew people thought of thirty-three, her age, as their Jesus year. "So is this your Hank year?" she asked. He only stared at her, and when he did, he looked way past twenty-nine, and she wondered, fleetingly, if that look was the only way he'd ever reach past the age Hank had lived, then dismissed this thought as the kind of dark notion she was prone to, dismissed it until later when she learned he'd done time for assault, twice, and after he told her the stories, she suspected the second time he'd meant to kill the man.

"Polly," she told him when he asked. It was a name she'd hated as a girl, thought too plain, simple, old-fashioned. But at eighteen, after she'd learned to play guitar so well that her parents bought her a Martin D-28, she first heard the song "Pretty Polly," and the beauty and tragedy of the hundreds-year-old murder ballad, its very intensity, made her hear her name in a new way that weighed heavy on her in a way she liked, felt connected to.

That first meeting had been eight months ago, though it seemed much longer. Now she was in the cab of his truck, their guitars stowed in hardshell cases in the bed, where they'd put them after playing at the bar on Fairview, and she wondered, not for the first time, if names could be destiny. Another dark thought. She knew their source, but that never made them go away.

They were headed again to the place they'd ended up that first night, Oakwood Cemetery, at the top of the hill where Hank was buried next to French pilots killed in training at Maxwell airbase during World War II. She remembered now, because she couldn't *not*, the feel of the cold marble slab against her ass as they fucked over Hank at four in the morning. Even as she heard the slap of his body against hers she realized he knew what a younger man didn't, that every stroke of his dick was a stroke against death, a futile one. Afterward, when they pulled their jeans back on, she told him about the French pilots, and that the French word for orgasm meant *little death*. "So did you die?" he asked. "Many times over," she answered. What she didn't say was that she'd been dying, many times over, for years.

When the light changed, he pulled off Fairview and onto Perry Street. He'd once joked about their moving into one of the big houses there, maybe next to the governor's mansion, when he sold a song that ended up a hit. She noticed he'd talked about *his* success, not hers. So far, none of their group had sold anything to a Nashville publisher, which is why he'd said they should call themselves Songwriters Anonymous.

He reached toward the dash and turned off the Steve Young song, "Montgomery in the Rain," that had been playing. Hi, as she often called him—because she didn't want to disparage Hank's true name—had claimed Young was Hank's heir. After the silence between them had replaced the music, he said, "You don't have to do this."

Her first thought wasn't about his pleading tone, nor about the sound of too much whiskey mixed in his syllables, but rather how horribly predictable and unoriginal he sounded. He'd never allow such a line into one of his songs. That he thought he knew what she wanted did not surprise her. She'd counted on it. She had her ways of handling him, not the least of which, this night, was singing her harmonies off-key on every song, and that was a hard thing for her to do, took great effort, and he knew that too.

"I don't understand why you did it. On 'Seven Bridges Road' you sounded like you'd never sung it before, never even heard it, when you know it backward and forward. Hell, you even know the road it's about, know it like absolutely nobody else does, I'd say."

"Fuck you for that last remark. Just fuck you." They were passing the governor's mansion now, heading up the hill to the bridges over I-85, which came to its end a mile farther down. "And I keep telling you, the song's about a mythical road. That's the only reason I can sing it at all."

"How many bridges does Woodley Road have south of town?" he said.

"Seven."

"And where was Steve Young living when he wrote the song?"

"Here."

"You even knew the man whose backseat Young was riding in when he started writing the song." He stopped talking, appeared to swallow against a dry throat, then opened and drank from the flask between his legs. "Let me tell you something else." His voice began to shake now, not out of anger, she knew, but fear, afraid like a child, because that's what he was, had always been, no matter how many men he'd beaten. She'd need to hear enough of both fear and anger in his voice before the night was over.

He took another drink. "You say you can only sing that song because it's mythical. That's bullshit. You live on that road, the real one, the one you can't leave. Instead of you try-ing to break up with me at Hank's grave—because that's what you want, *that's* what you were telling me with all your shit harmonies, *that's* what I been feeling from you—why don't we just go to your dead husband's grave, the one you killed, and you can try breaking up with me there? How 'bout that?"

"Fuck you, Hi. Just take me to where we're going, and then you can do whatever else you want."

"Take you where you died up under me?"

"That's right. Where I died over and over."

"How often do you die? Every time you think of him?"

"Yes, and every time I think about how he died."

They were headed downhill now, still on Perry, about to cross Dexter where parades and protesters marched their way to the capitol on Goat Hill, where politicians had once sent boys off to slaughter for reasons they little understood and where the politicians were still no better than the rutting ani-mals that once grazed on its slopes.

"You say *how* he died. You mean how you killed him, don't you? Just how drunk were you that night?"

"Not as drunk as you now."

"Drunk enough, then."

She had been drunk, enough so that she could not deny it or let go of the fact, but angry too, more angry than drunk. She'd been playing a dive way down Woodley Road, past its miles of Spanish moss and seven bridges. Her husband knew how rough the place was, so he'd gone with her. He sometimes turned jealous, ended the night by accusing her of playing up to the men, wanting more ones and fives thrown into her open guitar case, implying a woman with a guitar in a place like that was no better than a stripper, and some strippers, he told her, would take it outside, burn their knees on the carpet inside a truck. Was jealousy a sin punishable by death? She didn't think so, but she had punished him, had killed him. A circle of red as bright as her anger hanging over them, her hands raised above ten and two, the impact slamming him against the door, and her husband's body twisted into an impossible shape, dead on arrival, and the child she hadn't known about would never arrive. All lost, lost as she was on Woodley Road and on Hank's lost highway, but she knew the destination she sought, a place a man named Hiram might take her.

They were on Upper Wetumpka Road now, passing the backside of the police station and city court, and just on the other side of the station stood the main entrance to Oak-wood, where the bodies of Confederate dead and Union prisoners lay.

After he'd told her about his time in prison, first as a juvenile and later as an adult, he'd finally unburdened himself. A man inside Kilby would not leave him alone. Out in the yard others had crowded around the predator, knew what was coming. Hi joined the gathering, entered it with talk and laughter, and a sharpened piece of plastic, his first shiv, broke it off deep in the man's stomach, and edged away with the crowd, the body left lying on the ground in their wake. The story had not frightened her, had only drawn her closer to him.

Just past the main entrance lay the graves of lost children, and beyond them the site where Hank's body had first lain before he'd been moved to another hilltop and French pilots dug up to make room, punished in death for one man's tortured fame and immortality.

"Say my name," she said now into the silent cab, needing the reminder of who she was, her identity something older than her age. "Please, say it."

"Why? You already know your name."

"Don't be smart. Just say it."

"Polly."

"No. *Say* it. Say what I want to hear." He turned onto the narrow asphalt drive that led up to the dead. Then she said, more quietly, "Sing it." He would have to understand now, at least what she wanted to hear if not yet what she really wanted from him, what she knew he was capable of delivering.

"*Polly, pretty Polly*," he sang and then began to hum the harrowed tune. "You want to end things with me the way the man ends things with Polly in the ballad? You want to kill me? That what you do to men? Because your breaking off with me will be my death. And why? Why do it? Aren't we good together, or have been? Can't we be again?"

The pleading was back in his voice, which meant the kind of fear a child feels was showing itself again. She half expected him to whimper, and realized if she did hear it, that's when he would be at his most dangerous. He'd need to whimper.

He stopped the truck at the end of the French graves, where the final pilot had not had to give up his rest in peace, like the others, to the teeth of a backhoe. Hiram lowered his window and cut the engine. The hum of nighttime air filled the now-dark cab, a timeless song of crickets, a soft wind, distant frogs from the bank of the Alabama River, unseen but not far from them, down the far side of this hill they sat atop.

"You're a child," she said. "And it's way too late for you to be a child at your age. Don't you know that much?"

He surprised her by simply opening his door and stepping out of the truck. Then she heard him pulling his guitar case from the bed and dragging it over the side, as if something heavier than a guitar lay within.

She opened her door, closed it behind her, then walked around and closed his, watched the light inside the truck again dim and disappear. A three-quarter moon lit the white marble of the first of the two large, towering headstones, the grave on the left belonging to the first wife, who'd been determined to join her husband in death if she couldn't lie beside his wrecked body while it still had life—and that's why his grave had been moved, easier to dig up Frenchmen than the dignified locals from wealthy families in order to make room for a headstrong ex-wife. Hank's stone and marble slab lay to the right, and a low, white marble border wall surrounded the plot's artificial turf, put down to prevent seekers from digging up pieces of hallowed ground. Beneath the moon the turf was subdued to a more natural, darker color. Hiram walked over to the marble bench, a dark figure but more than a shadow. He carried his guitar case, and then sat down, facing the stones. She slowly walked toward him, said his name, Hiram, quietly to herself, unsure why she now had that name on her tongue, felt as if maybe she were trying to conjure the spirit of something she couldn't truly give name to. She sat down beside him, close enough so that in the warm night she felt the heat from his body.

He bent over, opened the case before him, and pulled out his guitar, a prewar Martin that had first been played before those pilots, with shouts or with silence, had met their deaths, most probably country or Appalachian songs echoing out of the guitar's sound hole in some 1930s honky-tonk, or maybe more than one murder ballad. There were so many to choose from, such an ancient and timeless form. He began to play a quiet melody out of single notes, his fingers moving across the fretboard, his palm hard against the neck. He played so slowly it took time before she recognized the bare melody of "Cold, Cold Heart." He always knew overplaying was sense-less, could kill a song's beauty.

"Why leave me now, why tonight?" he said as the melody disappeared into the dark reaches of two a.m.

"It's the right time for me," she said, and didn't want to answer further, though she could have. But his knowing to-night was the ten-year mark of her husband's death wouldn't have been an explanation that made any sense to him as a cause for *their* end. Better to not offer him any explanation, leave him all the more frustrated.

"Have I not treated you good?" he said quietly over the sound of a diminished D chord.

"You have," she said, "mostly."

"Maybe that's your problem with me. You're a woman who wants awful treatment. Be careful what you wish for. I can give it to you. But you know that, don't you?"

At first she remained quiet, gave herself time to think, to judge the moment. "Yes," she said finally. "I do."

"We didn't have to come here tonight. You wanted this, whatever *this* is. Like in that song you love, when the man takes Polly riding into the night, toward her death, she knows where he's taking her. He even tells her that her guess is about right, but it wasn't a guess. It's what she wanted."

"That's one version," she said.

"It's *your* version. Child that I am, as you say, I know you better than you think."

"I don't think you do," she said, ready to push him now, goad him, play on his anger for the moment, later on his fears.

She knew them, including one he'd never given voice to but was there, waiting for her to use.

"I've seen pictures of you as a teenager," he said, "the ones you showed me where you're wearing all that black, the crazy hair, the black makeup and fingernails. You were all Goth. Death as pretend. Little death. You've been drawn to it all your life, like some drug you want. Killing your husband and baby was the closest you've come. It wasn't enough, was it? Just made you crave it more, thought it gave you all the more reason for wanting it. Fucking over a grave was foreplay for you."

She waited to speak, bided her time, wanted to steel herself for all that would come. Then he began to play simple notes again, and she recognized the song she needed to hear but didn't realize it until she heard the title line in the melody as he played "I'll Never Get Out of This World Alive." She could not look at him now, but she began, hesitantly. "That man in prison," she said, "the one who wouldn't leave you alone."

He stopped playing. "What about him? Why bring him up now?" He looked toward the two headstones, appeared to read the engraved words, but she knew it was too dark for him to read them. He then began to sound two notes on the fretboard, the second note flat, the D string out of tune. He turned the tuning peg, tightening the string, hit the two notes again, waiting on her, she knew, looking for comfort inside the sound of the instrument.

"It wasn't the way you told me, was it?" she said, ready now to push him beyond an irrevocable point. "He didn't force you. You wanted it, and kept wanting it."

He tightened the string again, hit the note that now grew sharper, and sharper again with another turn of the peg, and he kept striking the note, the sound climbing.

"You liked it. But you couldn't live with wanting a dick. That's why you killed him. So nobody would know."

He twisted the peg hard, the sound beyond sharp, and she heard the sudden, awful *snap* of the metal, bronze-wound string. It sprang from the neck, and he caught a broken end, pulled its other end from out of the body of the guitar and held the two ends of the heavy-gauge string in his closed, tightened hands. She knew what he now wielded, and her blood surged and then seemed to thin, and she felt as if she were being lifted higher, climbing her way toward something without effort. All she had to do was let him bear her, not fight.

He raised his hands, the string taut between them, and in one motion threw it past her and toward Hank's grave where it landed on his engraved marble slab, rolled toward the far edge.

She didn't speak at first, waited only to see if his anger would show itself, but he neither moved nor spoke.

"You broke it on purpose," she said. "For no reason? Just to throw it away?"

He took a slow breath, as if to mark the end of contemplation. "You know it wasn't like that. The man did me harm, like you can't imagine, unless you've suffered that and haven't told me. Have you suffered it?"

"No," she said, "not that."

"Then why claim what you just claimed to know about me?" He lowered his guitar into the case, sat upright again, his back rigid, as if he were bracing or preparing himself for something he expected from her. "You had a reason. I want to hear you say it."

Now she felt afraid, not of what he might do, but afraid to articulate the lie she'd told herself, afraid to reveal some empty, unfillable place within her for him to judge.

"You can't answer. It's all right." He placed his right arm over her shoulder, gently. "I know the reason, and I know where you want to go." He drew his arm higher, closer, pulled her toward him, intoning her name, and began to squeeze, his forearm now tight against the side of her neck, his bent elbow the spring-loaded hinge in a closing wedge. "I'm going to take you past where you want to go. Do you hear me? Are you prepared?" She felt his left hand upon her bare throat, felt his fingers tighten. She could not move her head, did not try. "*Past* it, and you'll awake with breath. Are you ready?"

She could not answer with words, could only feel his hand closing, cutting off any form of utterance he might understand. All she could do was whimper.

ABOUT THE CONTRIBUTORS

ACE ATKINS was born in Troy, Alabama, in 1970 and attended high school and college in Auburn, where he played football. Atkins has been nominated for every major award in crime fiction, including the Edgar three times. He has written nine books in the Quinn Colson series and continued Robert B. Parker's iconic Spenser character after Parker's death in 2010, adding seven best-selling novels in that series. He lives in Oxford, Mississippi, with his family.

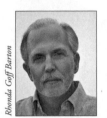

MARLIN BARTON lives in Montgomery. He has published three story collections: *Pasture Art*, *Dancing by the River*, and *The Dry Well*; and two novels: *The Cross Garden* and *A Broken Thing*. His stories have appeared in *Prize Stories 1994: The O. Henry Awards* and *The Best American Short Stories 2010*. He teaches in a program for juvenile offenders called Writing Our Stories, and he also teaches in the low-residency MFA program at Converse College.

D. WINSTON BROWN was born at Holy Family Community Hospital in Ensley, Alabama, a neighborhood on the west side of Birmingham, and he grew up in nearby Bush Hills. He went on to graduate from Ramsay High School, and later from the University of Alabama at Birmingham. He has published both fiction and creative nonfiction. He now works in Florence, Alabama, but still lives and writes in Birmingham.

KIRK CURNUTT was born in Lincoln, Nebraska, in 1964 but has lived in Montgomery, Alabama—the hometown of Zelda Fitzgerald—since 1993. He is the author of three novels: *Breathing Out the Ghost*, *Dixie Noir*, and *Raising Aphrodite*, as well as nonfiction studies of F. Scott Fitzgerald, Ernest Hemingway, William Faulkner, Gertrude Stein, and the 1970s. Every day he travels the route outlined in his contribution to this volume while commuting to nearby Troy, Alabama.

TOM FRANKLIN, from Dickinson, Alabama, is the author of *Poachers: Stories* and three novels, *Hell at the Breech*, *Smonk*, and *Crooked Letter, Crooked Letter*, which won the *Los Angeles Times* Book Prize for Mystery/Thriller, the Willie Morris Prize for Southern Fiction, and the UK's Gold Dagger Award. His most recent book is *The Tilted World*, cowritten with his wife, Beth Ann Fennelly. Franklin lives in Oxford, Mississippi, and teaches at Ole Miss.

Edward Garner

ANITA MILLER GARNER, born in Coosa County, Alabama, is a descendant of Alabama pioneers. She attended Coosa County High School and the University of Alabama and is Professor Emeritus of English and Creative Writing at the University of North Alabama. Garner is the author of the story collection *Undeniable Truths*, and fiction editor at Mindbridge Press in Florence, Alabama.

Anna Ritch Photography

THOM GOSSOM JR. was born and raised in Birmingham. He has written a memoir, *Walk-On: My Reluctant Journey to Integration at Auburn University*; and *A Slice of Life*, a three-volume collection of short stories. He received his BA from Auburn where he was the first black athlete to graduate from the university. Gossom is also a playwright and working actor, perhaps best known for his recurring roles on *Boston Legal* and *In the Heat of the Night*.

Squire Fox

WINSTON GROOM, a native of Mobile, graduated from the University of Alabama, served in Vietnam, and worked as a newspaperman. He is the author of eight novels, most famously *Forrest Gump*, and most recently *El Paso*. Groom has published twelve books of nonfiction, largely military history. The most recent is *The Allies: Roosevelt, Churchill, Stalin, and the Unlikely Alliance That Won World War II*. He lives in Point Clear, Alabama.

JD Scott Photography

ANTHONY GROOMS married into a Titusville family more than thirty years ago. Among the oldest black neighborhoods in Birmingham, Titusville has proven to be a rich source of stories for him. It is the setting of his prize-winning novel *Bombingham* and of several stories in his collection *Trouble No More*. Like these works, his novel *The Vain Conversation* explores race, civil rights, and the fight for justice. His story "Selah" appears in *Atlanta Noir*.

John Adams/Adams Imaging

CAROLYN HAINES was born in Lucedale, Mississippi, and currently lives in Semmes, Alabama. She is a *USA Today* best-selling author of mysteries and crime fiction. Along with writing full-time, she has been the director of fiction writing at the University of South Alabama. She has published over eighty books and been honored with the Harper Lee Award for Distinguished Writing and the Alabama Library Association Lifetime Achievement Award.

Beri Irving

RAVI HOWARD is the author of the novels _Like Trees, Walking_ and _Driving the King_. He was a finalist for the PEN/ Hemingway Award and winner of the Ernest J. Gaines Award. Howard has received fellowships and awards from the Hurston/Wright Foundation and the National Endowment for the Arts, and his short fiction has appeared in _Salon_ and _Massachusetts Review_. He was born in Montgomery in 1974, and he lived in Mobile from 2006 to 2011.

Kevin D'Amico

SUZANNE HUDSON was born in Columbus, Georgia; grew up in Brewton, Alabama; and is a longtime resident of Mobile and Fairhope, Alabama. She is the prize-winning author of two novels and two collections of short stories. Her latest book is _The Fall of the Nixon Administration: A Comic Novel_. Hudson lives near Fairhope, at Waterhole Branch Productions, with her husband, author Joe Formichella.

Greg Hagler

DON NOBLE is the editor of twelve volumes, three of which are collections of short fiction by Alabamians. He has received a regional Emmy Award for achievement in screenwriting and is the recipient of the state prizes for literary scholarship and service to the humanities, as well as the Governor's Arts Award. Noble is host of the TV literary interview show _Bookmark with Don Noble_ and reviews books weekly for public radio.

Jennifer Horne

WENDY REED, an Alabama native, is an Emmy Award–winning writer and producer, whose work includes the series _Discovering Alabama_ and _Bookmark with Don Noble_. An Alabama State Council on the Arts fellow, Reed's books include _An Accidental Memoir: How I Killed Someone and Other Stories_, _All Out of Faith_, and _Circling Faith_ (coedited by Jennifer Horne). Reed teaches in the University of Alabama Honors College and lives in Hoover, Alabama.

Nick Elliott

MICHELLE RICHMOND was born in Demopolis, Alabama, raised in Mobile, and is a graduate of the University of Alabama. She is the author of two prize-winning volumes of stories and five novels, most recently the thriller _The Marriage Pact_, which has been translated into thirty languages. Richmond is the recipient of the Truman Capote Prize for Distinguished Work in Short Fiction and the Grace Paley Prize.

DANIEL WALLACE was born in Birmingham in 1959. He is the author of many novels, including *Big Fish: A Novel of Mythic Proportions*, which was made into a feature film by Tim Burton, and then a Broadway musical. Wallace's most recent novel, set in Birmingham, is *Extraordinary Adventures*. He now resides in Chapel Hill, North Carolina, where he directs the creative writing program at UNC. Wallace is the 2019 winner of the Harper Lee Award for Distinguished Writing.

BRAD WATSON was born near the Alabama border in Mississippi and moved across the state line in 1978. His work has received honors from the National Book Foundation, the PEN/ Faulkner Foundation, the Southern Book Critics Circle, and the American Academy of Arts and Letters. He has won the Harper Lee Award for Distinguished Writing. He is the author of two volumes of stories and two novels, *The Heaven of Mercury*, short-listed for the National Book Award, and *Miss Jane*.

Also available from the Akashic Noir Series

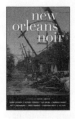

NEW ORLEANS NOIR
edited by Julie Smith
288 pages, trade paperback original, $15.95

BRAND-NEW STORIES BY: Ace Atkins, Laura Lippman, Patty Friedmann, Barbara Hambly, Tim McLoughlin, Olympia Vernon, David Fulmer, Jervey Tervalon, James Nolan, Kalamu ya Salaam, Maureen Tan, Thomas Adcock, Jeri Cain Rossi, Christine Wiltz, Greg Herren, Julie Smith, Eric Overmyer, and Ted O'Brien.

"*New Orleans Noir* explores the dark corners of our city in eighteen stories, set both pre- and post-Katrina . . . In Julie Smith, Temple found a perfect editor for the New Orleans volume, for she is one who knows and loves the city and its writers and knows how to bring out the best in both . . . It's harrowing reading, to be sure, but it's pure page-turning pleasure, too." —*Times-Picayune*

MISSISSIPPI NOIR
edited by Tom Franklin
288 pages, trade paperback original, $15.95

BRAND-NEW STORIES BY: William Boyle, Megan Abbott, Jack Pendarvis, Ace Atkins, Dominiqua Dickey, Michael Kardos, Jamie Paige, Jimmy Cajoleas, Chris Offutt, Michael Farris Smith, Andrew Paul, Lee Durkee, Robert Busby, John M. Floyd, RaShell R. Smith-Spears, and Mary Miller.

"In these stories, from Biloxi to Hattiesburg, from Jackson to Oxford, the various crimes of the heart or doomed deeds of fractured households are carried out in real Mississippi locales . . . [A] devilishly wrought introduction to writers with a feel for Mississippi who are pursuing lonely, haunting paths of the imagination." —Associated Press

NEW ORLEANS NOIR: THE CLASSICS
edited by Julie Smith
320 pages, trade paperback original, $15.95

CLASSIC REPRINTS FROM: James Lee Burke, Armand Lanusse, Grace King, Kate Chopin, O. Henry, Eudora Welty, Tennessee Williams, Shirley Ann Grau, John William Corrington, Tom Dent, Ellen Gilchrist, Valerie Martin, O'Neil De Noux, John Biguenet, Poppy Z. Brite, Nevada Barr, Ace Atkins, and Maurice Carlos Ruffin.

"[An] irresistible sequel to Smith's *New Orleans Noir* . . . Anyone who knows New Orleans even slightly will relish revisiting the city in story after story. For anyone who has never been to New Orleans, this is a great introduction to its neighborhoods and history." —*Publishers Weekly*, STARRED REVIEW

HOUSTON NOIR
edited by Gwendolyn Zepeda
256 pages, trade paperback original, $15.95

BRAND-NEW STORIES BY: Tom Abrahams, Robert Boswell, Sarah Cortez, Anton DiSclafani, Stephanie Jaye Evans, Wanjikū wa Ngūgī, Adrienne Perry, Pia Pico, Reyes Ramirez, Icess Fernandez Rojas, Sehba Sarwar, Leslie Contreras Schwartz, Larry Watts, and Deborah D.E.E.P. Mouton.

"Editor Gwendolyn Zepeda has cannily divided the collection into four separate areas of the city, which only serves to multiply a reader's certainty: Like the sodden sheet covering a much-lacerated corpse, all of Houston is pretty much dripping with crime. Best to experience it, we suggest, only between the covers of this new paperback."
—*Austin Chronicle*

DALLAS NOIR
edited by David Hale Smith
288 pages, trade paperback original, $15.95

BRAND-NEW STORIES BY: Kathleen Kent, Ben Fountain, James Hime, Harry Hunsicker, Matt Bondurant, Merritt Tierce, Daniel J. Hale, Emma Rathbone, Jonathan Woods, Oscar C. Peña, Clay Reynolds, Lauren Davis, Fran Hillyer, Catherine Cuellar, David Haynes, and J. Suzanne Frank.

"All in all, the stories in *Dallas Noir* have an unsettling, slightly creepy presence . . . If you think Dallas is boring or white-bread—well, perhaps you haven't gotten out much and seen the dark edges of Big D for yourself.." —*Dallas Morning News*

ATLANTA NOIR
edited by Tayari Jones
256 pages, trade paperback original, $15.95

BRAND-NEW STORIES BY: Tananarive Due, Kenji Jasper, Tayari Jones, Dallas Hudgens, Jim Grimsley, Brandon Massey, Jennifer Harlow, Sheri Joseph, Alesia Parker, Gillian Royes, Anthony Grooms, John Holman, Daniel Black, and David James Poissant.

"Jones, author of *Leaving Atlanta*, returns to the South via Akashic's ever-growing city anthology series. The collection features stories from an impressive roster of talent including Jim Grimsley, Sheri Joseph, Gillian Royes, Anthony Grooms and David James Poissant. The 14 selections each take place in different Atlanta neighborhoods." —*Atlanta Journal-Constitution*